and walked past Izzy, purposely brushing her elbow with his. Startled, she jumped and looked at him.

"You hangin' in?" he said.

"Guess I'm a little shell shocked."

They crossed the room and met Cal at the fireplace. He was bent over, examining the body.

"Cal, Moreno, you'd better take a look at this," said one of the techies. He motioned them over to the blood-soaked couch.

Izzy hadn't been called over, so she stayed at the fireplace. The scene was gruesome and the stench wafted up her nose. She gingerly touched the body with a stainless steel probe. It crunched. She steadied her queasies and took a deep breath. *Get back on task.*

She scrutinized the area, searching for fibers and trace evidence. When she picked up the fireplace poker that lay nearby, a blood-soaked packet tumbled off the hearth and plopped on the carpet. Izzy glanced around to see if anyone else had noticed. When she realized she was the sole recipient of this piece of evidence, her heart skipped a beat. This could be her first break—her way to show those seasoned guys that this newbie knew her stuff.

Praise for Jocelyn Pedersen

"*AN EYE FOR AN EYE* is one of the best thrillers I've read in years. No truly rough stuff that's hard to read before bed, it's an engaging suspense thriller with plenty of blind alleys and a killer who can't be found or stopped. The main characters are unique and lovable, you won't find any like them in other thrillers, and the possible romance between our main character and her partner sizzles. The best of all reading worlds!"

~Win and Meredith Blevins

An Eye for an Eye

by

Jocelyn Pedersen

The Izzy O Crime Files, Book One

An Eye for an Eye

Cover Art by *Angela Anderson*

The Wild Rose Press, Inc.
PO Box 708
Adams Basin, NY 14410-0708
Visit us at www.thewildrosepress.com

Publishing History
First Mainstream Mystery Edition, 2016
Print ISBN 978-1-5092-0950-7
Digital ISBN 978-1-5092-0951-4

The Izzy O Crime Files, Book One
Published in the United States of America

Dedications

This book is dedicated to my late mother,
G. Isobell Pedersen, and my dad, Curt A. C. Pedersen,
who both helped instill in me a love of language.
~*~

I also dedicate this book to my three children,
Jordan, Elise, and Al Miller,
who put up with a mom in grad school
and lived to tell the tale.
I love you more than you'll ever know.
~*~

Thanks to my mentor and friend, Deborah Chester,
whose pen bled on my work until the day
she turned several pages without making a mark,
looked over her glasses at me and said, "Good job."
I probably still owe you some ink.
~*~

I'd be remiss if I didn't mention my sweet friends
Win and Meredith Blevins, whose comments
I incorporated into the book and from whom
I have learned a lifetime's worth of writing tips.
~*~

And of course, my editor, Anne Duguid Knol,
who patiently pointed out that Moreno can't be
two places at once, and much, much more.
~*~

Last, and by no means least, I dedicate this book
to my very own Apple, Erin Moore,
without whom this book would never have happened.
Was plotting this book in our jammies
while we were both sick as dogs the best, or what?

Chapter One

She had sinned. He knew what had to be done. He had watched her with a twist in his lips as she scolded her children, ignored them, ignored their needs. She had brushed them off when they tried to get her attention. Then, when the little girl said she had to go to the bathroom, the mother snapped at her for interrupting and made the little girl cry.

This woman was impatient and mean. She had to die.

He drove to her house. She'd be alone. Her husband would be at work and the kids were at a Mother's Day Out program, because it was Friday. Then grandma would pick the kids up from Mother's Day Out and keep them overnight so she and her husband could have their precious date night. That was the Friday routine at Polly Fullerton's house. He knew this.

He pulled into her driveway, opened the door to his car and the Miami humidity stuck to him like plastic wrap. He looked up at the morning sun and walked to her door. A thrill shot through him and he rang the doorbell. He flexed his hands while he waited for her to answer, adjusted the knife in its sheath at the small of his back. He heard footsteps. A pause. The viewer on the door darkened, and she was there, looking out at him through the peephole. He managed a smile, one that was easy to conjure. He had a duty, after all. Then the peephole brightened and the lock clicked and turned.

She opened the door. They always opened the door. Why wouldn't they? They knew him.

She smiled, stepped back, and invited him in. The look on her face was pleasant, but perplexed. *Why was he here?* She'd soon find out.

He got through an eternity of mindless chitchat. Would she *ever* shut up? But if he interrupted, she might get suspicious. Probably wondering why he'd come, she rattled on and on, tapping her toe against the tile floor. It sounded like a woodpecker hammering away at a tree. So very impatient. Didn't she know that patience is a virtue?

His blood ran hot and eager. He struggled to stay calm. If he let her rush him, he'd be no better than she. He sent up a silent prayer for patience and imagined the words wafting out of his head, up to the ceiling and through the roof, up to the ears of the Almighty, the One he wanted to serve and obey. Her phone rang and mid-sentence, she cut away from her conversation with him and rushed to the sofa where her purse lay, the phone dingling inside it.

This was his chance. He pulled latex gloves from his pockets and put them on. She was madly digging through her purse to find her phone. His need intensified—the moment had come. He quickstepped over to her. She looked up at him in surprise, clinging to her phone. He knocked it out of her hand. It skittered to the floor and across the carpet. Her purse fell, a female calamity.

At last. He raised his hands and jammed them

around her throat. Her eyes widened. He squeezed. Her fear was a banquet of ozone and sweat. She tried to pull his hands away, but she was no match for him. He held pressure. Steady pressure. She tried to scream, no luck. She scratched at his gloved hands. He pressed harder and felt her blood pulsing. She kicked him. He laughed out loud and held on. She thrashed, hair flying, eyes gaping. The tendons in his hands strained taut and he looked straight into her eyes. Her eyes darted from side to side, searching for someone to save her. The whites gleamed. His gaze was implacable. She'd look back at him. Her eyes would beg for the mercy he would never give. It always happened that way. *Wait for it. Wait...* Then, there it was. Her eyes stared into his.

She's almost done. Here comes the moment of surrender. He smiled at her.

Her eyes swamped with fear, now. He liked that. Her face contorted, a still-living mask. She kicked at him again, tried to hit him in the groin. *You fool. You're no match for me.* She flailed, clawed at him, and he refocused, pressed harder.

Her pathetic thrashing weakened. Her body turned limp and loose. A surge of joy rushed through him. He was strong enough to do the right thing, his grip fierce against her throat. She went limp, but she was still breathing. He never went too far. He never strangled them to death. Unconsciousness was the key.

He picked her up and laid her on the couch. She looked like she was taking a nap on the deep yellow cushions with a blue and white floral motif. It was time for the ceremony.

He opened the front door—stepped out, looked toward his car, then skyward and said, "It's time for the cleansing." He walked back in and admired his handiwork. He stroked her locks away from her neck. He carefully slipped his polished knife from its sheath and slit her throat from ear to ear.

Blood squirted from her neck. It stained the flowers on the couch, covered her phone and pooled onto the floor. The sight of it thrilled him. He touched it, warm and slippery. Blood always seemed warmer than human skin. He stroked her hair with his bloodied hand. He was helping to deliver and cleanse her from her sins. Helping society by ridding it of this horrible, impatient creature. He should be thanked, applauded, honored.

The blood only trickled now. It was over.

The cleansing ritual demanded that the mortal part causing the evil be removed. It was her ears that had proved her impatience. She could hear, yes, but she wouldn't listen. When her ear was gone, the cleansing would be complete. She'd go to heaven and live an eternally virtuous life. It was his duty to help her, his job to save her.

Cutting the ear off was much easier than rendering her unconscious. But each step of the ritual had to be done in precise order.

He removed a piece of parchment from his pocket and unfolded it. He'd taken considerable time looking through Brother Hamor's notes, reviewing the ritual yet again, and searching through his Bible for the proper verses. He wrought each letter with care using ink and a porcupine quill he'd fashioned himself. He then typed and printed them before placing the handwritten copy in his Bible for safekeeping Now he would put the verses to use.

James 1:19, "Know this, my beloved brothers: let

every person be quick to hear, slow to speak, slow to anger."

1 Corinthians 13:4, "Love is patient and kind; love does not envy or boast; it is not arrogant."

Ephesians 4:2, "With all humility and gentleness, with patience, bearing with one another in love."

He laid the paper on the couch next to Polly Fullerton's body. He placed her ear on the words and wrapped it up. He left the package on the couch, lifted Polly and carried her to the fireplace.

This was always the hard part. Brother Hamor had a pyre on which to place the cleansed, but he himself would have to use the fireplace. Large marble tiles framed its opening. It would be difficult to fit her whole body inside. He folded her into a repentant kneeling position as best he could and shoved. Next, he poured alcohol on the body. He lit the match and with a poof, flames burst up.

He watched for a moment to make sure the fire caught. Fire took the thin fabric of her blouse, first. Then the flames flashed down to her Capri pants and up to her hair. It sizzled with the blood he'd left there while caressing her. When the smell of burning flesh filled the room, the familiar tumescence coursed through him. He knew he had done God's work. He would be elevated for this. He placed the wrapped ear next to the fireplace and took his leave.

Brother Hamor would be deeply pleased.

Chapter Two

Izzy O'Donnell loved driving the unmarked Toyota Avalon. As the newbie on the team, she didn't get to drive much, but today she got lucky. It didn't look like a typical cop car, not the standard fleet-mobile. It was *truly* undercover, and she liked that. She loved being a cop. Like everybody else, she'd started on the streets where she wrote speeding tickets and broke up marital disputes. Recently she'd earned her wings and been switched from vice to homicide. At times, it was important to be invisible on the job, whether that meant wearing four-inch stilettos and a skin-tight, gold lame mini skirt and blouse that only covered the essentials, or driving an unmarked car.

As she drove, she noticed *For Sale* signs in front of houses, but house hunting would have to wait. She pulled up along the curb and parked in front of a two-story stucco house. Her place could fit three times over inside one of these houses. She felt a little out of place in this fancy neighborhood, but at least the car fit in.

Izzy was the first to open the car door and find herself swimming in Miami's humidity. She looked around. *Nice neighborhood.* You'd have to have a great job to live here. Beemers and Benzes in the driveways. These folks definitely brought down more than civil servant pay. The shrubs were manicured—some even cut into dolphin-shaped topiaries. *Sheesh. Must have more dollars than sense.* Everywhere she looked, shutters were freshly painted, front doors tinted in a complementary hue to the house stucco and trim. Windows gleamed with the care given only to homes whose children and pets were never allowed to make anything dirty. The very grass looked polished. Beautiful. Even the people standing around gawking were beautiful. She swiped at her brow as did some of the gawkers. Heat and humidity. The great levelers. Even beautiful people sweat.

Pete Moreno and his partner, Cal Callahan, slammed their doors making her jump. Moreno walked up carrying latex gloves and a black plastic forensics kit that looked like an overgrown tackle box. "Here, rookie," he said, handing each of them a set of gloves. "You'll need these."

She took hers and nodded her thanks. *Rookie*. Once again she was reminded of her place in the food chain—at a level somewhere near the nematodes. At least they broke the regular protocol and didn't call her the FNG—F-ing New Guy. It was great being sent to homicide only a few years after graduating from the academy, but not so great being assigned to the team with Moreno and Cal. Cal had changed her diapers. He used to be her dad's partner. Terrific. It was like being on a team with a big brother or her dad. And Moreno? Jeez. The ultimate macho cop with looks that could melt the Arctic Circle.

"Why you daydreaming?" Cal said, staring her in the face.

Embarrassed, Izzy looked up at him. "Sorry. Just thinking how strange it is to have a murder scene in a nice neighborhood like this."

"Honey, people get themselves killed in alleys and castles alike," Cal said. "Ever hear of Hamlet?"

Izzy ignored him, reached into her pocket and pulled out a ponytail holder and quickly scooped her long, dark auburn hair into it. They each snapped on their gloves. Izzy glanced around and saw a couple of uniformed officers standing on the porch with a distraught-looking man. She turned to Moreno.

His gaze met hers. "That's probably the husband," he said. "Let's get going. We'll need to see how far the forensics team has gotten and then we'll have to talk to the husband ourselves." He studied her. "Izzy O., this is your first big one, isn't it?"

"Yeah," she said.

"You gonna be okay?" he asked.

Wow. Actual concern? She squared her shoulders. "Of course I am," she said, hoping she'd be able to keep her word and not mess up.

Cal slapped her on the back, a little too hard, and said, "Okay then, kid. Let's see if you have the same stomach as your old man. When he was my partner, he could handle the worst."

Cal and Moreno headed up the sidewalk. Izzy rubbed her shoulder, which smarted with Cal's expectations. She shook it off and fell in line behind them. A mental eye roll later, she wondered how many paces she should stay back—just to prove she knew her place. The three of them approached the front door where the officers and husband stood. One of the officers moved away from the others and approached them. Cal shoved Izzy to the front of the pack. She read the uniform's name tag and gave him a nod.

"Officer Bradley, I'm Detective O'Donnell,

Homicide." She showed him her badge and indicated her partners. "Detective Callahan and Detective Moreno."

Officer Bradley nodded in acknowledgement.

"When did the call come in?" Moreno said.

"About fifteen minutes ago, when the husband came home." He gestured in the direction of the porch where Bradley's partner was consoling a tall, blond man with red eyes and a tear-streaked face.

"My partner and I got the husband away from the crime scene and secured the area. My partner's made sure he stays in one place until you got here."

"Thanks," Cal said.

"How bad is it?" Moreno said.

"It isn't pretty," Bradley said with a shudder. "This is a two bucket job."

Cal looked at Izzy and Moreno, sighed and said, "Let's do this. Moreno, you and Izzy start inside. I'll talk to the husband. Be there in a sec."

Izzy took a few steps, looked at the husband and said, "I'm sorry for your loss." She picked up her kit and walked to the threshold.

Moreno opened his kit and pulled out booties and caps.

"Here's a set for you Izzy O."

Izzy nodded her thanks and donned her gear. It was then that the smell of burned flesh met her nose. Her insides flip-flopped. She looked toward the fireplace and saw the body stuffed inside it. A garish scene with the victim's limp, crusted hand draping out of the confines of the firebox onto the hearth. Her face and neck were charred and black. Her stomach and knees were scorched, but the fire had apparently died down before it could consume her back and upper torso.

Izzy gulped hard and turned her attention to the couch and carpet.

All the blood had soaked into the sofa. Droplets of blood stained the cushions, walls, and coffee table where a picture of the victim and two young children sat. It splattered the frame, and a trickle had dried before making its way all the way down the glass to the table. Izzy's gut turned over twice when she looked back at the body. She'd seen plenty of pictures of crime scenes at the academy, and smelled plenty of piss and shit when working vice, but this pungent scene, with so much blood and scorched human flesh, hit her in the face like a heavyweight's sucker punch.

Moreno was already on his knees near the body with a forensics team member.

"You finished taking pictures?" Cal said shoving his way past Izzy into the room.

"Yes. All the pictures are in. We're looking for trace evidence and prints now," the techie said. "We haven't spent a lot of time with the body yet. The medical examiner is on his way. You can take a look if you like, but just follow protocol."

"Right," Cal said, shooting the techie his best *duh* look. The techie shrugged and moved on. Cal turned to Moreno. "There's a lot of blood. Call the spatter guys and get them over here."

"Sure," Moreno said. He pulled out his cell and dialed.

Izzy still stood in the entryway, transfixed by the scene.

"C'mon, kid," Cal said. "Show us what you're made of."

"Comin'," she said, pausing to look around the room.

The blood had dried, indicating it had been a while since the murder. Cal waved her into the room on his way to the fireplace.

Moreno hung up the phone and walked past Izzy, purposely brushing her elbow with his. Startled, she jumped and looked at him.

"You hangin' in?" he said.

"Guess I'm a little shell shocked."

They crossed the room and met Cal at the fireplace. He was bent over, examining the body.

"Cal, Moreno, you'd better take a look at this," said one of the techies. He motioned them over to the blood-soaked couch.

Izzy hadn't been called over, so she stayed at the fireplace. The scene was gruesome and the stench wafted up her nose. She gingerly touched the body with a stainless steel probe. It crunched. She steadied her queasies and took a deep breath. *Get back on task.*

She scrutinized the area, searching for fibers and trace evidence. When she picked up the fireplace poker that lay nearby, a blood-soaked packet tumbled off the hearth and plopped on the carpet. Izzy glanced around to see if anyone else had noticed. When she realized she was the sole recipient of this piece of evidence, her heart skipped a beat. This could be her first break—her way to show those seasoned guys that this newbie knew her stuff.

She fished around in her kit and found an evidence bag, leaned over the object and picked it up. It was heavier than she expected, and cold. Blood smeared the paper and streaked her gloved hand. Trying hard not to think about it, she held it up.

"Look at this," she said.

Cal and Moreno rushed over. "Open it," Cal ordered.

Izzy opened the paper revealing an object that was short and small and very bloody. A gemstone dangled underneath it. The contents of her stomach headed north. She coughed and choked down bile.

Moreno stated the obvious. "I believe that's an ear." He looked up at Cal and then over to Izzy. "What you want to bet our vic is missing hers?"

That was it. Izzy took off at a dead run for the door but she didn't make it. Her lunch spewed all over the carpet.

Chapter Three

It was a couple of hours later when Moreno pulled the Avalon into the parking lot and maneuvered into a space under the neon sign that featured a blinking green shamrock and the words "O'Donnell's Irish Pub." It was poker night, and although Izzy was tired and still embarrassed about heaving at the crime scene, she felt she could use a drink and some camaraderie, so she hung in.

"Well, here you are, Izzy O. Home." Moreno said, his face and short, dark hair alternating from green to mocha with the reflection of the shamrock.

Home. But for how long? Just yesterday, the waitress at the coffee shop had introduced her to Mark Traesk, a realtor, and she'd made an appointment with him later in the week to talk about finding a new place for her dad. Dad didn't know that yet, and she wasn't about to tell him today.

"Home," she said absently.

"Yeah. Your dad will want to hear about the case," Cal said.

Izzy nodded. "He misses his detective days and working with you, Cal. He enjoys hearing our stories. Keeps him young." She paused. "Do you have to tell him I blew chow?"

Moreno laughed and slapped his thigh. "Of course we're going to tell him. The question is do Cal and I

13

have to arm wrestle to see who's going to do it?"

Cal said nothing, and Izzy was glad about that.

"Everyone has a hard time on the first bad one," she said, defiantly.

Cal snorted and got out of the car.

"What's with him?" Izzy said.

"Dunno," Moreno said.

They followed Cal toward the bar. He opened the door. A wedge of light and rock and roll from the jukebox spilled into the parking lot. The door slammed behind him in Izzy's face.

"Nice of him to hold the door for a lady," Moreno said.

"Forget it," Izzy said. "Something's eating at him."

"Allow me," Moreno said, opening the door and bowing.

She flashed him a flirtatious smile. "Thanks."

They were practically run down by a waitress carrying an over-laden tray of beer and frosted glasses. Her long, curly red hair looked like it had met its match with a hurricane, and her large black glasses clung to the end of her nose for dear life.

"Sorry, Izzy, Moreno," the wild woman said. "Didn't see you." She wriggled her nose and tipped her head back in an effort to scootch her glasses back to the top of her nose.

"It's okay, Apple," Izzy said. "Hold still a minute and I'll fix your glasses."

Apple paused and turned her head toward Izzy. She reached over and pushed Apple's glasses up to their proper place.

"Thanks," Apple said. "Gotta get this beer over to table five. See you in a minute." And she was off like a cyclone, red hair streaming behind her in curly banners.

A smiled tugged at the corners of Izzy's mouth. She looked up at Moreno.

"Apple's a mess," he said shaking his head, dark eyes twinkling.

Izzy grinned. "Yeah, but we all love her."

"Everyone except Cal," Moreno said.

Izzy shrugged. "They have a love-hate thing going on. Whatever. You ready for a beer?"

"Man, I thought you'd never ask," he said.

Izzy shimmied behind the long, mahogany bar, reached into the cooler and grabbed a couple of bottles of beer, wiped them dry, and handed one to Moreno.

"I love it that you and your dad own this place," he said.

She tipped her bottle to him. "Stick with me, Toots."

"I'm glad I know you, Izzy," Moreno said.

Was that a blush? Did Moreno actually blush? It was hard to tell, his mocha latte skin didn't reveal much, especially in the dim pub. Izzy felt a rush of heat sweep over her. Surely he didn't mean anything by his words. She brushed it off and took a pull of her beer, dodging his gaze.

"Let's head to the back, it's a little quieter there. We can start setting up for the game," she said.

They crossed the bar to the door under the stairs that led up to the apartment Izzy shared with her dad, Spencer. Izzy opened the door and switched on the Tiffany light over the game table. She was surprised to find Cal there.

"What are you doing sitting here in the dark, Cal?" Izzy asked.

Cal harrumphed and took a swig of his beer.

"Sitting. Anything wrong with that?"

Izzy arched an eyebrow. "No. Nothing wrong with sitting. You okay?"

"I'm great. I'm absolutely perfect. Marvelous, in fact," Cal said. He swept the table with his arm. "I pulled the table out already. All we need are a few more chairs."

Izzy didn't quite know what to say. "Great," she offered. "Thanks."

She looked at Moreno. He shrugged. They picked up a couple of chairs and put them around the table.

Moreno looked around the room.

"Where'd the cards go?" he asked.

"They're upstairs," she said. "Why don't you go get Dad and have him bring the cards?" she said to Cal.

"Forget it," Cal grumbled. "Moreno, you go. You're younger. I'm tired."

Moreno raised a dark, bushy eyebrow at his older and portly partner, but didn't respond. He glanced at Izzy who gave him her best *please* look, and he turned and walked through the door.

The stairs overhead thumped as Moreno climbed, and soon Izzy heard muffled voices. She didn't like her dad to take the stairs alone any more. It was good of Moreno to go get him. Ditching Moreno was good on two counts. Now she had Cal alone.

"What's up?" she asked. "Why're you grumpy?"

Cal's blue-gray eyes met hers. He raised a silver eyebrow at her, thought a minute, shook his head and dropped his gaze.

"C'mon, Cal. I'm your friend. What's up?"

"Friend, yeah. Long time. Lillian and I babysat

you." Cal harrumphed again. "But I'm also your boss, now. Forget it. Nothing's wrong."

"Boss or no boss, that *nothing* sounds like *something*, and we're not on the job right now."

"Look, Izzy, I know you mean well, but things have changed since last week. I'm not just your dad's old partner. We're dancing a new waltz. Why, out of all the homicide teams, did the captain put you with me? I'll never know."

"Maybe because he knows you're the best and the most experienced. Is that what it is, Cal? Do you want me to ask to be assigned to a different team?"

"No, no, Izzy. We can work together. It's not that." He drew little circles on the table with his index finger. "Thing is, if I tell you, you'll tell Moreno and he doesn't need to know. I don't want anybody's sympathy."

Sympathy? Something must really be up.

Cal drew more circles on the table, then added, "Besides, if I tell you and not him, he'll be mad at me. So there's nothing to talk about."

"Cal, I'm not going to say anything to Moreno or anyone else for that matter. Would you have told my dad when he was your partner?" she said.

"That's different."

"Yeah? How?"

"He wasn't my rookie."

"I don't know what difference it would possibly make if you tell me what's bugging you," she said. She reached over and poked him playfully. "Come on, Cal. You've known me all my life. And I won't tell anyone. Cross my heart." She made an X on her chest.

Cal eyed her suspiciously, his gray brows knit

17

together. Finally, he sighed and blurted, "Lillian lost her job to a reduction in force. We may have to move," he said.

"Move? Where?"

"Friggin' Minnesota. You know how *cold* it gets in Minnesota?" His head bobbed with animation, and light flickered off his bald spot. "Damn cold," Cal said. "I'm almost ready to move to a desk job as it is. I'm getting up there and my arthritis bothers me. How am I going to deal with arthritis in Minnesota? My joints hurt just *thinking* about it."

Izzy felt bad for him but didn't really know what to say. "I'm sorry," was all that came out.

Cal shrugged, then continued. "Jeremy's off to college, so it won't really affect him, but Heather is a junior in high school this year. She's going ape about the possibility of having to move. Drama, drama, drama."

"Ouch," Izzy said.

She put her hand on Cal's arm. She wondered what life might be like without him. She couldn't remember a time without him. It would be so strange. So empty.

She heard Moreno and Spencer coming down the stairs. It was a slow descent. It really was getting hard for her dad to take those stairs. Her mind wandered off for a moment in worry, but she was brought back to the present problem when Cal moved away from her.

"I have a feeling it will all work out," she said.

"Oh, no. Not that again. What kind of feeling? One of your woo-woo feelings or just a regular feeling?"

Izzy opened her mouth to answer, but Cal interrupted. "Never mind. I don't want to know. You know I don't go for that stuff."

Izzy nodded and took a swig of beer. "Cal, let me know if there's anything I can do to help. And don't worry, you can think of me as 'Take it to the grave O'Donnell'."

Footsteps were growing closer.

Cal raised his beer to her. "Not Moreno, for sure. Got that?"

Just then the door opened and Moreno walked in. "What's going on?" he asked. "Not Moreno what?

Cal turned his chair slightly and said, "Nothing." Under his breath, Izzy heard Cal mumble, "Told you he'd be mad."

Feeling a little awkward and strangely guilty, Izzy looked at Moreno. "It's nothing. We're just chatting."

Moreno eyed her suspiciously.

"Mind your own business," Cal snapped.

Moreno's face fell. His dark eyes flashed at Izzy and then at his partner. He opened his mouth but before he could get anything out, Spencer shuffled through the door holding a deck of cards. Cal continued to glare at Moreno.

Izzy grinned and walked over to greet her dad, giving him a hug. Tonight he seemed frail for someone in his late fifties, but that's how it had been since he was injured in the line of duty.

"Hi, Dad."

"Izzy-O," he said, patting her on the back.

"How was your day?" she offered, too brightly.

"My day was right as rain, filled with lively customers and conversation, daughter."

Izzy's lips twitched into a smile. She loved the sound of her dad's Irish lilt.

"Are you ready to lose your money?" she asked.

"Take yours," he said.

"Come sit by Cal." She helped him over to the table and showed him to a seat next to his former partner. She poked Cal, who was avoiding Moreno's eyes.

Jeez! Izzy thought. *So stubborn.*

She held the back of the chair while her dad took his seat.

"Spencer," Cal said, nodding, forcing a smile that still revealed his raised shoulders and pinched face.

"Is something wrong?" asked Spencer.

In unison, Izzy, Cal and Moreno said, "No."

Spencer blinked in confusion.

Izzy looked daggers at Cal and Moreno. "Everything's fine," she said. "Hard day. Let's play some poker and relax."

Spencer poked Cal on the shoulder.

The tension in the room softened a bit, but the bewilderment on Spencer's face was unmistakable. He knew something was up.

Izzy wished her dad were well enough to share Cal's burden. Down deep she worried for the two of them. Moreno sat nearby looking wounded and put out. She worried about him too. And herself. How was she, the kid rookie, the daughter, the poker hostess, cop partner, and friend, supposed to keep this confidence from Moreno and keep peace all at the same time?

Chapter Four

"I'll see that and raise you five." Izzy tossed a domestic bottle cap onto the pile of caps already in the middle of the table. They were well into the first hour of playing, and everyone was feeling good.

Moreno looked at her from across the table, dark eyes twinkling on his very *guapo* face. He rolled a cocktail skewer in his mouth. "You're bluffing," he said.

"Think so?" she asked, deadpan. "You can either fold or put up and see me."

"Izzy, you're killing me," Moreno looked at his cards.

Cal muttered something under his breath, but Izzy couldn't make all of it out. The only thing she knew for certain was that it was a snide remark aimed at Moreno.

Moreno glared at Cal.

"Make a move, Moreno," Spencer O'Donnell's Irish lilt sang in his words. "My daughter may be painin' you boy, but you'll have to make a decision just the same."

Izzy smiled at her father. Sometimes he was his old self.

Dan Walker, the medical examiner, wore his poker uniform. His favorite TV show was M*A*S*H and he wore a fishing vest *a la* Colonel Blake when he played poker—called it his lucky vest. The difference was that instead of fishing lures dangling off a hat like his TV hero, Dr. Dan's vest was festooned with tack and lapel pins he'd collected from various places he'd traveled, volunteered or donated time or money. He picked the plastic sword out of his drink and swished it at Moreno, ending with a mock lunge in his direction. "Yeah, make a move already, before we plug ya and put you on my slab," he said, blue eyes flashing.

"Get with it, Moreno. I'm growing a beard over here," Cal muttered impatiently, rubbing his bristly chin.

"C'mon, Moreno," Izzy said. "Play already."

"All right, all right," said Moreno. "You guys can put in to see Izzy if you want. Me? I'm folding."

He tossed his cards down. Izzy's eyelid twitched a little. She might actually pull this one off.

"Okay, daughter," said Spencer O'Donnell. "Let's see your hand, then."

Spencer, Dr. Dan and Cal plopped their cards down. The best anyone had was two pair—queens over eights. Izzy grinned broadly and turned over a straight.

"Shit!" said Moreno, tossing his head back. "I can't ever tell if you're bluffing. I have a flush. That pot should be mine!"

Izzy laughed out loud and Moreno collected the cards to shuffle and deal.

Apple, the bartender, burst through the door. Her frizzy red hair flapped behind her, as usual. The oversized glasses that made her eyes look like they were in a fish bowl were once again slipping down on her nose. She held a large white rabbit with gray ears in her arms.

"Jeez, Apple"—Izzy put her hands up

defensively—"Where's the fire?"

"Sorry." Apple held the rabbit out to Izzy. "Norman wanted to say hi."

Izzy set her cards down on the table and took the rabbit. "Hi, Norman," she said. The rabbit settled himself on Izzy's lap.

Spencer grinned broadly and said, "Norman, are you in?"

Norman wriggled his nose and buried his head in the crook of Izzy's elbow. "Guess not," said Spencer. "Who else is in?"

They each tossed in a light beer bottle cap—worth a dollar. Apple pulled a chair up next to Izzy and plopped down. Norman raised his head and looked at her. She made a lap for him and he hopped over. Apple rubbed his head behind his long ears, and Izzy thought if rabbits could purr, Norman would.

"How's your hand?" Apple asked, peeking over Izzy's shoulder.

Izzy shielded her cards from Apple. "Why do you ask? You're supposed to be the psychic one. You tell me," she said.

"Very funny," said Apple. "You know it doesn't work that way." She closed her eyes and made circles with her fingers, imitating a yoga stance. "I just meditate and channel. But I have a feeling that you're cleaning these guys out tonight."

Izzy rearranged the cards in her hand and patted her pile of bottle caps. "True, true, but you don't have to be psychic to know that. Just look at my pile of caps." She wiggled her eyebrows.

Moreno groaned and tossed a domestic cap onto the pile. "Yeah, yeah, yeah. Whatever. You seem to know everything tonight." He glared at Izzy.

Cal raised his eyes to Moreno, "She knows what she needs to know. And I know that you need to bet or fold," he said.

Izzy saw Moreno's nostrils flare slightly, the way they did when he was making a concerted effort to keep the lid on his anger. The stir stick in his mouth rolled quickly from side to side. She watched him. He turned his gaze away from Cal, tossed in a domestic beer cap and said, "I raise you five."

Izzy studied Moreno for a moment. Their eyes locked for a second and she knew he was annoyed with her. And it wasn't because of the card game.

Dr. Dan looked at the two of them suspiciously and tossed a cap into the pile. "I don't know what's going on, but I sense tension. Did everything go okay at the crime scene today?" Dr. Dan asked.

The corners of Moreno's mouth twitched into a smile. "Izzy blew chunks at the scene."

Everyone looked at Izzy. Her face suddenly felt wildfire hot. "So?" she said. "It was a bad scene. Besides, I did just fine until that ear plopped on the floor."

Dr. Dan frowned, Spencer scrunched his nose in disgust and Apple grimaced.

"Yuk," Apple said. "I wouldn't have made it either."

Moreno turned to Apple. "Hey Apple, we may need you to meditate on this case if we don't catch a break soon," he said.

"Oh?" she said, perking up a little.

"Never mind," Izzy said. "We can solve this forensically."

Apple deflated a little.

"A bad one today?" Spencer said.

"Sick one," Cal said.

"Yeah," Moreno said. "Another woman—scumbag slit her throat and stuffed her in the fireplace. Just like the others. Only this time he cut off her ear and wrapped it in paper. That's what made Izzy blow."

Izzy lowered her cards and launched daggers at Moreno. He'd already told everyone that she vomited. Couldn't he just leave it?

Spencer reached over and patted Izzy on the arm.

"Ignore him, daughter," he said. "We've each one of us lost a lunch at a crime scene. Even Dr. Dan. Sadly, you'll get used to it."

"Thanks, Dad," Izzy said, zapping Moreno with her best drop-dead-now look.

Moreno twitched a sly grin. "It's lucky Izzy didn't puke on the paper because something was written on it," Moreno said. "The blood smeared the ink badly. Ink jet, you know. Forensics thinks they can reconstruct what it said, though."

"Wrapped in paper," Cal pondered aloud. "This is the third victim we've found like this. Throat slit, body part removed, stuffed in a fireplace. The only difference this time is the body part was wrapped in paper. You guys think it's a copy cat job?"

Izzy looked up from her cards. Everyone had stopped playing for the moment. "What if it's not a copy cat? What if the murderer is evolving?" she said.

All eyes moved to her. Izzy had a sudden case of stage fright.

"It was just an idea," she said, backpedaling.

"This isn't *Criminal Minds*, newbie. Maybe you

should just concentrate on your cards," Moreno said.

Izzy fiddled with her cards. She felt about two inches tall. *Dumb, dumb, dumb.* When would she learn to just keep her mouth shut?

They played the rest of that hand out without talking much and then they called it a night. It was late and Apple had closed the bar a half hour earlier. Dr. Dan helped Spencer up the stairs before taking his leave, Apple and Norman headed for their apartment a half block away, leaving Cal, Moreno and Izzy to stash the table and chairs.

Izzy placed a chair in the corner. Moreno brought another one over and slammed it down on top of the first.

Izzy picked up another chair. "Moreno, you got a problem?" she said.

Cal looked at the two of them.

Moreno blinked. "Yes, Izzy, as a matter of fact, I do," he said. "Are you trying to edge me out and become Cal's partner? Because it seems to me you might be having private conversations with him about that when I'm not around."

She felt like a giant spotlight glared at her and she was blinded. "What?"

Cal set his chair down. "Moreno, Izzy doesn't want your job. If anything, she wants *my* job. I'm the old one. She's probably ticking off the days until I retire."

Izzy put her chair down and held her palms up in a wait-just-a-minute gesture. "Hey, guys, I don't want *anybody's* job. I was *assigned* to your team, remember? I didn't request it. What's going on here?"

The three exchanged glances.

Moreno was the first to break the silence. "All I

know is I was called upstairs to purportedly get Spencer and a deck of cards and when I return, you two are deep in conversation and Izzy looks guilty."

Cal piped up. "We were just talking about something that doesn't concern you, Moreno."

Moreno wasn't buying it, Izzy could tell. That Latino *machismo* air about him was thick. She hated that. She always told him to get a grip on his irritable side when he pulled that attitude, but now she felt it would only exacerbate the problem.

Both men were glaring at each other and at her.

Izzy looked at the two of them. Tolerating the whole male head-butting thing wasn't her forte. She knew it, and she had no patience for it.

"For the record," she said, "the only job I want is mine." She turned to Cal. "If my being assigned to this team is going to be a problem, then either you, as senior detective, need to put in for a transfer for me, or I need to do it. Make a decision and get back to me on that."

She looked at Moreno. His nostrils were still flared. "And you, Moreno, need to back off and pocket your ego. Not everything is about you," she said.

They both looked at her like toddlers and blinked.

She gave each of them a rough shove toward the door. "Stop acting like kids and get out of my bar," she said. "This conversation is over."

Moreno turned and opened his mouth to say something.

"Moreno!"

Moreno turned and walked out the door. Cal followed.

Izzy stood in the empty room and listened to the blissful quiet. After a few minutes, she locked the door, turned the lights and neon sign off, and went upstairs. *Men*!

Chapter Five

Dear Brother Hamor,

Since the time we were forced to leave the Hevite colony and join the unclean world, it has been difficult to find people who understand our ways. I continue to look for them.

I have performed a cleansing ritual to the best of my abilities without the help of my brothers, sisters and elders around me. Even though it wasn't performed in the precise manner you taught us, all the ritualistic elements were present and I believe it was effective.

I watched this woman, just like the others. She was impatient with those around her, with me, even—but being a Hevite, I knew I had to forgive her for her slight against me. I knew in my heart that I had to save this woman from her impatience, so she could be cleansed and go to heaven.

You were right, Brother Hamor, there are few virtuous people in the unclean world, and women in particular, are weak.

During the ritual, there was a lot of sinful blood. Her very soul must have known that the blood was vile because it raced from her body and pooled on the floor.

I didn't put the impure part of her on her body, rather on a piece of paper. But it wasn't just any paper, Brother Hamor. I made it special. My Book is now well worn, and in its pages I found several verses about the virtues of being patient. I wrapped the offending part in the verses and set it aside for the unclean to find so that they might know why the cleansing ritual was performed. In the news they say someone is murdering women. Why don't they understand that a cleansing is not a murder? Performing rituals isn't easy in the morally blemished world. The unclean don't understand.

Since I lack elders around me to share in the ritual, when my work was done, I came home to write to you, Brother Hamor. I only hope that my small detraction from the ceremony as you taught us will not make it any less effective—for the poor woman's sake. I know that you will send me a sign if slight variations, in any way, make the act less potent.

I am blessed to know that you understand me.

Your Hevite Brother,

Seth

Chapter Six

The next night, Spencer walked past the flashing neon shamrock, and Izzy helped Apple load the last of the beer glasses into the dishwasher. The Saturday crowd had left the bar about forty-five minutes ago. Spencer insisted on sweeping up. Recently, he declared this would be his nightly job. He wanted to pitch in, and because Izzy was so busy working during the day, running the bar at night and looking out for her dad, she didn't argue with him. Even though sometimes he seemed to have a hard time with the work, at least he was where she could see him. He'd seemed pretty alert this evening, so she figured it was okay to let him sweep. The doctor had told her it was best for him to keep active.

Izzy bent down to get a soap tab for the dishwasher. Dizziness flooded her and a stabbing pain shot through her temples. *Not again,* she thought. White streaks flashed in front of her eyes, and she went to her knees. She reached up and grabbed her head in an effort to steady it. She felt suddenly cold as death and she was only vaguely aware of Apple rushing to her side. Her voice sounding like a jumble of contorted words.

"Are you all right? What happened?" Apple said.

Izzy wasn't really sure what was happening. She steadied herself against Apple and the counter. Her head began to clear and she looked up at her friend, confused.

"What happened?" Apple said again.

"I don't know. I've had a few dizzy spells, or whatever you want to call them, like this over the past few days. It's weird."

"Are you okay?"

"Yeah, thanks," Izzy said, nodding, but in truth, the freckles on Apple's nose were still swimming. "It's over now," she said.

Apple picked at a strand of Izzy's hair and put it in place on top of her head. "Tell me about it," she said.

Izzy rolled her eyes. "Not much to tell. Truly. I'm sure it's just the pressure of the job. That's all."

Apple eyed her suspiciously. "Any dreams?" she said.

"Nothing that makes any sense," Izzy said. "Why?"

"You know the last time you had dreams when you were under pressure it was something more. It was your inner oracle talking."

"Inner oracle? Apple, I'm fine. Truly. A couple of dreams and a few dizzy spells do not a psychic issue make," Izzy said.

"Give me your hands," Apple demanded, extending her hands, palms up.

Izzy sighed. She shook her hair back and obediently placed her hands on Apple's. She looked into Apple's green eyes. Apple slowly closed them and began to concentrate. Izzy closed her eyes too. The silence in the room was broken only by the sound of Spencer's broom swishing the floor off in the corner.

"You know how this works," Apple said. "Clear your mind. Let me channel. Let me see."

Izzy swept away the thoughts of how crazy this

felt. She knew that sometimes when she had one of *those* feelings, she'd better listen to it. Didn't every woman? Sometimes they were omens, sometimes warnings, and sometimes it was a great big nothing—especially when she ate spicy food. This episode was probably nothing more than a reaction to the spicy Italian meatball sandwich she'd had for lunch—the only thing she'd eaten all day.

"You're not concentrating," Apple scolded. "I'm not interested in your meatball sandwich."

Izzy's eyes flew open. "How did you know—?"

"Close your eyes. Clear your mind!"

Izzy drew a few deep breaths in through her nose and out through her mouth. She wondered if the garlic on her breath had tipped Apple off. Her shoulders moved down away from her ears by about an inch and she began to relax. Her mind cruised back through her day. Through yesterday's poker game and her talk with Cal. Before that, the crime scene. Her mind froze. A nebulous vision came to her. A crowd of people. What were they watching? A fire? She had the sense of a little boy. Was he in trouble? No, that wasn't it. He's watching something, she thought. Watching with all those other people. He likes what he sees.

Apple jerked suddenly and Izzy opened her eyes.

"What?" Izzy said. "What happened?"

"Your mind's eye quit seeing," Apple said.

"What's *that* supposed to mean?"

Apple fluffed her red hair and pushed her glasses up on her nose. "It means that your mind closed off. Either there's nothing more to see, or you're not supposed to see any more than that for now." She picked up a bar towel and matter-of-factly hung it over a towel rack to dry.

"Have you gone loopy on me? What are you talking about?"

"Tell me what you saw," Apple said.

Izzy looked around the room. Spencer was off in the opposite corner, still sweeping. She didn't really want him to hear this. No need to make her father worry about her. The less stress, the better.

"Well, what did you see?" Apple prodded.

"I saw a crowd around a fire. And a boy. But he wasn't scared or worried. He was just watching. It seemed like he was enjoying himself."

"Anything else?"

"Nope. That's it. Nothing else," Izzy said.

Apple took her glasses off and polished them in her apron. She looked funny without them. Izzy was so used to seeing her with them on, magnifying her green eyes, that to see them a normal size seemed odd. Apple replaced her glasses and her eyes grew three sizes larger.

"You didn't see anything else at all?" Apple said.

"I told you no already," Izzy snapped.

"Do you think this is related to the killings?"

"How could it be?" Izzy said. "Simple forensics dictate that the murderer is larger and stronger than an adolescent boy. And there's no evidence of a crowd being present at any of the murders. The only common denominator is that there was a fire at each crime scene, but certainly no bonfires. I'm sure my subconscious is just piecing things together and maybe even running away with me a bit."

"Forensic facts aren't the only kind of facts out there," Apple said. "There are other truths in the universe. There may be a connection." She hung three wine glasses on the rack over the large mahogany bar. "I'm not the one seeing the visions. I just channel to make them stronger, clearer. Only you can see what you see." She paused, looked at Izzy and wagged a finger at her. "I really think you should consult your inner oracle."

Izzy rolled her eyes. "This is going nowhere. I think I've just been trying so hard to get a handle on this guy that I'm experiencing weird stuff. My subconscious is working overtime and it's causing me to have these spells. I really want this guy. And *soon*, before he kills someone else." She paused. "I'll damn well prove to myself and everyone else that I can do it."

"Of course you can do it," Apple said. "No one doubts that—except you."

Izzy gave a half smile and looked down at her toes. "Maybe," she said.

Apple smiled at Izzy and scooped her up in a big hug. Izzy hugged her back.

"You don't have to try so hard, Izzy. You got that promotion because they know you can handle it. You *earned* it. I believe in you," Apple said. "So believe in yourself."

"Thanks. You're a great friend."

Apple let Izzy go and said, "I'm not just a great friend, I'm your *best* friend. And don't you ever forget it."

Izzy smiled. "I know."

There was a large crash and Spencer let out a yelp. Both women snapped their gaze in the direction of the stairs. Spencer lay in a heap at the bottom.

Izzy ran to him and nearly screamed, "Dad? What

happened?"

Spencer looked up at her. His eyes combusted with anguish and embarrassment, his brow was bleeding and a nasty lump was forming over his eye.

"I guess I tripped on the stairs," he said.

Izzy grabbed the dishtowel she had draped over her shoulder and dabbed at his eyebrow. Apple emerged from behind the bar with a bag full of ice. She handed it to Spencer, and he put it on his eye.

"Thanks," he said.

"Apple, let's get him upstairs," Izzy said.

They got on either side of him and lifted. They half carried, half guided him up the stairs, into the apartment, and onto his bed.

Izzy checked his brow. It had stopped bleeding, and it wasn't deep enough to require stitches, but the bump looked to be reaching adolescence—it would continue to grow.

"Dad, you're going to have a nasty bruise. I think you should keep that ice on there for a while, okay?" she said.

Spencer nodded and sank into his pillow.

Apple threw an embroidered caftan over him. "If you think you'll need me tonight, I can come back after I bed Norman down," she said. "I know you're tired. Let me help."

Izzy smiled at her friend. She knew that for Apple to offer to leave her beloved pet rabbit for the night was a sign of true affection.

"Thanks, but no. We'll be fine. I'll call if I need you."

Apple hesitated, wrung her hands, and then said, "Okay." She reached over and kissed Spencer on the cheek. "Get some rest, Spencer. I'll check on you in the morning."

"Thanks for your help, Apple. Good night," he said.

Apple turned to Izzy and said, "Remember to call if you need me. Just because I'm off tomorrow doesn't mean I'm not around."

Izzy smiled her thanks, walked her downstairs, and watched her get into her car to drive the half block home. This was their nightly routine. No matter how safe the neighborhood, Izzy didn't want Apple walking home alone after dark. She waved goodbye.

Izzy locked the door to the bar behind her, turned off the neon shamrock and the other downstairs lights and went back up to check on her father. Spencer was snoring lightly with the ice pack still on his forehead. Izzy decided to leave it there. It couldn't hurt.

She was bone tired, but she pulled up a chair and sat next to her father. She couldn't leave him. Sitting there watching him sleep with that lump on his head reminded her of when he'd been injured in action. He had been so strong and vibrant before his accident. Then, when he fell off a wall and hit his head, it all changed in an instant. Izzy remembered all the sleepless nights she spent by his bedside in the hospital wondering if he'd ever wake from his coma. He had, but the epidural hematoma had claimed part of him forever. She rearranged his blanket and wondered when she'd lose him. She knew she would. It was only a matter of time. The doctors made no promises and had few answers. The only thing she knew for sure was how much she'd miss him. She wondered if today's fall, this latest bump to his head, would be his undoing.

Izzy sighed and pulled a throw around her shoulders. She couldn't sleep. Her mind was buzzing with questions from the day. What was she supposed to do about Spencer? The answer came as quickly as the question had. It was time to move him out of the apartment above the bar. He didn't need to maneuver those steep stairs any more. He was not going to like it, she knew. That's why she'd been looking at places for sale in the newspaper and watching for realtor signs along streets. She wasn't looking forward to the confrontation.

And what was with Moreno? And Cal? Everyone doubted her. Then there was Apple. Why had she asked about Izzy's dizzy spells being related to the killings? What kind of a question was that?

Izzy's head started to swim. She was awake, but only semi-conscious in that place between sleeping and awakening. Her temples seared and she saw him again, the boy, watching the fire. He walked over to a woodpile and picked up a piece of wood. He put it on the flames. Something was already burning there. Izzy strained to see, but she couldn't quite make it out. She felt a chill, a moment of shadow. Then her head cleared and she was back beside her father.

Confused and afraid to close her eyes again, she stretched her leg and kicked an empty glass of water at the edge of her father's bed. It fell over with a clatter. Spencer rolled over. The ice pack fell to his pillow. Izzy retrieved it and put it on the nightstand. She sighed and watched her father, and fell into a dreamless sleep.

Chapter Seven

Monday morning, Izzy drove to the homicide offices of Miami's finest. She'd stewed most of the weekend over what had happened between Cal and Moreno. Moreno wouldn't just let it go, so she'd have to talk to him. But she worried about Cal's reaction. Would he chew her out? Maybe he'd pretend it didn't happen. *Whatever*, she thought.

She squared her shoulders, strode through the office, put her purse in her desk drawer, and set out for the morgue. She wanted to get this meeting with Dr. Dan over with, the sooner the better. She'd worked hard to steel her stomach for it. The guys had quit picking on her for vomiting at the scene, and she wanted to keep that forward momentum going. She had stacked the cards in her favor by not eating breakfast or having any coffee. Nothing there meant nothing to toss up.

From the corner of her eye, she saw Moreno walking toward the door. He fell in step behind her and trailed her down the hall like a puppy.

"Hey, Izzy," Moreno said.

Izzy didn't look at him; she just kept walking. "Hi, Moreno."

He touched her elbow. "Slow down a sec. I want to talk."

She turned to face him. Moreno looked serious. He removed the ever-present toothpick from his mouth and tucked it behind his ear. It protruded from beneath his short, buzzed haircut. This must be serious. Moreno never took the toothpick out of his mouth. He probably brushed his teeth with it in, she thought. She raised a questioning eyebrow at him. "What?"

His dark brown eyes went all soft when he looked at her, and she let down her guard a little. "So, I think I owe you an apology," he said.

Well! She'd figured he'd want her to apologize for tossing him out of the bar, but she knew she'd stand her ground on that one. Cal and Moreno were the ones who had acted like two-year-olds. Izzy crossed her arms. "Oh?"

"Yeah," he said. He retrieved the toothpick and fiddled with it between his fingers. "I shouldn't have accused you of trying to get my job."

Izzy almost fainted—she hadn't expected a real apology from Moreno, Mr. Tough Guy. "Thanks," she said. "I appreciate this."

Moreno shifted his feet. Obviously, apologizing placed him outside his natural habitat. "I know you were assigned to our team, newbie. In fact, Cal and I could have said no, but we agreed."

Izzy was sure her shock showed on her face, but Moreno didn't react to it.

"Anyway, I'm sorry," Moreno said. He put the toothpick back in his mouth and Izzy knew the apology was over. She decided to throw him a bone.

"Moreno," she said, "you grovel well." With that, she punched him on the shoulder and turned to resume walking down the hallway.

"What I'm still annoyed about is that you won't tell me what you and Cal were talking about before the poker game," he said.

Izzy sighed and rolled her eyes. She had known this was coming. She'd had a couple of days to think of a response, but none had occurred to her. She'd have to wing it.

"Look, Cal's just concerned about something personal. It'll get better," she said, forging down the stairs.

Moreno double stepped to catch up to her. He grabbed her by the elbow and turned her toward him.

"Look, Cal's my partner. I need to know. If he won't talk to me, maybe that means he doesn't trust me. Partners have to trust one another. Our lives depend on it," he said.

A strange compassion swelled inside Izzy.

"Oh, Moreno, it isn't anything like that. Cal trusts you and he isn't unhappy with you," she said, then hesitated. "At least not about anything you've done. He sure seemed annoyed that you won't let this go, though."

"Let *what* go?" he said.

"The fact that he's not ready to tell you what's going on in his personal world," Izzy said.

Moreno's dark chocolate eyes filled with concern.

"Are he and Lillian all right? Izzy, you have to tell me. I know what it's like to lose someone you love because of this job. I've been there. You know that."

Izzy patted his solid arm. Moreno had come home one night to find an empty house and a note from his wife. It almost did him in. It had been three years ago and he was still visibly hurt. "I know you do. But quit worrying. Everything is okay between Cal and Lillian. He's just..." She paused to think a moment. "He's just got a speed bump in the road and he's taking his time to get around it," she said, feeling satisfied that she hadn't divulged anything.

Moreno raised his hands over head in exasperation. "Izzy, why won't you tell me?"

Annoyed at his persistence, Izzy folded her arms across her chest and tapped her toe. "Enough with the machismo. I've told you. I'm not going to say anything. If and when Cal wants to make it your business, he will. Think of it this way if you must: Cal confided something in me. I'm keeping that confidence. Now think about how safe you'll feel if you ever confide in me knowing that I'll be able to keep my mouth shut."

Moreno softened. His eyes twinkled respect. "Okay. You win. I can appreciate that. Just promise me one thing?"

Izzy narrowed her eyes at him. "What's that?"

His eyes pleaded with her like a puppy. "Just promise me that if there's something *really* wrong with Cal, you'll let me know."

A smile tugged at the corners of Izzy's lips. "Don't worry, Moreno, I'd find a way to keep my confidence but let you know if something were horribly wrong. For now, just give Cal some space and try not to chew his head off if he barks at you. He's on edge."

Moreno looked simultaneously stunned and hurt. "You think I'd chew his head off?"

Izzy closed her eyes, took a deep breath, and turned to continue her trek to the morgue. She looked over her shoulder and said, "Look, Mr. Tough Cop, since when did you mince words?" She thought she heard his teeth clack when he closed his gaping jaw, but she continued down the hall.

Moreno fell in step behind her. "Never," he said, defiantly with a somewhat grudging tone.

Feeling a little sorry for him, she said, "You know what?"

"Hmm?"

"Down inside, I can tell you've got a marshmallow for a heart. When it gets warm, it puffs up and gets all gooey and sweet."

Moreno raised an eyebrow at her. She forged forth. "But I won't tell anyone." She lowered her voice to a whisper. "It can be *our* little secret."

She cracked the door to the morgue open with her back before he had a chance to reply. Izzy knew it wasn't over, though. She might have won the round with him, but the battle was still on. And she hadn't even seen or talked to Cal yet. Before she turned to enter, she saw Moreno blink at the cobwebs of his confusion before falling in behind her.

"Izzy—," he said.

"Moreno, it's time to get to work," she said without looking back at him. She walked into the room and heard his footsteps behind her, his tension taking up real estate.

Dr. Dan Walker stood at a table examining the blackened remains of Polly Fullerton, Friday's vic. The bright overhead light shone on his gray hair, the corpse reflected in his small glasses. The body, once stiffened by death in a crouched position was now facing up. Dr. Dan was inspecting the worst of the charring on the remains. The stench of burned flesh filled her nostrils.

Moreno looked at the corpse and then at Izzy.

"You gonna be okay with this, rookie?" Moreno said. "You're not gonna blow again, will ya? Maybe you should stand over here by the door."

"I'm good," she said but in reality she willed her stomach down. She wondered what kind of perv would do this to a young mother.

Dr. Dan continued speaking into a small digital recorder. "Victim is twenty-six years old. Bruising around the throat and neck indicates strangulation, but the deep laceration to the neck indicates cause of death as exsanguination. Victim's left ear was cut off, wrapped in paper and found near the body at the crime scene. Victim's body is badly charred on the anterior and ventral side. Lividity suggests she was placed in the fireplace after death—to look like she was kneeling—and mainly the underside of her body was severely burned."

He clicked off the recorder and looked up at Izzy and Moreno. As he did, the corpse mirrored in his glasses disappeared and his blue eyes came into view.

"Detectives, good morning," he said.

"Hi, Doc," Izzy said.

Moreno nodded in greeting and indicated the corpse with a gesture. "What have you learned?"

"I just started. I had to finish up another autopsy before this one," he said. He was still in his examination zone, Izzy could tell. He'd left his poker-playing persona back at the bar last Friday night. He was all lab coat and business here. He studied the victim again. Then, he swung the arm of the magnifier over the body and really studied. He touched her throat with a gloved hand and the crisp skin crunched.

Izzy choked. It was bad enough seeing the scorched remains of the woman again, but to smell the body and see chunks of ash disintegrate and fall off her body onto the table when Dr. Dan examined her, made Izzy's stomach remember the day her cousin ate the fish eyeball in front of her.

Dr. Dan looked at her over the rims of his glasses. "You look a little pale, Izzy. Why don't you go sit on that stool over there? It's the report that's important. You don't have to be in the middle of this."

"Thanks Doc, but I'm working on it," she said.

Dr. Dan pointed a gloved finger at a nearby drawer and said, "Moreno, get some orange oil out for her and put it in a test tube."

Moreno did as he was instructed and handed the tube to Izzy. "This should help," he said.

"Thanks." She tried to sound matter-of-fact rather than grateful. She wafted the container under her nose. The smell was strong, and it was better than the smell of seared death. Moreno, who had been all about looking tough and unbothered, leaned over toward her and took a whiff.

He was crowding her now and in order to keep from being nudged closer to the table, she shoved him away with her elbow. "Get your own, tough guy; this is mine."

Façade cracked, Moreno stood up straight. Izzy figured he'd never get his own tube. That might be construed as a sign of weakness. Fine. At least *she* hadn't hurled this time.

Izzy took another whiff. "How do you ever get used to it?" she asked Dr. Dan.

He shook his head but tended to his work. "You never get used to it. If you get used to it, desensitized to the brutality of it all, you're hardly better than the monsters who do this to people. No, you just learn to compartmentalize everything. And use it. The smell of death is part of what motivates me to keep looking, to find every clue. If I miss something, if I fail to tell you detectives one little thing that could help find a victim's killer, then I'll likely have another victim on my table very soon, and that's not acceptable."

Izzy nodded. "I feel the same. I want this guy. And I want him before he kills again."

"We all do," Moreno said.

Dr. Dan leaned over the body and scrutinized the throat. "Look at this," he said, moving his lab-coated arm out of the way.

Moreno took a long step forward and leaned over the corpse. Izzy's brain dared her to lean over the table, but her stomach warned her not to. Her toes compromised and edged her a little closer.

"Gloves. You have to wear gloves," Dr. Dan said.

Moreno pulled a pair on and handed some to Izzy. They were a couple of sizes too big and the fingertips flopped over the ends of her hands. It was hard to hold the tube of orange oil.

Dr. Dan looked up at Izzy. "Remember, you look. I touch," he said.

"You don't have to worry about me touching," Izzy said, squeezing the tube of orange oil.

Dr. Dan cleared his throat. "As I was about to say before our little interlude, the victim's hyoid bone is broken. See?" He indicated a small white bone in the midst of all the blistered flesh.

"That little white thing is a bone?" Izzy said.

"Yes. And it's broken, see? When it's intact, the hyoid bone is u-shaped. It's not attached to any other bones in the body. It's supported by surrounding muscles and ligaments."

"So, if it's not connected to anything, why is it so important?" Izzy said.

"Basically, it's what makes speech for humans possible. It supports the tongue's weight, enabling vocalization." Dr. Dan indicated his throat with one lean hand.

Moreno looked at the bone through the magnifying glass. "When it's broken, it's a sign of strangulation."

"Very good, detective." The doctor nodded his approval. "Since the hyoid bone is extremely hard to break, when we find it broken, forensically we see it as an indicator that the victim was strangled."

"I don't understand. You just said that cause of death was exsanguination. Now you're saying she was strangled," said Izzy.

"Ah," said Dr. Dan. He looked up and the bright light reflected off his glasses. "I see your confusion. Not all forms of strangulation cause death. Controlled strangulation, sometimes used in martial arts or even in law enforcement, can be used to suppress a victim without killing him or her. I think that's what happened in this case."

"So she was unconscious before he slit her throat?" Izzy asked, covering her throat with her gloved hands.

"Yes. She was still alive, as evidenced by the blood spattering. The arterial spray at the scene doesn't indicate movement or struggling on her part. The blood's all in one general area—on the couch, the nearby wall and then, of course, on the floor. Her heart was still pumping, but she wasn't conscious."

Izzy heaved a sigh of relief. "At least she didn't know what was happening."

"So, you've dismissed the blood spatter folks on this one?" Moreno asked.

"Yes. I feel confident that I'm right. Besides, Batina, the blood spatter specialist, went out to the scene and she concurs that it's pretty cut and dried," he said.

"Nice choice of words, Doc," said Izzy.

The doctor's face flushed red. "I didn't mean..." He shrugged it off and resumed his duties.

"What about the ear?" asked Moreno.

Dr. Dan set the magnifying glass aside. "It was cut off after she was dead. No evidence of blood circulating when it was removed."

"Thank heaven for that," Izzy said.

"Did you find any prints? Any sign of struggle?" Moreno said. "*Anything* for us to go on?"

Dr. Dan shook his head. "Not yet, anyway."

Izzy tapped her chin with a gloved finger. "So, Polly Fullerton knew her attacker."

Moreno nodded in agreement. "Looks that way," he said. "Do you think we have a copy cat murderer on our hands?"

The doctor looked at the remains and shook his head. "All the evidence shows the same *modus operandi*," he said, examining the throat again. "All three of our victims so far have been rendered unconscious before their throats were slit. All three had a body part cut off. The post mortem mutilation takes a different form each time." He indicated the corpse on his table. "Aside from that, everything is consistent with two exceptions."

Izzy leaned in as close as she dared. "What?" she said.

"This time, the body part was wrapped in paper," said Moreno.

"Correct."

"And the other difference?" Izzy said.

"Look here," Dr. Dan said. He took a stainless steel probe and lifted the victim's hair near the nape of her neck.

"What are we looking at?" Izzy said.

"Just like the other victims, a piece of scalp has been removed along with the hair," Dr. Dan said. "But the area removed is much larger on this victim."

"So?" Moreno said.

Dr. Dan pulled off his examination gloves. "So either our perp got clumsy or purposefully took a larger souvenir this time. In short, I think Izzy might have been right the other night. It's possible our perp may be evolving."

Izzy shuddered. "And becoming even more dangerous."

Moreno leaned over the body and pointed at something shiny in the victim's hair.

"What's that?" he asked. "Why is this patch of hair different than the rest?"

Dr. Dan scrutinized the patch of hair.

Moreno and Izzy watched. Dr. Dan's gaze rose slowly from the shiny area to Izzy's face. He didn't look happy.

Uncomfortable now, Izzy said, "What?"

With a scowl on his face, Dr. Dan asked, "Where's that tube of orange oil, rookie?"

"Right here," Izzy said. She raised a gloved hand. The test tube was gone. Her gaze shot to Dr. Dan's. His eyes were narrowed to slits and his lips were one thin line.

"That's right," he said, in an icy tone. "You dropped your test tube. You'd better be thankful that it didn't spill on anything more than a patch of hair, or some defense attorney would have a real axe to grind."

Izzy's heart stopped. She wanted to crawl into a refrigerated corpse locker and hide. How could she have messed up again? Compromising evidence was bad. Real bad. She could get written up for this. "I'm so sorry," she said.

Dr. Dan looked like he might explode. He squared his shoulders and looked at Moreno. "Detective," he said, "get your rookie out of my morgue."

Chapter Eight

Mark Traesk drove his late-model Lincoln Navigator into the circle driveway of a large, two-story home painted pale yellow. It was a luxury neighborhood on the southwest side of Miami, houses costing nearly a million dollars on average. He looked at the client in his car and thought of the tidy commission she could bring. And he definitely could use the money. He made sure he parked under the large palm tree growing in the middle of the driveway. He wanted his client to notice the beautiful landscaping.

"This house is a peach," he said. "There's lots of room for entertaining inside as well as out back. Let me show you. I think it's exactly what you're looking for."

He got out of the car and walked around to open the door for the woman sitting in the front seat. She sat there, touching up her lipstick, poofing her hair, making no attempt to leave the car. She was clearly waiting for him to open the door for her. That was okay with him. He was used to the kind of high-end, high-needs clients who wanted to be waited on when he showed them houses. He'd even had one who wanted him to serve champagne to her while she looked through homes. He'd declined, not wanting to get a ticket for having an open container in his car and not thinking that his client could make a good choice on a home while inebriated. He didn't have that client anymore. Oh well.

He smiled at this client, Lolly Glad. What a name. Her real name was Lolita, "But all my friends call me Lolly—and I'm sure we'll be great friends," she had told him. He opened the door to the car for her, but she had her face in the mirror, as usual, applying even more mascara—if that were possible.

"I'll just be a sec, Mark," she said. "I'm touching up. You know the expression, 'Be as cute as you can be.' But for me, it's more than an expression. It's my motto."

She closed the mirror on the visor, put her makeup back in her purse, placed her knees firmly together, turned toward the open door and put her perfectly-manicured feet adorned in four-inch high-heeled stilettos on the driveway. It was a good thing she kept those knees together, thought Mark. If her skirt were any shorter, she wouldn't need it.

"Where to first?" she asked him, making an effort to adjust her very round, very plastic bosom.

He had to make a conscious effort to keep his eyes on her face. "Let's go inside first," he said.

He indicated that she should walk in front of him. He was only trying to be polite by asking her to precede him, but the tall, slender blonde walked like a woman in a beauty pageant—deliberately placing one foot in front of the other to make her hips sway. Her form-fitting clothing left little to the imagination, and Mark felt himself getting hard. He felt guilty about it too. It wasn't right. But he wasn't lusting after her—it was just a natural thing, he thought. He watched her walk toward the door and was glad he had baggy pants on. Maybe she wouldn't notice. He tried to think of something bland to get his mind elsewhere. It wasn't easy. She exuded sex from her very pores as if it were cheap perfume.

He excused himself and reached in front of her to open the lock box on the door, which held the key to the house.

"As you can see, Mrs. Glad, the spacious entry way leads directly into the large living room. That's great for entertaining," he said.

She took a step inside the door and looked around. "I like the French doors leading from the living room out onto the back patio," she said.

Mark's spirits leapt. He might actually sell this house. It was about time. He'd been dragging this woman all over Miami for days. And it was embarrassing and frustrating to have her constantly flirt and carry on with him like she did. He'd just have to continue to redirect her when she came on to him. He would never make a pass at a client, it could ruin his business. And he needed the money. Yes, a sale of this size would be sweet. He wasn't broke, but he was supporting his mother, his disabled brother, and his church. The Lord had never let him down yet, surely a sale would come soon.

Lolly was roaming around the living room, examining the Italian tile floors, the tall white pillars, the ornate doorknobs, and other custom touches.

Mark led the way to the left. "The bedrooms are this way," he said. "How many children did you say you and your husband have?" he asked, hoping three large bedrooms would be sufficient.

"Oh, we never had any children," she said. "Having children ruins a woman's figure, you know, so I never wanted any of the little beasts."

Mark's shock must have shown on his face because Lolly laughed and said, "Don't worry. That's a perfectly normal reaction. Most people think I'm quite strange when I tell them that. But the truth is, my husband is a plastic surgeon and he's very busy. He didn't want children either, and he was quite content with my decision not to ruin my body." She posed for Mark, then continued. "You see, I've already had a tummy tuck. That was quite painful, and to think that I'd have to have one after each child—well, that just wasn't acceptable," she said.

Mark didn't know what to say, so he didn't respond.

"How about you, Mark Traesk? Any kids?"

"No, I've never been married."

"I didn't ask if you'd been married, I asked if you had kids." She dabbed at the corner of her lipstick with her pinky.

Embarrassed, Mark looked at his shoes. "No, never married, no kids," he said.

She walked over to him and ran her finger with a long, polished fingernail down his chest. "A good boy," she said. "An innocent one, I like that."

He turned away. "I'm uncomfortable with this conversation, Mrs. Glad," Mark said. "Let's look at the house."

Lolly sniffed a laugh. "You must think I'm a despicable flirt. Well I am, but don't worry, I'm a happily married woman. I don't cheat on my husband. I was just having a little fun. I like to tease men and then go home to my husband."

"I'm happy for you both," Mark mumbled. He crossed the living room to the right and indicated the kitchen. "Let's look in here," he said.

Lolly abandoned the hallway leading to the bedrooms and followed him. The counters were marble and the cupboards had a hand-rubbed finish. The refrigerator took up real estate of its own and the eight-burner gas range had a warming drawer beneath it. Four drawer-type dishwashers were next to the sink. If she didn't love this kitchen with all its fancy bells and whistles, Mark didn't know what she'd like. She was picky—this was the thirtieth house he'd shown her. He was getting a little tired of her constant primping and bragging. A dose of humble pie would do her good.

"I love the kitchen," she said finally. "And the laundry room is very spacious. I like that it's down by the kitchen. I'm not a fan of houses where the laundry room is near the bedrooms. Bedrooms are for relaxing." She winked.

Again, he ignored her flirting and opened a door leading outside. They walked through and explored the covered patio complete with a wet bar, a built-in gas grill and a fire pit. A circular pool lay beyond the patio and a hot tub was nestled in a corner just outside the master bedroom.

"Nice pool," she said. "I like the high fence, too. I don't like tan lines."

Not knowing what else to do or say, Mark simply nodded.

Lolly walked over to the hot tub. She slipped off a shoe and stuck a manicured toe into the gently swirling water. "It's hot." She sounded surprised. "I guess I figured they'd turn the heat off."

Mark crossed the U-shaped patio and joined her. "I like to show homes that are set up and move-in ready."

Lolly continued across the patio and turned the doorknob to the master bedroom. It was unlocked, and Mark followed her in. The room was as large as most living rooms. An adjoining sitting room was tucked into one corner. The bathroom offered a claw-footed tub perched in front of a spacious walk-through shower sporting multiple body jets and a rain bonnet showerhead. His and hers closets were at opposite ends of the shower, each with built-in chests of drawers and three levels of hanging space for clothing.

Lolly pouted. "The closet is so small, I'd have to use one in one of the other bedrooms."

Mark tried not to let his amazement show.

"I have lots of pretty clothes," she said. "I don't believe in wearing the same outfit more than once in any two-week period." She pouted again. "You can't be as cute as you can be if you're recycling outfits."

"I see," Mark said, and then, in an effort to change the subject, "You said you like to entertain? What type of entertaining?"

Lolly walked over to him and put her hand on his arm. Her long, acrylic fingernails were adorned with tiny gems, strategically placed so they wouldn't chip off.

"I'm a saleswoman," she said. "I hold parties where ladies do makeovers and if they want a little extra something to make themselves beautiful, my husband will perform a minor procedure right then. He smooths out the wrinkles. There's never any obligation, of course."

She looked around the room and her gaze fell on Mark. "You look so surprised," she said. "Think of it this way. Ladies put their lips on to look extra pretty.

56

Jewelers take diamonds and if they have a slight flaw, they may laser the flaws out so that the diamonds really sparkle. This treatment does the same thing. That's why we want three bedrooms. One room will serve as a small surgical suite and the other will be a guest bedroom."

Stunned, Mark managed, "I see. I suppose turning a bedroom into a surgical suite will require a major renovation."

"Money isn't an issue. We'll have it done in a matter of weeks."

Lolly looked around the room. She stood unnaturally straight and her breasts protruded even farther, her bulbous silicone inserts swollen to almost bursting. Mark thought that although her chest looked fake, it was still lovely and creamy. He started to get hard again and guilt swept over him.

"They are nice, aren't they?" Lolly said, daintily caressing her bosom with a finger.

Jarred back into the moment, Mark said, "Excuse me?"

"I saw you looking. It's okay. If I didn't want men to look at me, I wouldn't have gone to the trouble to make myself so beautiful," she said, posing again.

Mark cleared his throat. "I'm sorry. I shouldn't have…I was just…I'm sorry."

Lolly laughed out loud. "I bet you've never been with a woman, especially one like me."

Mark felt his face grow hot. "Mrs. Glad, being humble is a good thing. And so is patience. I'm trying to be patient with you. Please stop making remarks like that, or I'll have to end our professional relationship."

Lolly's eyes flew wide in disbelief. She took a step

backward. "I've offended you," she said. "That's a first. I apologize."

Mark nodded graciously. "Apology accepted. Now, let's stick to task. What do you think about the house?"

"House? No, let's not talk about that yet. It's your turn to apologize," she said.

"I'm sorry," Mark said. "Apologize?"

Lolly put on a pouty face.

"Yes. I'm offended too. I'm offended that you won't play my little game."

This woman was certifiable, Mark thought. But he didn't want to lose this sale.

"I didn't mean to offend, Mrs. Glad. But I do wish to stick to business. What do you think about the house?"

Lolly snorted slightly.

"I think it has potential," Lolly said. "We'll put it on the short list to show my husband."

Mark's heart sank. He'd shown her so many houses already and now they had one more—for a total of ten—on her so-called short list. He wondered if he'd ever actually make a sale to this woman. He wanted to and needed to, but he knew he couldn't bank on it. He'd seen high-end clients like this before. Some just pretended to be looking for a new home when really all they wanted was to see the latest in expensive decorating trends. Needing a sale, he decided he'd have to put up with this hideous woman and her husband at least a little while longer.

Mark had one more home to show her today. He held the car door for her while she got in. He had plenty of time to walk around to the driver's side, because he knew Lolly would have to check her lipstick in the mirror. He only prayed that prancing around in those stiletto heels hadn't shifted her bosom. He didn't think he could bear to watch another adjustment. He put his sunglasses on and pulled out of the driveway.

Chapter Nine

He was well dressed in his favorite lightweight suit. It was a shade of blue somewhat deeper than navy, but lighter than black. His white shirt was tucked neatly into his waistband, and the pale blue and white striped tie coordinated with his gray eyes. His blond hair was swept to one side. His black shoes looked good from the top. He'd gotten a marker pen and colored in the scratches on the toes. Unless you were really looking, you wouldn't notice them. The holes in the soles of his shoes weren't obvious unless he crossed his legs when he sat down. He was careful to keep his feet flat when sitting. It was important to Paul Winters that he look good at all times. He might be out of a job and homeless, but he didn't have to dress the part.

He paused to gaze at his reflection in the plate glass window of the department store. Yes, he looked very put together. He entered the store and walked toward the TV section. A clerk in hardware nodded to him.

Paul smiled and nodded. He walked over to the TVs, Bible in hand. This was his daily routine. He came every day, at precisely 4:55 p.m. to hear Brother Gideon preach. He changed the channel on all the television sets and turned the volume up so he could be surrounded by God's word.

The twenty-five-member choir dressed in red

cottas and white surpluses sang "Amazing Grace" while the camera faded in. Soon, a tall, thin man, Brother Gideon, took the stage. He thanked the choir for their music ministry.

"Today's lesson is about patience," he said. "Have you ever known anyone who was not patient?"

Paul nodded at the TV.

"Let's read from our Bibles what God says about patience," Brother Gideon said.

Paul clutched his Bible, ready to turn the pages.

"Turn with me to Romans, chapter 12, verse 12," Brother Gideon said.

Paul turned quickly to the chapter and verse, ready to follow along.

Brother Gideon looked out into the studio congregation then straight into the camera.

"Be joyful in hope, patient in affliction, faithful in prayer," Brother Gideon said.

"Amen, Brother!" Paul shouted.

"Now, follow along in your Bibles to Psalms 37:7-9," Brother Gideon said. "The Bible says, 'Be still in the presence of the Lord, and wait patiently for him to act.' Don't worry about evil people who prosper or fret about their wicked schemes. Stop being angry! Turn from your rage! Do not lose your temper—it only leads to harm. For the wicked will be destroyed, but those who trust in the Lord will possess the land."

Paul held his hands in a prayerful gesture. He stood listening to every word that Brother Gideon had to say.

A middle-aged woman wearing a white blouse and a blue polka-dotted skirt approached. Her bounteous hips set her skirt swaying. She stopped right in front of him, blocking his view.

"Sir?" she said.

Paul looked at her, then tried to see the TV around her.

"Sir, I'm the manager here, and I'm going to have to ask you to leave," she said.

"Why?" Paul asked. "Don't you like the Lord?"

"It doesn't have anything to do with that," she said. "But every day you come in at the same time, you blast every TV on the same channel and you watch the same show. Sir, we are not a living room. Perhaps I could interest you in a TV set? We have payment plans, if you'd like."

The blood in Paul's veins turned hot. "You're just like the rest. You say you love the Lord, but when someone like me wants to share the word, you try to shut me down."

"Sir, please. I'm not trying to argue."

Paul paced back and forth along the row of TVs. He pulled at his hair and stopped in front of her.

"They didn't want to listen to me when I told them about God at my office, either. They told me I should stop. Finally they made me leave. Now they're sorry."

The manager walked to a nearby service desk and picked up the phone.

"Ninety-nine to Electronics, please," she paged.

Paul's gaze darted from the TVs to the woman. Brother Gideon wasn't finished talking about God yet, but Paul knew the manager had called security. He looked at her and indicated the television sets.

"He's talking about patience. In Proverbs, the Bible says 'A man's wisdom gives him patience; it is to his glory to overlook an offense,'" Paul said. "You should listen to Brother Gideon. You should overlook my offense and let me stay."

The manager shook her head at him, hands on hips.

A security guard turned the corner and walked over to Paul. His heart quickened in his chest. They were really going to make him leave. They were going to keep him from listening to God's word.

"Is this man causing you trouble?" the guard asked.

She nodded.

The guard pointed at the door. "You're going to have to leave."

Paul shook his head. "But Brother Gideon isn't done talking."

The guard took a set of handcuffs off his belt and showed them to Paul. "We can do this the easy way or the hard way."

Paul started singing loudly. "Lift high the cross, the love of God proclaim…"

A crowd of onlookers started to gather.

The security guard moved toward Paul, cuffs extended. Paul gripped his Bible tight to his chest.

"You may want to persecute me," he said. "But God is on my side and he will smite you. Romans 9:22 'What if God, choosing to show his wrath and make his power known, bore with great patience the objects of his wrath—and prepared for destruction?' God will destroy you."

The guard took another step closer. Paul dropped to his knees and said, "Forgive them, Father, for they know not what they do."

Chapter Ten

Izzy and Moreno stood behind Cal, each leaning over one of his shoulders looking at the report the forensics lab had sent over. Izzy was a bit nervous. This was her first encounter with Cal since the altercation at the bar.

Cal pointed to a line on the report. "The perp used an inkjet printer."

Izzy watched as he pointed and flipped the page. Obviously he wasn't mad at her—at least he didn't seem to be—but then again, maybe he was just saving it for when they were alone. He tapped his finger on the page and Izzy was drawn back into the now. She read quickly to catch up. She didn't want them to know she'd been snoozing. She knew that the lab could identify the brand of printer based on the lay of the ink on the paper and by the font formation. Determining the exact printer however, was another story. "An inkjet printer? Not much to go on," she said. "Lots of people have those."

Cal turned the page with a chubby hand. "Well, at least we have this," he said, pointing to a paragraph on the page. The lab had run the paper through the electrostatic detection device, which revealed unique physical markings left on documents by any given printer.

"Yeah," said Cal. "Those markings are good and

this particular printer is missing a few pixels of ink in the top left quadrant. So we should be able to match pages printed by that machine forensically."

Moreno looked exasperated. "I just want something more than a printer to go on. Anything to go on," he said. The ever-present toothpick twirled in his mouth.

Izzy nodded. "Me too."

"We'll check suspects' printers," Cal said. "If the printer markings match the ones on the paper we have, we've got a piece of hard evidence."

Moreno nodded. "Now all we need is a suspect."

Cal looked up at Moreno. "Most people know their killers. You and Izzy go talk to friends, relatives, neighbors. Collect samples from printers and bring them to the lab for examination."

Moreno nodded.

"What about the ink?" asked Izzy. "Did the lab have any luck making sense out of what was printed under all that blood?"

Cal glanced at all the papers in disarray on his desk. He ran a chubby hand over the bald spot on his head. "I know I have that report here somewhere," he said. He rifled through several piles on his desk. Finally, he picked up a folder and flipped through it. He ran his finger along as he read. "Blah, blah, blah, solvent evaporation, blah, blah—Here it is."

Izzy leaned in closer. She could smell Cal's aftershave. He was such a dyed-in-the-wool cop. He never, ever changed his spice island scent. It made her smile for a moment, then she focused again on what she was supposed to be reading. She raised a critical eyebrow.

"Bible verses?" she said. "He wrapped the ear in

Bible verses?"

"Okay. That's strange," said Moreno. "What did they say?"

Cal flipped to another page in the report and a printout of a page with faded, reconstructed print emerged. He read,

"Ephesians 4:2 'With all humility and gentleness, with patience, bearing with one another in love.'

"James 1:19 'Know this, my beloved brothers: let every person be quick to hear, slow to speak, slow to anger.'

"1 Corinthians 13:4 'Love is patient and kind; love does not envy or boast; it is not arrogant.'"

Moreno ran a hand through his short, black hair. "Wow, that's weird," he said. "What do you think it means?"

Cal snorted. "It means this guy's a religious nut case."

Izzy stared at the paper and felt the familiar flash of excitement that accompanied one of her plausible theories. "Look at the theme," she said. "There's a reference to patience in each verse." She put her hand on Cal's shoulder and leaned in a little closer, his aftershave wafting toward her again. "Obviously this guy's a nut job, but what if he thinks he's doing God's work?"

Moreno's dark eyes met hers and then shifted to Cal. "Our newbie could be onto something, you know." He shuffled through a file on Cal's desk.

Izzy beamed inside. Moreno had said *our* newbie. Plus he had said she might be right. She was determined not to show her excitement. "Any radical clergy in the area that we know about?" Izzy said.

Moreno shook his head. "None that I'm aware of. You, Cal?"

Cal furrowed his brow in thought. "I haven't heard anything or seen any reports to that effect." He picked up his pen and made a note. "But it's something we should definitely look into."

Izzy's heart leapt. They had taken her seriously. She had to stick to task and not blow anything. This could help turn things around for her. Right here, right now.

Moreno's fingers rifled through files. "The other women linked to this killer, what body parts were removed?"

Izzy shuddered. "Let's review. The first victim, Mary Hanson, a strawberry blonde, had her left hand chopped off."

Moreno pulled a picture out of the file. "Yeah, I remember," he said, pointing to the severed hand in the picture.

Cal huffed. "Robbery obviously wasn't a motive. Look at the size of the rock on that ring," he said.

Izzy steeled her stomach to the gory pictures, flipped through the file and continued. "An African-American woman, Lakisha Brown was next. Dr. Dan said her heart was cut out." *Ugh.* She was glad in a way that she had just made detective when that murder was committed a couple of months ago and she hadn't had to process the scene. She wrinkled her nose and remembered reading the particularly grisly details and recalled the crime scene pictures with all the blood.

She regrouped and went on. "Polly Fullerton, our most recent victim, was blonde and is missing an ear," Izzy absently rubbed her lobe. "I don't see any physical connection. Most serial killers have a type they like. This guy is all over the place with his hair trophies—strawberry blonde, black, blonde—there's no connection. What's the type here?" She paused for a beat and then continued. "And what's the significance of the body parts he's cutting off?"

Cal drummed his fingers on the desk. "It just seems so random. But it can't be."

His voice trailed off to nothingness. She ached to know the answer. She pushed her long hair behind her ears and leaned forward to look through the files. Although she'd done it a hundred times before, she filtered through the files yet again, hoping that some clue, *any* shred of a clue would come to her.

"We're missing something," she said. "There's got to be something right here in front of us that we're just not seeing."

Cal shifted in his seat and rolled his chair a few inches away from the desk. The overhead fluorescent light reflected off his bald spot. "Three murders in just a couple of months." He looked at Moreno who stood over the desk with his brow furrowed. "Now it looks like he's taking a bigger trophy—you know, the bigger chunk of scalp Dr. Dan found missing? If Izzy's right and he's evolving—or at the very least getting braver—he might step up the pace of the killings."

Moreno shook his head slowly and shrugged. "How is he identifying his victims?"

Izzy taped pre-murder pictures of each of the victims to the white board in Cal's office. She took a pen and labeled each one with the date that she was murdered, then moved a step back and looked at them. Each vic looked so different.

Moreno twirled his toothpick. "What's the connection?" he said.

Cal tapped his pencil on the desk. "Well, not race. This guy seems to be an equal opportunity killer, that's for sure."

Moreno shrugged. "I'm going to state the obvious. They're all women."

Izzy picked up her cup of coffee and took a sip. "And of various ages," she said. "A mixture of married and single. Some had kids, some didn't."

Cal shook his head and rubbed his bald spot. "I don't think that's the connection."

"Me either," Izzy said, pushing a stray lock of auburn hair behind her ear with her empty hand. "I don't see a thing but the cutting after they're dead."

"And what about the burning?" Cal said. "Didn't the neighbors smell anything?"

"These women were all found either in remote areas or in their own homes in neighborhoods that are basically abandoned during the day because people work," Izzy said. "Nobody would smell flesh burning, and the Miami wind always blows, so fireplace smoke would dissipate quickly."

Moreno looked at her and pursed his lips in thought.

Izzy's vision blurred suddenly and her temples blazed with fiery white pain. She dropped her mug. It hit the floor with a crash and coffee splashed everywhere. Her knees buckled and she sank to the floor holding her burning temples in her hands, the knees of her slacks soaking up the lukewarm coffee on the floor.

"Izzy!" she heard Moreno say.

She looked in the direction of his voice, but all she could see was a blur of tawny skin, swimmy muscled arms reaching toward her and another voice—Cal's? It sounded like it was being played on an old tape recorder in extreme slow motion. Strong arms laid her down gently and held her hand. Other hands put something under her feet to raise them up.

Her head began to clear and she could make out Cal's words. "Get some water," he shouted over his shoulder into the bullpen office.

"No," Izzy protested, her vision returning. "I'm okay. Really." She tried to sit up.

Moreno gently pushed her back down to the floor. "People who are okay don't suddenly drop coffee mugs and land on the floor next to the ceramic bits."

"Where's that water, damn it?" Cal yelled.

"On its way," called a voice in the background.

Izzy succumbed and lay back down. In Moreno's eyes, she saw true concern. He held her hand and she let him.

"What? Did you faint?" he said.

"No, I don't think so," Izzy said. "I've had a few of these sudden headaches lately—and I just got dizzy."

"When's the last time you ate, Izzy?" Cal said.

"Lunch. I had lunch," she said.

"What? A diet Coke and a carrot stick?" Cal scoffed.

"No," Izzy said indignantly. "I had a burrito from the man on the corner."

"We grabbed lunch together. I had the same thing," Moreno said. "It was good. His burritos are always good. It wasn't anything she ate."

Cal looked at Moreno who was still holding Izzy's

hand. "You pregnant?" he asked.

Shocked, Izzy dropped Moreno's hand and glared at Cal. "No, Cal, I'm not. In case you missed biology class that day, you have to have sex to get pregnant."

Cal looked away from her and said, "Hmph."

Clattering sounds came up behind him. He stepped out of the way, and a tall stranger with soft blue eyes crouched over her, carrying a glass of water. Someone else carrying a first aid kit knelt down on the other side and checked her pulse.

She tried to sit up.

"Take your time," Moreno said, resting a reassuring hand on her shoulder. "Don't get up too fast, Izzy O."

She rested on her elbows.

The tall man with the water gave her the glass. She thanked him, took a sip and handed it back.

"You say you've been having episodes like this," Cal said. "Maybe we should call the paramedics."

Her pride bruised and her clothes soggy from the coffee, Izzy pushed Moreno, the tall man and the pulse taker aside. "Look, I'm just fine. I don't need the paramedics and I don't need medical care," she said. "It's probably just a migraine."

The guys tending her glanced at each other and up at Cal seeking guidance.

Cal stood with his hands on his hips. "She's really stubborn," he said.

Moreno nodded. "You have no idea."

Izzy harrumphed. "Look, I'm all good," she said. "Now, let me up." She struggled a bit and sat upright. Her head swam a little, but she didn't want to admit it.

"She seems okay," the tall guy said. He turned to

Izzy. "I don't see any sign of trauma—no bumps or bruises—I'm no expert, but if you've been having episodes like this, you should probably see a doctor."

Izzy brushed her shoulders off with her hands. "I'll bear that in mind. Now, if you gentlemen will excuse me, I have work to do." She stood up and started through the assembled crowd.

"Not so fast," Cal said, extending his palm to her in a "stop right there" gesture. "You need to go to the hospital and get checked out, *now*."

"No I don't. I'm okay," Izzy protested. "I'm not going to the hospital."

Cal looked agitated.

"You can't work cases in this condition," he said.

"Cal, if it will make you happy, I'll make an appointment to see my doctor, but I'm not going to the hospital. Look at me. I'm all right," she said. "Good as new, with a bit of a headache."

No one spoke. Moreno's face was filled with concern. Cal had sunk back into his chair and was rubbing the crown of his head. Izzy wondered if that's how he went bald. She was irked she just couldn't get a break. Just when she did something right on this case, she had to have one of her blasted headache spells.

Moreno reached his hand out toward her. She stepped away and said, "It's all good. See?" She shot him her very best "back off" look and he withdrew his hand.

"We have a perp to catch. Let's get on it," she said.

"Not so fast," Moreno said in his best macho voice.

Oh great, Izzy thought. Here it comes.

He wagged a finger in her direction. "You don't get to hit the deck like that and then expect us to believe that nothing happened," he said. "Give. Tell us."

Cal swiveled in his chair and looked at Izzy. "You heard the man. Give."

"If I tell you, you're not going to like it," she said, looking at Cal. "And you'll make too much out of it," she said looking at Moreno.

They stared back at her. Four eyeballs slowly drilling holes in her façade, perforating her tough cop veneer.

"All right," she said. "I've been having these spells lately. I get this searing pain in my temples, I get weak-kneed and then it's over."

"Yeah, we got that much. What's the rest of the story?" Moreno said, hands on hips.

She glanced sideways at Cal. "This is the part you won't like," she said. She looked at Moreno. "When I have the pain, sometimes I see things."

"Like little pink elephants?" Cal scoffed.

"No, like vision things," Izzy said.

Cal tossed his head back and guffawed. "Not that again. Please, anything but that again."

Izzy looked at Moreno for help. "I told you," she said.

Seriously, Moreno said, "What do you see, Izzy?"

"Never mind," she said, sorry she'd mentioned anything in front of them. "Cal's right. I see pink elephants. Let it go. I'll go get some ibuprofen and move on."

"Yeah. Move on. You can't see bullshit," Cal said. He slapped the palm of his hand against his forehead. "And to think I was going to call the paramedics. I should call the loony bin." His steely gaze swung to Moreno. "Both of you, out of my office. Now! Get outta here. I don't have time for this bullshit. I have a murderer to catch."

Moreno took Izzy by the elbow and led her to the door. Cal followed and stopped in the doorway.

"Get yourself checked out by a doctor," Cal said. "If there's nothing wrong with you, then quit eating spicy burritos for lunch. We have work to do. And for God's sake—"

Here it comes.

"Requisition some gloves in your size," Cal bellowed. "Dr. Dan called up here screaming that you'd dropped a tube of orange oil on his victim. Took me ten minutes to calm him down. You owe me for that one, rookie. Compromising evidence—I'll report you myself if it happens again." He closed the door roughly behind them. It was barely this side of a slam.

Izzy looked up. All activity in the bullpen had ceased. All eyes stared at her. Horrified that everyone had heard about her *faux pas* in the morgue and embarrassed by her latest little stunt here in the office, she thought again of crawling into a corpse locker. But, she'd have to get past Dr. Dan to procure one, and there were sharp instruments in the morgue that he might use against her. This was definitely a day from hell. She should have stayed in bed.

Moreno's grip on her elbow tightened slightly. She wiggled, trying to break free from him. He squeezed it a little tighter yet. She indicated that people were staring and snapped him a glance that made him let go. She nodded for him to follow her down the hall and was grateful that he took her meaning. They walked a few steps away from Cal's door and out of everyone else's view.

"Izzy," he whispered, "what do you see, really?"

She softened a bit and looked into his dark, coffee eyes. She ached to tell someone. Her best shot at having anyone believe her would be Moreno. His grandma was a *curandera*, so mystical wasn't mystery to him.

"Fire, mostly," she said. "And an adolescent boy. But he doesn't seem to be in danger. He likes it by the fire. It's a bonfire. After poker the other night, I had an episode and it looked like the kid might have been stoking the fire. It all went blank pretty quick."

"Did you see the same thing just now?"

"No. I saw the number seven," she said.

"What does it mean?" he said.

She shook her head but held his gaze. Ego and pride bruised, she wished she had an answer other than the one she was about to give him. "I have no idea," she said.

Chapter Eleven

There she was again. Dressed in those slutty clothes. He sat and watched her now like he'd been doing for weeks, learning her patterns, her movements, her life. It was important to know, to be certain that a cleansing was necessary.

Brother Hamor always took his time in selecting those who needed help. He would never rush in to do God's hard work. It was easy to tell people about God, but when it came to cleansings, people misunderstood and used words like murderer, killer, and freak. That wasn't right or fair. Doing God's will was a duty, a privilege, and as such, it took a great deal of time to be sure.

He knew it was time for the cleansing. Besides, he was tired of following her around the streets of Miami until she picked up a john. Surely this woman could find another way to make money.

A car pulled up to her alongside the curb, the passenger window went down. She bent over and leaned in, her heels so tall and skirt so short all that was left was legs. She and the driver exchanged some words; she straightened, opened the car door and got in.

It was over. He decided not to follow her and wait outside some sleazy hotel all night to verify her activities. By now, he knew the drill. She'd be there all night.

He pulled away from the curb and made a U-turn. Yes, it was time for prayer and a cleansing.

Chapter Twelve

Izzy and Moreno sat at their desks that took up real estate in homicide. Research, phone calls, and paperwork were all part of the job. They were both deep in thought when Izzy's phone chirped.

"O'Donnell," she said.

Moreno looked up from his computer screen.

"We'll go check it out," Izzy said and closed her phone.

"What we got?" Moreno said.

"That was Lieutenant Boggs. He said the manager at Rico's Electronics called to say she's been following the accounts of the murders and read about the religious references surrounding them. She apparently had to have security escort a religious fanatic out of the store a couple days ago. When she read we were asking the public to report anything unusual she decided to call."

"So where are we headed?" Moreno said.

"The place is just off Dixie Highway," she said.

They made their way to the car and headed in the direction of the store. When they arrived, Moreno and Izzy found the manager, Lupita Vazquez, and the electronics clerk, Karl Freedman. They walked over to the TVs to get a visual on how it all went down.

"He always dresses real nice," Karl said. "He comes in every day precisely five minutes before his show. Like it was a religion. Guess that sounds funny since he was watching that TV preacher."

"That guy's a lunatic," Lupita said. "Every day, same thing. Tune every TV to the same channel—the one with that televangelist. He'd turn the volume up so high that people were covering their ears and moving to other parts of the store. I couldn't have it any more. He wasn't buying, and the paying customers wanted to leave."

Izzy smiled. "Sounds like a real character. You know his name or where he lives?"

"No—he lives on the streets around here some place. Sometimes he'd talk to me when I went on break for a smoke," Karl said. "You might check St. Joe's shelter down the street."

"St. Joe's? Even they wouldn't want a nut case like that guy," Lupita said.

Izzy glanced at Moreno. "We'll check it out anyway," he said. "May we have a copy of the picture you got off the surveillance cameras?"

"Yeah," Karl said. "Here it is."

"Just look at him," Lupita said. "He's a freak. Look at him kneeling on the floor, praying like that in the middle of all these TVs."

Izzy took the picture from the clerk. Lupita was right. There was a guy kneeling in prayer surrounded by TVs all tuned to the same channel. Expecting grunge and rags, she was surprised when the picture showed a man who looked like he belonged in a corporate office. She gave Lupita and Karl her card and asked them to call if they thought of anything else.

Izzy and Moreno left the store and walked down the street toward St. Joe's. They stopped in shops and businesses along the way but nobody recognized the man. When they got to St. Joe's, Moreno approached the reception desk with the picture in hand. He showed his badge to the clerk and asked if she knew the man in the picture.

"Sure, that's Paul Winters," she said.

"Does he live here?" Moreno asked.

"Live here? Nobody lives here. You can only stay here for two weeks at a time. Then you have to move on to give someone else a chance to stay here and get on their feet."

"Is he here now?" Izzy said.

"He's in and out. He stays for two weeks, then he has to move on like the rest. After a while, he's back for another two-week stint," the receptionist said.

"When was the last time you saw him?" Izzy said.

"He left about three days ago," the receptionist said. "Said something about having to do God's work. And then he was gone."

"Did he mention what that meant?" Moreno said.

"Sort of," she said. "He said he was going to help a Brother Gideon."

Chapter Thirteen

About six thirty that evening, Izzy blew through the door of the bar. She was in a rush to make sure her dad wasn't around. Today was the day to meet Mark Traesk, the realtor, to discuss looking for a one-story place for him. She didn't want her dad to know, though. After her passing-out episode at work today, she didn't need any more drama. The only thing she lacked for becoming a complete drama queen was a coronation ceremony.

The door closed behind her and she swept the room with a glance. Apple was washing glasses in the sink behind the bar and Izzy was relieved to find Spencer nowhere in sight. She walked behind the bar.

Apple looked up from the sink, her large glasses steamed over. "Hi, sweetie," she said. "How was your day?"

"It was awful," Izzy said.

"How so?"

Forgetting the arrival of the realtor for the moment, Izzy recounted the events of the day: dropping the tube of orange oil and compromising evidence, Cal chewing her out in front of everyone and how embarrassed she was when she had a searing headache spell. Of course, Apple thought Izzy had a psychic spell and she hated it that Cal was such a skeptic and how he poo-pooed everything whenever the topic came up.

"What I hate most is that I don't know what any of it means."

Apple dried a glass and placed it in on the shelf over the bar. "Don't worry about Cal. If he doesn't believe you have the gift, you can't change his mind," she said.

"Gift, schmift," Izzy said. "Cal thinks I'm a flunkie."

"Cal probably thinks you had a headache. But let's get real. What did you learn from this psychic episode?" Apple said.

Izzy sighed and drew circles on the bar with her finger. "I've been exposed to lots of violent images lately. Death, burned bodies, severed body parts. My subconscious is just working overtime. Anyone's would. There's nothing psychic about any of this."

"I beg to differ," Apple said. "There must have been something that came through. Wasn't there anything that didn't seem to fit in your so-called subconscious workings?"

"Nothing."

"Work with me here, Izzy. Work with me."

"Okay, okay," Izzy said. "All I got was the number seven."

"The number seven? What were you doing right before you got the flash?"

Izzy looked at Apple and shrugged. *Flash? Never mind.* "I was reviewing the victims' photos with Cal and Moreno. I was just doing what I do—being a cop."

"Have there been seven murders?"

"No, three."

"That you know of—or maybe three so far…" Apple's thought trailed off and it seemed to Izzy that it went down the drain with the sink water. Apple hung her towel up.

"So why the number seven?" Izzy said.

Apple ignored her and wriggled her glasses up with her nose. "Maybe we should channel again. Give me your hands." She reached toward Izzy.

Izzy looked around. The bar was mostly empty. She thought about Apple's suggestion and was about to extend her hands when she noticed the time on the large clock mounted on the wall behind the bar. It was nearly 6:40 p.m. "Oh!" she said, pulling her hands back. "I can't do this right now. Where's Dad?"

Apple blinked in confusion. "Upstairs," she said. "Why?"

"I have a meeting in twenty minutes with a realtor named Mark Traesk."

Apple's mouth gaped open. "Whatever for?"

"Dad scared me the other night when he fell. I've been doing a lot of thinking. I think it's time for him to move into a one-story place," Izzy said.

Apple shook her head making her wild curls bounce. "He'll never leave this bar. It's his life. He loves this place. Since his accident, it's what gives him purpose."

Izzy glanced at her watch again. "I know, Apple." She glanced around the room. "Look, I need your help. I just want to talk to this realtor for a minute—before I tell Dad about my idea. I want to know if it's even feasible to think about finding a place for him. You know, cost wise, and all that. Plus, it would have to be near the bar." Izzy glanced toward the stairs. "If he comes downstairs, can you distract him for a few minutes while I talk to this guy?"

Apple scrunched up her nose. "I don't like this idea. Not one bit."

Izzy put her hands together in a pleading gesture. "Please?"

Apple picked up a dishtowel and tossed it over her shoulder. "I *really* don't like it," she said. "But I'll do it. However, I won't lie for you. If your dad asks any direct questions, I'll answer him honestly."

Izzy nodded and tucked an auburn strand behind her ear. "Fair enough," she said.

Apple harrumphed. "You're making a mistake, mark my words."

Izzy looked at her friend, but didn't answer. Usually she took Apple's advice to heart, but this time, she felt she knew what had to be done.

The door to the bar opened and a ruggedly handsome man with short, black hair entered. He was dressed in khaki pants, a short-sleeved button-down shirt and loafers. He wore no jewelry. He didn't have to. This guy was knock-down-dead gorgeous.

Apple leaned over the bar toward Izzy and said, "Hottie alert."

Izzy slapped Apple on the shoulder and said, "Hush! That might be the realtor."

Momentarily blinded from coming into the darkened pub from the sunny street, the man paused in the doorway, but turned toward their voices. He took off his sunglasses and took a step toward Izzy and Apple. He reached into his pocket and pulled out a business card.

"Good afternoon, ladies," he said. "I'm Mark Traesk. I'm looking for Izzy O'Donnell."

Izzy stood and extended her hand to shake Mark's.

"I'm Izzy," she said.

Mark shook hands and gave her his card. "Pleased to meet you," he said.

Izzy indicated a barstool. "Have a seat."

Mark sat facing Izzy. Apple stood next to her on the opposite side of the bar.

Mark looked around. "Nice place," he said. "I've never been in here before."

While his gaze was averted, Apple fanned herself and mouthed, "He's sooo hot," in her friend's direction. Izzy clandestinely pinched her elbow.

"Ouch," Apple squealed.

Mark's gaze snapped to her. "Something wrong?" he asked.

Izzy shot Apple her well-practiced stink-eye look.

Apple rubbed her elbow and said, "It's nothing."

"Oh." He sounded confused. He extended his hand to Apple and said, "I'm Mark. I didn't catch your name."

"Apple," she said, still holding his hand.

Mark smiled. "Cute nickname. What's your real name?"

Apple stared at him all goo-goo eyed. "That *is* my real name," she said.

Mark wiggled his hand to break free of Apple's grasp. "How'd you get a name like Apple, if you don't mind my asking?"

Izzy sat back on her bar stool to watch the show. Whenever Apple was introduced, it was the inevitable question. And judging by the way Apple was carrying on with Mark, this could be an interesting telling of the tale.

"It's really pretty simple," Apple said. When my

mom went into labor with me, my dad called a cab. Mom's labor went really fast and I was born in the back seat of a New York taxi. Nobody had anything to wrap me up in, so the cabbie pulled over to the first T-shirt vendor he found and bought one that said, "New York, the Big Apple" on it. So, being born in New York, wrapped in a Big Apple T-shirt and being the apple of my dad's eye, well, the name was inevitable."

Mark flashed a broad smile that could cause blindness. Izzy thought Apple might swoon right there. She caught her friend's eye and pointed to the watch on her wrist.

Apple picked up a dishtowel and said, "Nice to meet you. I gotta get back to work."

"A pleasure," Mark said.

Izzy couldn't believe it. She was stuck in a flirt fest and couldn't get out. She shrugged and sat back to watch the show.

Mark grinned and reached out to shake Apple's hand again. "Nice to meet you, Apple."

"Charmed," she said, holding on a little too long before taking her leave.

Izzy turned to Mark. "Never mind my friend," she said. "She's harmless. So, how long have you been in the real estate business?"

Mark turned his attention away from Apple and back to Izzy, cleared his throat and said, "About two years. I like it and, as you know I suppose, I'm not associated with any brokerage firm. I work alone and find my clients by word of mouth. My clients appreciate my personalized service and refer me to new clients."

"That's impressive," Izzy said. "Especially in

Miami. There's a lot of competition here."

Mark shrugged. "May I ask who referred me to you?"

"Amanda, over at Joe's Brew House."

"Ah, Amanda Shackelford. She's very nice. We found a cozy place for her and her husband. Just in time for their new baby. So, how can I help you?"

She quickly glanced around the bar and felt relieved her dad was still upstairs in the apartment. "My father and I own this bar," she said, then realized that she hadn't offered Mark anything to drink. Feeling foolish, she added, "Would you like something to drink?"

"No thanks," said Mark. "I'm good."

Izzy smiled and tucked her hair behind her ear. "We live in the apartment above the bar. He suffered a brain injury a while back and it affects his balance sometimes."

"I'm sorry to hear that," Mark said.

"Thanks," Izzy said. "Recently, he's been having some trouble maneuvering the stairs and I'm wondering about options. That's where you come in."

Mark flashed her a dazzlingly white smile. "How so?"

Izzy immediately understood how Apple had been swept up by this man's charm. He was good.

"Maybe you can help me find a one-story place for my dad," she said. "It's dangerous for him to stay here. The stairs are tough. So maybe something small and easy to maintain, perhaps with a small yard for a dog. I've even considered a duplex where he could live on one side and I could live on the other—so that I can keep track of him." She hesitated. "He doesn't know that I'm thinking about any of this. He's not going to want to move out of the bar. I wanted to see if it's even a possibility before I broached the subject with him."

Mark nodded. "I hope I can help. And I admire the fact that you're looking out for your dad."

Izzy felt a little uncomfortable. "It's nothing really. Dad and I take care of each other."

"I'm kinda in the same boat," Mark said. "My mother is retired and I take care of her. We live together with my disabled brother."

Izzy liked him. He seemed to really get it.

"It can be challenging," she said. "I love my dad, but sometimes it's hard to juggle work, helping out with the bar, helping him, taking care of all the bills, and all that. But mostly, I worry about him falling all the time."

Mark smiled at her. "So what's your time frame?" he asked.

"I don't really have one," Izzy said. "I'm more interested in finding the right place than making all this happen quickly."

"Great. It's easier to find just what you're looking for if you're not in a hurry," Mark said. "I'll start looking. I'm assuming that you'd like to stay fairly close to the bar?"

Izzy nodded vigorously. "That would be great. Do you really think it's possible?"

Mark appeared to be thinking. "Off the top of my head I don't know of many houses close by. At least not anything small. There are some medium-sized homes, and of course the apartments about a half block away, but they're nearly impossible to get into and you've indicated a preference for a house with a yard."

"That's right," Izzy said.

"I'll have to do my homework," he said, flashing that five-hundred-watt smile again.

"And I'll have to do mine. I need to talk to my dad," Izzy said.

"I hope it goes well."

She smiled. He seemed like a good guy. Aside from being hot. "Thanks," she said.

He got up to leave. "It might take some time, but I'll be in touch." He turned in Apple's direction. "It was nice meeting you."

Apple waved goodbye as he walked out. "That guy's easy on the eyes," she said.

"You weren't very subtle with all that flirting."

"I didn't mean anything by it. I was just having a little fun. After all, eye candy is eye candy," Apple said. "And that guy could cause cavities."

Izzy grinned. "At least the scenery will be good when I go looking for a house."

Apple picked up her bar tray and became suddenly serious. "All kidding aside, Izzy. I'm telling you, I don't like this idea one bit. You're making a big mistake by calling that realtor. I can feel it in my bones."

Chapter Fourteen

Heading home from the office a couple of days later, Izzy suddenly remembered she was supposed to meet Mark Traesk to look at a house. It wasn't too far from the bar, only about three miles. Even though she was exhausted she figured it wouldn't hurt to look at one house on her way home. She had to keep the housing ball rolling now that she'd pushed it.

She got off the highway and turned into a neatly manicured neighborhood. She'd wanted to meet Mark at the property rather than have him pick her up at work. Sharing the fact that she was a homicide detective was something that she did on a need-to-know basis. Not everyone needed to know what she did for a living. People treated her differently when they knew she was a cop. When Traesk inquired about her profession, she'd told him that she and her dad ran the bar and that she worked for the city. That was all the information he needed for now. And, it was the truth.

Izzy arrived at the address Traesk had given her. The front yard was small, and professionally landscaped with tropical flowers, a yucca plant, and some rocks. A lizard sunned itself on one of the larger stones but scampered off when she opened her door to get out of the car. A tall gardener wearing a hat was weeding a garden around the side of the house. He didn't acknowledge her, and being tired, she put aside her urge to make polite conversation.

Looking around, she saw that the house was of typical Miami architecture: cinder block and stucco, which withstood hurricanes better than wood. It was painted a pale green. That was something that Izzy really liked about living in a tropical environment—all the houses were painted pastel colors. It just seemed fresh to her. She drew in a deep breath and let some of her stress go as she exhaled. This was a nice, quiet neighborhood. Spencer could be happy here—assuming she could convince him to move. She shook the thought from her mind.

Traesk pulled in behind her car. Izzy caught her breath when she saw him. He was so handsome. She had to remind herself not to stare, and not to make a fool of herself flirting like Apple had. At least she wouldn't have to worry about Apple embarrassing her this time. He got out of the car. "Sorry to keep you waiting," he said.

Izzy cleared her throat and pushed a strand of hair behind her ear. "No problem," she said. "I just got here."

Traesk waved to the gardener and walked toward the door. "Let me show you around. Let's go this way."

He approached an iron gate that led into a small courtyard and beyond it, the front door. There was a little bench and table in the courtyard, which was shaded by one of the shorter varieties of palm tree. Izzy followed, taking everything in. Her mind was on home maintenance, and so far, there wasn't much to maintain. That was good. She didn't have the time or the inclination, and she knew her dad didn't need to be on a ladder fixing little things. There would be a house payment, and that left little to hire maintenance help.

Mark opened the door and gestured for Izzy to walk in. She noticed his toned, tan arms as she walked by. The breeze caught her blazer and blew it open, exposing her weapon. She quickly grabbed her lapel to conceal it and shifted her gaze to a small foyer inside. Mark explained that the master bedroom was to the right and the living room, followed by the kitchen, second bedroom, and bathroom were all to the left. It was cozy. Just about the right size.

Mark showed her through the house. It seemed adequate, and the appliances all appeared to be in good condition. A door opened off the kitchen out onto a covered patio. A privacy fence surrounded the small yard, and birds and tree frogs chirped in the surrounding foliage. This would be where Spencer would spend his time, she knew.

"How old is the house?" Izzy asked.

"It's about twenty-five years old. But it's in good condition for its age."

Izzy nodded. "Hmmm," she said, not committing.

Mark looked at her and her heart skipped a beat. "What did your dad say when you talked to him?"

Izzy fidgeted a little, because she didn't usually feel like a schoolgirl. "Actually, I haven't done that yet," she admitted. "I decided it might be better to get a handle on what's available and have a few places in mind before I talked to him. I'm afraid he's not going to like the idea of moving, so having a few jewels ready to show him might be just the ticket."

In her heart she knew that waiting was a coward's way of buying time before approaching Spencer about moving.

"What do you think about the little house?" Mark said.

"I like it. It has potential, but I want to see others for comparison."

"Of course," he said. "I just want to make sure I'm on the right track."

"Yes, right on."

"There are several other houses in this price range. I'll be happy to set appointments to see them. A few are somewhat farther away from the bar than others, but I think you should look for comparison's sake."

Izzy pushed that stray piece of hair behind her ear. She'd have to ask the hairdresser to leave it longer next time. "I'd like to do that. The only problem is that sometimes I get called into work on a moment's notice, so I may have to cancel at the last minute."

"Tell you what," he said. "I won't worry about your having to cancel if you won't worry about it. I may have to cancel sometime, too."

She smiled and extended her hand. "Deal," she said.

Mark grinned and shook her hand, holding it a moment longer than necessary. Izzy looked at her toes. He let go of her hand and she looked into his eyes. He smiled without saying anything, took her gently by the elbow, and led her through the front door, opened her car door, then closed it behind her. "I'll be in touch."

"Thanks," said Izzy, looking into his dark eyes. Her palms were moist, and not because the steering wheel was hot.

As Mark drove off, Izzy steered around the small circular driveway and out onto the street. In her rear view mirror, she noticed the gardener packing up his tools. Her thoughts drifted back to finding a home for her dad. If the price were right, maybe she could even hire a gardener. Making this move might be pretty painless in the long run. Mark seemed nice, in more ways than one.

****

Later that night, Izzy lay in bed but couldn't sleep. She was trying to make sense of her sudden headache, or psychic moment, as Apple described it. What was the meaning of the number seven?

As usual, she'd had dinner with her dad, but she weenied out of talking to him about moving. How could she face tough situations on the job—okay, so she'd puked at a scene, but she'd still processed the scene, right?—and simultaneously be such a coward when it came to facing her dad? How was she ever going to convince him to move?

No, she wasn't looking forward to that conversation at all. And if he did move, how would she watch over the bar and be a homicide detective too? She couldn't ask Apple to live above the bar and watch over it. Apple was already leasing one of those coveted apartments half a block away from the bar while saving up to buy a place of her own. She wouldn't want to break her lease and move, and Izzy would never ask her to. No. There had to be another way. Time to face up to Dad.

Izzy rolled over, punched her pillow to fluff it up and lay there staring out her window. The palm leaves outside waved softly in the Miami breeze and the full moon threw shadows across her bedroom wall.

Why had she promised Cal that she'd go see her doctor? There wasn't anything wrong with her, she knew that. Just headaches. Apple always thought Izzy was a bit psychic, but Apple was Apple, an entity unto herself. Cal described flashes as nothing more than the subconscious working overtime and chiming in. The weird part was that most of the time, Izzy knew she'd be right about what she'd learned after a flash—unless she'd just eaten spicy food. That seemed to be the only deterrent to accuracy. Maybe her subconscious was telling her to avoid spicy.

Izzy rolled over on her side but couldn't get away from her thoughts. She didn't need a doctor, despite what Cal might think.

Frustrated that she couldn't relax, she pulled the covers up around her shoulders and punched her pillow again. Anything could be used for good or evil, she thought. Including something as innocent as a pillow. People had been killed with pillows. *Enough! I have to get up in the morning and work. I've got to get some sleep.*

Eventually, she felt blessed sleep seeping into her thoughts when her cell phone rang. She groaned, rolled over and picked it up from the nightstand and said, "O'Donnell."

"Sorry to wake you," Moreno's smooth voice said into the phone. "The killer hit again."

Izzy sat straight up in bed. "When?"

"Call just came in. Forensics team has been mobilized. Throw some clothes on. I'll come get you. Be there in ten. Cal said he'd meet us at the scene."

"Okay," Izzy said, and hung up.

She felt the adrenaline rush and liked it, especially since she hadn't slept. She rolled out of bed and pulled on a pair of slacks and fished through her closet for her favorite comfy white blouse. She pulled on her shoulder holster and mechanically checked the rounds in the cylinder. She clipped her badge to her waistband and pulled her shoes on. She tied them and walked down the hall past Spencer's room toward the kitchen. Seeing her dad was sound asleep, she jotted him a quick note telling him that she'd been called out. Heaven only knew how long she'd be gone.

She left the note on the kitchen counter and slipped through the door at the top of the stairs, being careful to close it quietly and lock it behind her. She always took the extra precaution of locking the upstairs door when she left at night. You could never be too careful in Miami—or any other big city—when you lived above a bar.

She made her way down the stairs and through the door to the parking lot. Even though it was 2:00 a.m., the night was muggy. She no sooner made her way to the pole holding the dark neon shamrock when Moreno pulled up. He was in his macho mobile, a sleek black Nissan GT-R. Such a guy thing, she thought. They could be giving sports cars away at the end of the block and she wouldn't go look at them—no place to put groceries—but that was Izzy, always the pragmatist.

She slid into the front seat. "Hey," she said.

"Hi," he said back. "You ready for another bad one?"

"Do I have a choice?"

"Not really."

"Then I guess I'm ready."

Moreno pulled out of the parking lot and turned right. He made his way to the highway and pulled onto the onramp. There was little traffic at that hour, and they merged smoothly.

"Who ID'd the vic?" Izzy said.

"Another woman," Moreno said. "Single, Hispanic. Don't know much else yet."

"I hope I don't puke again," she said. "Am I a total screw up as a cop, Moreno? You can be brutal. Tell me."

Moreno's dark eyes were soft when he looked at her. "Stop trying so hard. You're a good cop. If you weren't, you wouldn't have gotten promoted, and Cal would never have agreed to take you on his team. You know how he is."

"I figured he took me because I'm his former partner's kid," she said.

Moreno laughed out loud.

It startled Izzy. "What's so funny?" she said.

"I thought you grew up around Cal," he said. "You should know him better than that. His bullshit tolerance is zilch. If he didn't want you, he'd look you in the eye and tell you."

"I guess you're right," she said. She looked at her lap and twiddled her fingers. "I just keep screwing up."

"Everybody has a screw-up story. We just don't tell the newbies," he said. He reached over and punched her playfully on the shoulder. "It's an unwritten rule." He shook his finger in her face. "But don't, whatever you do, compromise evidence again. Cal almost blew a gasket on that one."

Izzy's eyes felt moist and she blinked hard to quell her emotions. "I'm trying, Moreno."

"I know you're trying," he said. "Too hard. Just let it happen. Do your job. You already know the drill. Don't sell your soul to the job."

"I understand," she said.

"Do you, Izzy? I lost the woman I loved because I let the job consume me."

"I know," she said. "Unfortunately, I don't have anyone in my life like that to lose."

"Yeah you do," he murmured. "Maybe you don't know who that is, yet, though."

Izzy just looked at him and didn't answer. This was one of those Moreno-has-a-gooey-marshmallow-for-a-heart-but-don't-tell-anybody times, she thought. Saying anything would ruin the moment with her partner and friend, so she just sat there.

He pulled off the highway and turned into a neighborhood. Izzy could tell that the scene of the crime was on the next street over. A halo of light above the houses gave it away.

A modest adobe-style house with arched doorways and a clay tile roof stood alight with police and searchlights. The wop, wop, wop of the police chopper with its searchlight buzzed overhead. The surrounding palm trees cast lanky shadows on the ground. A boom box blasted hip hop in the background and a small gaggle of neighbors wearing lounge clothing stood across the street talking in Spanish. A couple of uniforms were on crowd control and the forensics van was already at the curb.

Izzy reached for the handle to open her door.

"Izzy O," Moreno said, "Just breathe deep."

Izzy smiled to herself and nodded without looking at him.

They got out of the car and Cal met them in the driveway.

"How bad is it?" Moreno asked.

"Bad enough. It's the same killer," Cal said. "Come inside. The forensics team is working, but you need to see this."

Cal led the way through a small courtyard and into the house. There was blood everywhere. It wasn't a moderately tidy puddle like at the previous scene. Blood had spattered all over the walls in the living room and a large puddle was congealing next to the body. The woman had been stuffed into the fireplace, just like the others.

A techie leaned over a bloody shoe print, cutting the carpet around it. A toppled flower vase belched its contents on the coffee table. Saturated magazines sat in a puddle. An earring lay on the ground next to the couch, and a toppled plant near the window strewed potting soil across the carpet.

The stench from the semi-cremated corpse was sickening and Izzy was glad her stomach was mostly empty. She gagged at the sight, but didn't barf. After donning protective clothing and gloves so as not to transfer particulates or contaminate the scene, Izzy, Cal, and Moreno approached the body.

Body fluids seeped from pores on the woman's back. Under the stench of burned flesh, Izzy smelled the remnants of alcohol. It was a common accelerant. She made a note on her pad. One crisp ear displayed the mate to the earring that lay by the couch. At the foot of the hearth, a long fake fingernail sat painted-side down. Izzy picked it up with forceps and put it in a bag.

Steely eyed in the lamplight, Cal pointed to the hearth beneath the grate. Izzy turned her attention there. She was looking at a blood-soaked piece of paper.

"Has anyone opened it yet?" she asked.

"No, I was waiting for you guys to get here," Cal said.

Moreno grimaced. "Thanks, I think."

Cal picked the small blood-soaked packet up with a gloved hand and unwrapped it. It looked very dark and squishy.

"What is it?" Izzy asked.

Cal poked it with his thick index finger. "If I were guessing, I'd say it was a liver. Liver pretty much looks like liver, but we'll let Dr. Dan decide for sure. Let's bag it."

Moreno handed Cal an evidence bag, and he slid the bloody flesh inside it.

Izzy took the blood-soaked paper it had been wrapped in and gently spread it out, being careful not to tear it. "Look," she said. "I can still make out some of what's written. It's another set of Bible verses."

"What do they say?" Cal asked.

"I can only make out part of one verse," she said. "Looks like it's from Ephesians, but I can't tell the chapter or verse. It says, 'And do not get drunk with wine, for that is debauchery…' I can't make out any more," she said.

"Debauchery?" Moreno said. "What do an ear, Bible verses about patience, an organ and drunkenness have to do with murder?"

"Probably more with punishment," Cal mused.

Izzy looked up at Cal and then at Moreno. "Heaven only knows," she said. "But we're going to figure it out."

Cal thrust the evidence bag with the fleshy organ at her.

"Catalog this," he said.

It slipped around in its own blood in the bag. It was bad enough knowing that she was holding a human body part, but the fact that it was still warm repulsed her. She felt suddenly woozy and weak-kneed.

She scanned the vicinity for a way outside to get air. The nearest door was clear across the room. Afraid she might pass out, she took a slow, deep breath like Moreno told her to. Her vision cleared. She willed her stomach down. She had a fleeting sense of accomplishment for not puking.

Deciding not to take any chances, she got another evidence bag and put it in her pocket. Carrying the bag by the top so she wouldn't feel the squish of the liver, she walked over to an evidence collection box. She'd have to handle the slippery mass in order to put it in. She looked at the liver, steeled her stomach, and pitched it into the box.

In one swift move, she pulled the extra bag out of her pocket and threw up in it. Everyone turned to look at her. She was fairly sure she could see smoke coming out of Cal's ears.

"Moreno," Cal bellowed. "Get her out of here."

Chapter Fifteen

It was after 4:00 a.m. by the time Moreno dropped Izzy back at the bar. He waited until she found her key and made her way into the bar safely. She waved goodbye. He put the sports car in gear and headed off. They had driven in silence. Because she'd puked again, Izzy's pride was severely bruised. Maybe she wasn't cut out for this job. Cal had humiliated her in front of everyone again. Actually, she had humiliated herself.

Bone tired, Izzy took off her shoes and padded up the stairs. She unlocked the door to the apartment and let herself in, locking it again afterward. The apartment was lit only with the reflection of the streetlamp outside. The air conditioner hummed in the background. Even though it was fall, if you wanted a decent night's sleep in Florida, you had to cut down on the stickiness. The locals didn't use the air so much this time of year, but Izzy and Spencer preferred it a little dryer than Miami had to offer. She turned the thermostat down a notch.

She tossed her keys in the basket on the table, a little ritual she never failed to perform when she came through the door. Her dad had taught her if her keys were always in the same place, she wouldn't have to look around for them or fish in her bag to find them if she was called to a scene at a moment's notice. He also told her to always leave her service revolver near her bedside when she slept. Spencer once had a perp show up at his bedroom window and take a potshot at him in the middle of the night. The shot grazed Spencer on the shoulder. He returned fire, and the perp landed in the hospital for a while prior going to the penitentiary. Izzy remembered that night. She was just a kid when it all happened, but she never forgot the lesson of keeping her gun by her bed.

In her room now, she put her gun on the bedside table. She could smell death on her clothes. It permeated the fabric, and she was pretty sure it had seeped into her skin. As tired as she was, she ran a shower and stepped in. She replaced the stench of burned flesh with citrus body gel. She washed her hair and some of her weariness went down the drain with the shampoo. When she was finished, she pulled on her boxers and an oversized T-shirt and fell into bed. Maybe she could grab a few hours of sleep before she had to head to the office.

****

Thump, thump, thump.

Izzy awoke with a start. What was that noise? She looked around her room. It was morning. The sun shone through her window and the blue sky dotted with white clouds peeked through the slats of the window blinds.

Thump.

What *was* that? Izzy silently picked up her gun. She tried to piece the strange noise together in her foggy not-quite-awake state. Thump. Adrenaline rose, her hands gripped the revolver, ready to take any assailant head-on. She rolled over in bed and her nose touched something wet. Something wet with whiskers. And ears, long ears. The nose wriggled and the whiskers twitched. With a great leap, Norman was on her bed.

With a sigh of relief, Izzy un-cocked the gun. "Good morning, Norman," she said to the rabbit. "How did you get up here?"

Norman wriggled his nose.

"Does Apple know you've come upstairs?"

Norman wriggled his nose.

"You know I don't like it when you're on my bed, Norman," Izzy protested.

Norman nudged her arm with his nose.

Izzy smiled. In reality, she couldn't resist him. He was a great rabbit. She rubbed his floppy ears and his eyes grew soft with bliss.

Apple simultaneously knocked and blew through the door wearing a baby sling.

"Norman! There you are," she said. "Sorry, Izzy, I don't know how he got away from me. I put him down for just a minute while I took the trash out and when I came back inside, he was gone."

"It's okay." Izzy patted her lap and Norman snuggled in. "What time is it?"

"Almost 9:30," Apple said. "Don't you have to go in today?"

"Yeah. We were called out late last night to another murder and didn't get in until about four in the morning. Moreno and Cal decided we'd meet at the station about 10:30. Which means I need to get moving."

Izzy stirred. Norman protested by nuzzling her.

"You're going to have to move Norman. I know he likes my bed, but he already nibbled a hole in my favorite blanket, so he can't stay here."

"Sorry. Rabbits do that," Apple said, reaching over to pick him up.

"That's why he's not welcome on my bed."

Apple scrunched her nose and put Norman into the baby sling around her shoulders. "I'll take him downstairs." She turned to leave.

"Apple?" Izzy said.

Apple turned toward her, her red hair bouncing as she did. "Yes?"

"Why is Norman here at the bar? You know it's against health regulations."

Apple looked down at her rabbit. "I know but Rhonda called and can't work today because her son is sick, so I have to work a double. That means that Norman would be alone all day and you know how he hates that. He tried to chew through his cage the last time I left him that long. Chipped a tooth. The vet told me not to worry since it was one of the ones that grows all the time." Apple pulled her lips back exposing her top front teeth. She pointed at the middle two. "It was this one that he chipped," she said.

Izzy sighed. "I remember." She threw her covers back and said, "But we got a health citation the last time Norman spent the day here."

"All the customers thought he was great. Everybody except that health inspector, that is. I won't let him run around the bar like he did that time, I promise," Apple said, crossing her heart. "I brought his port-a-crib and litter box." Her eyes pleaded with Izzy.

"Port-a-crib?" Izzy said.

"Yeah, I switched him over to that because I didn't want him to chip another tooth. Please let him stay, Izzy. Please."

"Why do you do this to me? I can't believe I'm going to agree to this." She bit a lip. "You gotta, keep him out of the way and either in the back room under the stairs or up here—in his cage or crib or whatever it is, okay?"

Apple scooped her friend up in a big hug. "Thank you. I won't let you down."

Izzy smiled and hugged her friend back.

Apple stepped back and Norman poked his head out over the top of the sling and wriggled his nose.

"He's so cute when he peeks out like that," Izzy said. "Do you ever wonder what he's thinking?"

"I don't have to wonder," said Apple. "He tells me."

"Oh?" said Izzy.

"Yup. Norman told me that he smelled death on your clothes from last night."

"It doesn't take a psychic rabbit to know that," Izzy scoffed.

"Norman's not psychic. He's *telepathic*," Apple said, sounding a little wounded.

"Sorry, didn't mean to offend."

Apple patted Norman's ears. "He forgives you," she said.

"What else does Norman know?" Izzy said, trying to make nice.

"He says he's smelled that same smell before," Apple said.

"Death?"

"No, the killer."

"What? This is the first time he's been around when I've come back from a crime scene associated with this killer."

Norman pulled his head back into the sling. Apple pushed her glasses up on her nose and Izzy took the bait. "Now what's he saying?"

"He says he's smelled your serial killer before."

"That's crazy," Izzy said.

Apple shrugged. "He says he doesn't make the news, he only reports it." With that, she closed the door behind her.

Izzy sat on the edge of the bed and blinked hard a couple of times in bewilderment. Had she just had a conversation with a rabbit about a serial killer?

Chapter Sixteen

There was nothing they could do about last night's murder victim. Dr. Dan would be doing the autopsy, so Izzy and Moreno headed out to follow up on Paul Winters at Heaven's Gate Sanctuary. "Home to Brother Gideon and his Flock," the sign said.

Izzy pulled off her sunglasses so she could take the scene in, in all its apparent majesty. The white, circular building stood with a blue steel roof slanting upward to a point. On top of the point sat a large white cross, giving the impression it was suspended in a blue sky. The grounds were perfect. Symmetrically planted palm trees adorned each side of a long sidewalk that led up to the main entrance. There wasn't so much as a gum wrapper anywhere to be found on the ground.

Moreno led the way to the door. When they walked in, they found themselves in a large atrium complete with trees, flowers, a waterfall—a veritable Garden of Eden, Izzy thought. Off to the right, a sign pointed to the church. There wasn't anyone around, so Izzy led Moreno that way, thinking there might be someone in there.

She opened the door and found not just a sanctuary, but a huge auditorium. A stage was the centerpiece. It looked like the kind that could rise up and down. There was an elaborate fly system overhead and lights galore: red ones, blue ones, spot lights and foot lights. The controls were on the rails up on the catwalk. On the stage was a large set of risers, apparently for the choir. A conductor's platform stood in front of the risers with a music stand perched on the edge. Midway out into the audience, stood a large sound control board. Was this a church or a concert venue Izzy wondered.

Footsteps sounded in the wings, stage right. Two men meandered onstage.

"Greetings, followers, I'm Brother Gideon," said the taller, slimmer man. "Why has God brought you to me today?"

Izzy and Moreno walked down the aisle toward the stage.

"Brother Gideon, I'm Detective Moreno, and this is my partner, Detective O'Donnell."

They showed their badges to the men. Brother Gideon shook Izzy's hand. His skin was softer than hers, and his nails had been recently manicured. Definitely not something Izzy could relate to.

Brother Gideon indicated the man standing next to him. "This is Brother Paul," he said.

Paul Winters stood before them. Izzy's gaze shifted to Moreno. She could tell in an instant that he recognized the man from the picture, just as she had. He'd ditched the suit, but he still looked crisp. He sported a pair of khaki trousers, a red button-down shirt with a bamboo leaf pattern and new loafers. His blond hair, freshly trimmed and styled, blended with his gray eyes. He looked ready for a job, or at least ready to sell a car to someone.

"So, to what do we owe the honor of your visit?" Brother Gideon said.

Izzy wondered if people talked like that for real or if this guy had spent so much time on stage in this theatre that he actually thought it was the way normal people spoke.

"We'd like to ask you both a few questions," Izzy said.

Paul shifted his weight from foot to foot and his hands twitched at his sides. "Questions about what?" he said.

"There have been several murders lately." Izzy flipped her notebook open. "Some of them had a religious aspect. We're just doing routine follow up with people who might be able to shed some light on this."

"Paul," Moreno said, "have you been watching TV at Rico's every day?"

Paul's back stiffened. "Yes. I like to go there to hear Brother Gideon preach God's word."

Before Paul could say any more, Brother Gideon positioned himself in a protective stance between Paul and the detectives.

"Look," Brother Gideon said, "Paul is down on his luck. He lost his job. The Lord led him to Heaven's Gate Sanctuary and we're helping him help himself. We've fixed him up with some fresh clothes and shoes that don't have holes in them. Next we'll help him find a job. Just because someone is homeless doesn't mean he's a killer."

"No, homeless doesn't automatically equal killer," Izzy said. "But, I still need to know why you've been watching TV in Rico's store every day."

"God led me there to listen to His word. But that irreverent manager had me removed. It was just like the people at my old job. They didn't like it when I talked about God. They wouldn't let me share the word over my radio at work. Some people liked it. But the boss said my radio was disruptive. He made me leave. I got fired for Jesus," Paul said.

"And what was God saying that day in the store, Paul?" Moreno asked.

"He spoke through Brother Gideon, who taught about patience," Paul said. "That manager wasn't patient. God will smite her."

Izzy raised a mental eyebrow. *Smite*? "So you think God will, um, smite Lupita Vazquez, the manager at Rico's Electronics, because she threw you out of the store?"

Paul took in a long breath and let it out slowly as if to tame his temper. "Not for throwing me out of the store. For not being patient. He will smite her for not being patient. You'll see."

Chapter Seventeen

The next morning, Izzy walked into the office with a cup of coffee in hand. She had stopped to get her usual, a skinny latte with a shot of vanilla syrup. This time it was sugar-free vanilla syrup. Her waistband was a tad tight this morning. Too much paperwork and not enough gumshoeing. But, that's the price she had to pay for being the rookie on the team. Deep down, she knew her place. She glanced at her coffee. The barista had given her extra foam. Yum. It was going to be a good day.

Moreno walked toward her, sporting an open box of donuts. "Want a donut?" he asked.

She looked into the box and saw a maple cake donut. Forget the waistband. The sugar free syrup would cancel out a donut, right? "A maple cake. My favorite," she said.

Moreno smiled. She picked it up and took a bite. She closed her eyes slowly and savored it. Heaven. She rarely let herself eat pure, unmitigated sugar, but today was an exception. With extra coffee foam and a maple donut under her belt, she was certain she could turn her rookie luck around. "Thanks for the donut," she mumbled as she chewed. "I love maple cakes."

"My pleasure," he said. "When you're done with your donut orgasm, we're due in the morgue."

"You just spoiled my whole sugar moment," she

protested.

"Sorry," Moreno said. "Want another one?"

"Sugar orgasm? Is there another maple cake?"

"No more maple cake."

"No thanks," she said. "Not worth the calories if it isn't a maple cake. Besides, I'll be on a sugar high for an hour as it is. I don't eat this stuff very often, you know."

"Yeah, I know," he mused aloud. "It's a wonder they let you be a cop."

She popped the last bite into her mouth and licked her fingers. "They let me be a cop because I have abilities that exceed donut eating."

Moreno closed the lid on the box and set it near the coffee pot. "Right," he said. "Let's go, super cop. Dr. Dan awaits."

They walked down the hall and stopped by Cal's office to pick him up. The trio made their way to the morgue, Izzy the caboose as usual. *Sometimes you just have to suck it up. At least, I don't have to open my own doors when I bring up the rear.* A smile tugged at the corners of her mouth. Moreno opened the door to the morgue and they found Dr. Dan sitting at his desk poring over some notes.

"Hey, Doc," Cal said. His tone was too cheery. Like he was trying to hide his underlying grumpy mood. At least he was trying. Izzy hadn't seen any heads rolling in the hallway, so Cal hadn't bitten any off today—yet. "What's up?" He managed a smile.

The medical examiner barely looked up from the report on his desk. "Good morning, detectives," he said. "I have news. Good news. The forensics team found a partial print inside a glove that had been placed on your victim's body. Perp probably hoped the glove would burn along with the rest of the body."

"A partial print—that's great," Izzy said, enthusiastically. "Enough to match?"

Dr. Dan eyed her, obviously still steamed about the tube of orange oil the other day. In the end, he nodded. "There was enough of the print to run through the system, but there was no match."

Izzy's hope hit the floor and she wasn't sure, but she thought it made a thud.

"So it's really only sort of good news?" Cal said.

"No, it's genuine good news," Dr. Dan said. "Finding the glove gave us something to match on the other two bodies. We're still checking, but I'm pretty sure some trace evidence—threads that we found on the body with her hand cut off—will match the fibers on the glove. As for the victim whose heart was cut out, the lab is looking into a speck of dirt found on the heart. Obviously it was transferred. But now they're looking at the possibility that the killer didn't use clean gloves. If you can see it with a microscope, they'll figure it out.

"What about the earring and the fingernail we found at the last scene?" Izzy asked.

"No finger prints on those," Dr. Dan said. "But there was a little bit of skin under the fingernail. Like maybe she scratched him and that's how her nail popped off. The lab people are running it for DNA, but we all know that takes time."

"So, if he's using the same kind of gloves, then that's a solid pattern. And a solid lead," Moreno said.

Izzy nodded her head in agreement. Moreno thumbed through the reports on Dr. Dan's desk. "Any news on what was written on the blood-soaked paper?"

Moreno asked.

Cal glanced at Moreno then to Dr. Dan. "And whether this message was printed using the same printer as the last one?"

"Yes and yes," Dr. Dan said. "The same printer was used in this instance as in the last murder and, somewhere here"—he rifled through a stack of papers—"I have the report on what was written. Here it is—I'll read it."

"Ephesians 5:18 'And do not get drunk with wine, for that is debauchery, but be filled with the Spirit.'

"Isaiah 5:11 'Woe to those who rise early in the morning, that they may run after strong drink, who tarry late into the evening as wine inflames them.'

"Proverbs 20:1 'Wine is a mocker, strong drink a brawler, and whoever is led astray by it is not wise.'

"Galatians 5:21 'Envy, drunkenness, orgies, and things like these. I warn you, as I warned you before, that those who do such things will not inherit the kingdom of God.'"

Izzy frowned. Bible verses about debauchery?

"If this guy is killing people because they drink, all of Miami's in trouble," she said.

"Yeah, I'm thinkin' we better not invite him to poker night," Moreno said.

A smile tugged at the corners of Izzy's lips. The others nodded.

Moreno looked at Dr. Dan. "What was cut out of her?" he asked.

"Her liver."

Cal nodded. "That's what we thought."

Izzy's donut didn't seem so tasty any more. "Yuk," was all she could muster.

Dr. Dan raised an eyebrow. "Yuk, yes. But it makes sense in a way. The liver was sclerotic. Our victim was a heavy drinker."

Cal scratched his bald spot. "And the perp knew it, so—"

"So, do we have a stalker?" Moreno asked.

"Don't know that yet," Cal said. "But it's a safe bet, as usual, that the victims knew their killer."

Izzy looked at each one of them in turn. "And she knew him well enough to let the guy into her home. There were no signs of real struggle throughout the house. It looks like she let the guy in and then he took her by surprise. She obviously trusted him at some level."

Cal nodded approvingly. "Right."

Izzy smiled to herself, but kept her face blank. She didn't want Cal to know how pleased she was that he'd caught her doing something right.

"Next step, team?" Cal asked.

Moreno jumped in. "We have to figure out what they all had in common."

Cal nodded again. "That would be another piece of the puzzle found. Maybe not an edge piece, but a piece nonetheless," he said. He pushed the report back toward Dr. Dan. "Thanks for your time, Doc." He turned to Izzy and Moreno. "Let's go back to my office and see if there's a link between these women."

They trudged back to Cal's office and divided up file folders. The pictures Izzy had taped to the white board the other day were still there in all their ghoulish glory. After only a few minutes of sifting through notes, Izzy noticed something.

"Look," she said, "two of our victims—Alma Ruiz,

the latest victim without her liver, and Polly Fullerton, the blonde mom without her ear—were looking for new homes."

"Hmph," said Cal. "You figured that out all by yourself without puking?"

His words hit Izzy like a brick. She wanted to speak up about being dressed down in front of other people, but this was Cal, her dad's former partner. It was hard to razz him like she razzed Moreno. She refused to react.

"Yup, all by myself," she said.

"Good eye, Izzy," Moreno said, narrowing his eyes at Cal.

Cal ignored him and whipped out his phone. "Moreno, you call Fullerton's husband, I'll call Ruiz's sister. Izzy, keep scouring for more clues and try not to puke on the pictures."

Izzy narrowed her eyes at him. Dad's old partner or not, she'd had enough.

"It's time to give it up, Cal," she said, glaring.

Cal snapped her a glance but said nothing. Behind him, Izzy caught Moreno smiling. He gave her a clandestine thumbs-up.

The room filled with chatter as Cal and Moreno made their calls to the victims' relatives in search of information on realtors. Ten minutes later they each had a name. The same name. Mark Traesk.

Chapter Eighteen

Izzy was never so glad to get back to the bar and into the cool air conditioning. It wasn't baking hot today, just super muggy. Miami's standard afternoon rain shower had started after she left the office and followed her all the way to Mark Traesk's office, where she stopped to pick up a listing of houses he was showing. He'd stapled his card to it and handed it to her. She put them in her purse and zipped it closed so they wouldn't fall out for Spencer to find before she had a chance to talk to him. And, as much as she didn't like it, she now had the estate agent's finger prints on his calling card. She liked this guy. She could prove his innocence.

It was very humid now, and her skin felt like she'd been sitting in cooking oil. She was already tired from being a cop all day and with a sigh, she realized it was time to shift gears and get into bar owner mode. And depending on how her dad was today, maybe even caretaker mode. No wonder she didn't have a man in her life. Moreno's face popped into her mind. His dark eyes, mocha skin and broad smile, complete with twirling toothpick, looked at her in her mind's eye. She shook her head. Where did *that* come from? She conjured up the realtor, Mark Traesk's image. Then she smiled. If she weren't so exhausted at the end of the day, she might consider having dinner with a man sometime. But nobody had asked, and besides, she was simply too tired most nights to think about having a relationship. But there was Mark. She was so tempted it ached. But with a possible connection to two murder victims, he was out of the question until she cleared his name.

She looked around the room. There were a few of the regular clients sipping beer at the bar and a couple of guys playing pool in the corner. Apple was nowhere to be seen. Izzy walked to the door under the stairs and went into the back room.

Norman banged against his port-a-crib, obviously wanting out.

Izzy reached over the top and scratched the rabbit behind his ears. "Hi, Norman," she said. "You have to stay in there so I don't get another citation from the health department."

He wiggled his nose.

"Here you go, Norman," said Apple, appearing from nowhere.

Izzy jumped. "You startled me."

"Sorry," Apple said. "I was getting Norman a fresh pan of water."

"He seems to be doing fine."

"I think he's liked having the company today. I've been able to check on him off and on," Apple said, obviously pleased.

"I see he has a new toy," Izzy said. "What is it?"

Apple picked it up and showed her. "It's a rabbit. His name is Abner."

"Abner the rabbit? You got your bunny a pet rabbit named Abner?"

"Yes. Norman chews up everything I get him, so I

got him a rabbit. I mean, since bunnies aren't carnivorous, I figured this one might last."

Izzy did a mental head slap, but didn't say anything. She was afraid where the conversation might go.

Apple put the toy back in Norman's port-a-crib and looked at Izzy, her round eyes large behind her glasses. "Can I ask a favor?"

"Sure. What is it?"

"Well, since tonight is poker night, I was wondering if Norman could come out of his port-a-crib while you guys are back here," Apple said.

"You've forgotten about the Health Department?"

Apple's enormous eyes flashed behind her glasses. "I think he'd like some exercise and if you're back here playing poker, maybe you could keep an eye on him. When we got cited, I let him out on the bar floor. He'd be back here—not out there." She pouted a little. "Please?"

Izzy crossed her arms and sighed. "I can't afford another citation."

"I know," said Apple. "But if you watch him, and I'm careful when I come in and out, we can make sure he stays back here in the storage room where you're playing poker."

Exasperated, Izzy looked at Apple and sighed again.

"You know he'll use his litter pan," Apple continued. "There won't be so much as one marble on the floor."

"Okay, okay. He can come out when we're playing poker, but he'll have to stay in his pen a little while longer. I really need a shower before everyone gets here—and I can't risk him getting out of the storage room while I'm upstairs and you're busy. And, if he gets out and we get a citation, not only are you going to pay for it, I'll personally fix roast rabbit for dinner."

Apple hugged Izzy so tightly that Izzy thought she might hug the stuffing out of her. "Thank you, Izzy! No problem. Norman says to tell you thanks and he'll wait patiently until the game starts."

Honestly, a telepathic rabbit? Izzy loved Apple, but sometimes she seemed nuts, even to her. "I'm going upstairs now." She glanced back over her shoulder and saw a mass of curly red hair bent over the pen. Apple was talking to Norman.

When she got upstairs, Izzy found Spencer in the kitchen, cooking some supper that smelled deliciously like home when she was a child. He was concentrating on his work, hands to task stirring the wonderful concoction on the burner. His ruddy face was moist with the steam rising from the stove. It made his sun splotches look even splotchier.

"Wow, it smells yummy in here," she said, crossing the room to give him a hug.

"Supper's about ready," he said.

She slipped a finger into the pan and tasted the stew. "Tastes perfect, too."

"Thanks. Your Grandma Keyna taught me to make this stew," he said wistfully. "My mother was a good cook."

"Yes, she was," Izzy said. "Walking into the kitchen and smelling this stew takes me back to when I was a kid." The memory of Grandma Keyna taking over the cooking after Izzy's mom left mushroomed up a recollection of many Irish meals long past.

"My mother was a good cook," said Spencer. "Supper's about ready."

Izzy realized that he'd repeated himself—again. It was happening more frequently now. The doctor said along with coordination issues, forgetfulness and even motor system problems were common to people with brain injuries. At least he wasn't showing more severe signs of dementia, disorientation or aphasia. The symptoms of his disorder might arrest here or he might get worse. There was no way to know. Izzy thought how much she missed her Gran. If Grandma Keyna were here, she'd help out with Spencer.

Spencer turned on the faucet. The sound of running water brought her back. She shook the cobwebs of times past from her thoughts.

"Mind if I take a quick shower before supper? I can wait until afterward if you need help," she said.

"Nope, I've got it all under control," he said. "But be quick, we're almost ready to eat."

"Thanks," she said. "I'll hurry."

In the shower, Izzy started to relax. Her shoulders came down a notch and so did her stress. She dried off and hung her towel up to dry. She pulled on a pair of jeans. Ahh. Her favorite jeans. She didn't care that they had holes in the knees and a tear above the back pocket. She'd mended them with bright colored thread and they fit her like a glove. These comfy jeans and a beer to unwind seemed like just the relaxation ticket she so desperately needed. She smiled to herself as she pulled on a tank top and combed through her damp hair. She wound it into an auburn knot and put in a clip to hold it up off her neck. She glanced at herself in the mirror and thought about her dad. That fall. Repeating himself more. She decided with or without a house in mind for him, it was time to talk to Spencer about moving.

The only problem was that her courage for this conversation was hiding behind her fear. She sighed and rolled her shoulders.

Izzy walked into the kitchen and got three plates out of the cupboard. She knew there'd be enough food to share. Spencer always made sure that Apple got supper if she worked through the dinner hour. Apple was a member of the family. There was a pile of carrot peelings next to the stove on a paper plate. These were undoubtedly for Norman. Izzy smiled and thought about how much she loved her dad and Apple, with all their idiosyncrasies. She set the silverware around the plates and put the salt and pepper on the table. Even Dad liked ol' Norman.

"You sure are sweet to fix dinner, Dad. What else can I do to help?" she said.

"Nothing, daughter," he said. He brought a pot over to the table and set it down on a trivet. "Is Apple coming up?" he asked.

"No, there are a few customers downstairs. I'll go relieve her in a minute so she can eat," Izzy said.

"All right then," Spencer said. He took the top off the pot, and Irish stew it was. "You say the blessing."

Izzy said the prayer that Grandma Keyna had taught her as a child. She'd learned other ones over the years, but the old standby was still her favorite. She paused before the "amen" and added a silent plea for courage in the conversation she was about to have with her father.

Spencer dished braised beef and vegetables onto Izzy's plate. Steam rose and the aroma tantalized her nose. She took a bite and she suddenly felt eight years old again sitting at Gran's table eating the same meal. "This is really good, Dad," she said.

He looked at her over his fork. "Thanks," he said. And he took a bite. "The secret is in the gravy. I always add a dash of sugar to it." He wiggled his eyebrows at her.

"So *that's* your secret, is it?" Izzy said, pretending to have never heard it before.

The two of them fell into silence and ate, but Izzy's mind still buzzed with the essential conversation coming with her dad. After a while, she screwed up her courage and said, "So, Dad, I've been thinking."

"It's never good when you start a conversation like that," he said. "What's wrong?"

Izzy put her fork down. "I'm worried about you, Dad," she said.

Spencer didn't look up. He just kept chowing down on his stew.

"I was pretty scared the other night when you fell on the stairs," she said.

Spencer put his fork down and looked straight at Izzy. "I had a feeling this conversation would be coming," he said, stubbornly crossing his arms over his chest. "I refuse to do it."

Stunned, Izzy said, "To do what? You haven't even heard me out, Dad."

"I know what you're going to say," he said. "You want to move me to a nursing home."

"Dad, that never crossed my mind. You don't need a nursing home," she said.

"Then you want to have a nurse move in and watch me while you're at work." He banged the table hard with a large open palm to emphasize his point. Dishes rattled. "I won't have it!"

Stunned, Izzy said, "That's not what I had in mind at all."

Spencer looked confused.

"You don't need a full-time nurse," Izzy protested. "You need to live someplace without stairs." There. She'd said it. It was out in the open and into the ether. A wave of relief swept over her, but she knew it couldn't be this easy. She braced herself for the next wave.

Spencer's jaw dropped. Then he closed it hard. His five o'clock shadow bristled in the kitchen light. "I've been expecting a conversation of this sort after my fall the other night, but I thought you were going to move a nurse in," he said. "I was itching for a fight. But I agree the stairs are hard for me to maneuver. "

Izzy's heart leapt. He'd agreed!

"That's great, Dad. I'm glad you agree."

"Then it's all settled. I'll move downstairs into the back room."

A shock wave zinged through Izzy. That option hadn't occurred to her. But it wouldn't work. They needed the downstairs room for storage. It wasn't practical to have to go up and down the stairs for supplies all day. Plus, it wasn't cost effective to add on to the bar just to have storage. No, she had to nip this idea in the bud.

"Dad, if you moved downstairs, where would we store things?" Without giving him a chance to say anything, she forged forth. "I'd still live upstairs and your room isn't big enough for all the bar supplies, plus it's not practical to make several trips upstairs each day to fetch what we need to restock the beer coolers. I think we need to find you a one-story place outside the bar."

Spencer was animated now. He waved his hands in protest. His face turned red and the splotchy places turned crimson. "Outside of the bar? I'm not moving away from this bar. I've poured myself into it—given it my all—ever since I got hurt. It's my life! You know that."

Izzy flinched inside. "Yes, I know."

The red on Spencer's face spread to his ears. "Have you lost your mind, daughter?"

"No," Izzy said. "I know how important the bar is to you. Honestly, I do." She patted his hand.

He pulled it out from beneath hers. He wasn't shouting, but the vein in the side of his neck was pumping up, and Izzy could tell he was ramping up for a fight.

"What do you expect me to do? Go off and die quietly someplace?" he said.

Izzy was taken aback by this comment. "No, Dad. Not at all. I just want you to live someplace where you won't have to maneuver stairs every day. I need you to be where I won't worry about you."

"You're just tired of taking care of me. I can tell," he said. "The next step is to ship me off to a home someplace where you won't have to put up with me at all."

There it was again, spoken with his out loud voice and now squarely on the table.

"Is that what you think this is about?" Izzy said.

Spencer didn't answer. He chased a carrot across his plate. It made a little wake through his gravy.

"I want you to come to the bar and help out just like you do now. I can't run the bar by myself and be a detective at the same time. I just don't want you to live upstairs. That's all," she said.

He looked up at her and his blue eyes softened. The light caught a shock of his silver and brown hair and she thought he was coming around to see her side of things.

Izzy picked up her fork and chased a potato around her plate. It was something to do with her hands. "I was thinking that I—we—could find a one-story place that wouldn't require a lot of maintenance," she said. She put her fork down and looked at Spencer.

He met her gaze. "I understand and I appreciate your concern," he said. "But"—he popped the carrot into his mouth and started to chew—"I'm not leaving the bar and that's final."

"But, Dad…"

"No buts, Isobell Catharine. I'm not leaving, and this conversation is over." He stood and took his plate to the sink.

Chapter Nineteen

Izzy cleared her dishes and went downstairs.

"Apple, trade me places. You go up and eat, and I'll watch over the bar," she said.

Apple nodded. "Thanks. I'm hungry." She removed her apron and headed toward the stairs.

"Hey," Izzy called after her.

Apple looked over at Izzy, her red hair floppy and her glasses, as usual, perched on the end of her nose. "Yeah?"

"I talked to Dad. It's over-heated up there."

Apple turned back to climbing the stairs. "Thanks for the heads up."

Izzy busied herself washing glasses behind the bar and when she was done, she checked on her customers and headed to the back room to set up for the poker game. Norman looked at her, brown eyes bright. He held his toy bunny, Abner, in his mouth. She reached down and picked him up out of the port-a-crib. He nuzzled her neck. She ruffled his long ears before she put him down on the floor. He looked up at her.

"It's okay," she said. "You can go hop around. I'll put your litter pan right here."

Norman watched her put his food, water, and pan outside the port-a-crib. Then he hopped away and disappeared behind some boxes stacked in a corner. Off to do whatever bunnies do.

Izzy was pulling the table out away from the wall when Moreno walked through the door.

"Need some help?" he said.

Izzy glanced over her shoulder. "Sure," she said.

Moreno walked toward the table and stood next to her, ready to pull. *He smells yummy. New cologne.* His short, cop hair was slicked with a little gel and he wore a button-down shirt with a surfboard pattern. The top two buttons were open. Very Miami. Very *nice*. She could tell he'd caught her looking, and she looked down at the table. "Ready?" she asked.

"For anything," he said, suggestively.

She gave him a sideways smile and said, "Just pull on the table, stud."

He grinned and they pulled together moving the heavy mahogany game table into the middle of the room.

"How's it going with Cal?" she asked.

"A little better. He's calmed down a little, but he's still kinda edgy. Are you sure you don't want to spill?"

Izzy held up her hand. "Sorry I mentioned it," she said. "No dice. When he wants you to know, he'll tell you."

Moreno shrugged. Maybe he was finally getting the message. They worked together putting chairs around the table.

Soon enough Dr. Dan arrived in his poker uniform—his fishing vest festooned with pins and his well-worn sock filled with bottle caps ready to place his bets.

Cal showed up, grumpy as usual. He stood next to the table and shoved his hands deep into his pockets. A moment later, they emerged filled with bottle caps and he dumped them out, skittering them across the table in front of his place.

Spencer arrived with his bottle caps in a purple velvet bag swinging from one hand and the cards in his other. Apple held the door open for him and made sure he didn't stumble over the threshold. Everyone took a seat and they cut the cards to see who would deal first. They all had a small pile of bottle caps on the table in front of them and in short order, Apple arrived with a round of beer.

A few hands into the evening, Cal's pile of caps was substantially larger than it had been and his spirits seemed a bit brighter. Izzy wondered if they should let him win tonight so that he'd be easier to live with next week. But, then he'd probably just gloat over it. The rest of them did when they won.

Norman hopped over to Izzy and stood on his hind legs next to her chair. He was so cute when he did that. "Do you want up?" she asked him. He nudged her leg and she scooted her chair out a little. He took a great leap and landed in her lap. He sat there, quite content, watching her cards.

"Why is Norman here?" Dr. Dan asked. "I thought the last time he came to the bar you got written up on a health violation."

"Aye, we did," Spencer said. His tone was icy. "But Apple promised to keep him in the back room. The sweet lass had to work a double today and she was afraid he'd get lonesome."

Cal shook his head. "Only Apple would bring a rabbit to work," he said. "Why can't she just leave him at home and pat him behind the ears psychically from here?" He chortled at his own joke and rearranged the cards in his hand.

"Norman's special," said Izzy.

Cal scoffed. "Don't tell me he's psychic too?"

Izzy looked at Norman and remembered this morning's events when Apple said he had smelled the killer. "No, rabbits aren't psychic," she said.

Norman bit her, but not too hard.

"Ouch! What did you do that for?" she said.

Norman blinked.

Izzy arranged her cards. "Cal, you're not going to like this, but Apple says Norman told her he smelled the killer on my clothes before."

He tossed his cards down in exasperation. "Oh, for the love of Pete!" he said.

Dr. Dan burst out laughing and Moreno bit his lip, and probably his tongue, Izzy thought.

"I'm just reporting the news," Izzy said. Norman looked strangely dejected and jumped off her lap. Izzy watched him hop off toward a corner, then shifted her gaze to Cal. "By the way, I went to Mark Traesk's office on my way home to get a list of properties he's showing to see if there are any other connections."

Cal didn't answer, and an uncomfortable silence gathered like cloud cover.

Izzy looked around the table. All eyes were on her now.

"What?" she said.

"Why would you do that without Moreno or me along?" Cal said.

"Um, well, I kind of know that guy," she said. "When we discovered he was a common denominator to two of our victims, I just dropped by to get a property listing. He seems really nice." She left out the part where she inwardly wanted to meet with him over coffee. He could be an ally—after all, they both had jobs on top of caring for family members. Besides, there was no mistaking the fact that the scenery across the table would be nice.

"He may seem nice, rookie, but there may be a stronger connection to this guy," Cal said. "What if he's implicated in some way?"

"He doesn't strike me as a serial killer," Izzy said.

"Honey, anyone can be a killer," Dr. Dan said. "Look at Ted Bundy."

Izzy knew he was right, but still, Mark seemed so normal.

Moreno piped in. "And, you pulled that stunt without backup."

Izzy tossed in a bottle cap and looked at Moreno. "I was already seeing him before any of this came up, anyway," Izzy said. "Oh, and it's your go."

Moreno tossed a bottle cap on the pile.

Cal reached over to put another cap on the pile and the overhead light glanced off his bald spot. "Seeing him? Like on a date?"

"No," Izzy said, a little too fast. "Not like that. I went to his office."

"Well, going to his office was a stupid thing to do, Izzy," he said. "How do you know him, anyway?"

Izzy glanced at her dad. He gestured to her and said, "Go ahead, tell them. Tell them how you want to get rid of me."

Izzy put her cards down and looked directly at Spencer. "I don't want to get rid of you." She looked around the table at the others. "I originally met with Mark Traesk because I want him to show me some houses. I think it's time for Dad to move into a one-story place."

Izzy could have heard a pin drop. All eyes moved from Izzy to Spencer and back to Izzy. The tension in the room was thick enough to cut with a knife.

Spencer was the first to move and speak. "I told you, she wants to get rid of me."

Izzy started to protest, but Cal leapt in before she could say anything. "Spencer, Izzy's right. After that fall, it's time for you to move to a place without stairs—"

"Now you listen here—" Spencer interrupted.

"I'm not done," Cal boomed. Spencer closed his jaw and backed off. All eyes were on Cal now. "Can't you see that your safety is really important to Izzy?"

Spencer just stared at him.

Cal put his cards face down on the table. "Look, we all worry about you because we're friends. Izzy's your daughter. She *really* worries."

Spencer was bristling again. He shifted in his seat and said, "It's a conspiracy! Izzy put you up to this."

Cal pointed a hefty finger at Spencer. "Stop, you old coot. You know there's no conspiracy here. But there will be if you don't calm down. You're only proving Izzy's point for her—you're not your old self."

Looking defeated, Spencer slumped back in his chair.

Cal turned to Izzy. "Okay, and back to what Moreno said a minute ago. Izzy, Moreno's right. Where do you get off being alone with Mark Traesk?"

Izzy shifted uneasily. "There's no evidence that he's the killer," she said.

Cal's blue eyes were frosty. "That's not the point.

You broke protocol."

Izzy swallowed hard. She stared at Cal.

Cal's thick finger pointed at her now. "As the senior officer on the team, I'm informing you that I'm writing you up for this. Dan and I let it slide when you compromised evidence in the morgue. We saw that as an accident. But this—*this* can't be ignored. You know the drill, rookie. Two more and I'll have you reassigned. From now on, you have two shadows. Your own and Moreno."

Izzy groaned inwardly.

"Izzy," Cal said. "I'm talking to you. Do you understand?"

Izzy nodded. "Yes. I have two shadows. Understood, sir."

Chapter Twenty

The next morning, Izzy worked behind the bar prepping before opening. Having tossed and turned last night thinking about the rest of the poker game that had passed at a glacial pace, she felt horrible and hadn't wanted to get up this morning. She was still reeling from the humiliation of being dressed down by Cal in front of her co-workers and father during the poker game. Her dad hadn't leapt to her defense when Cal started to shred her publicly. Not one of her co-workers had said anything. Not even Moreno. And that hurt.

She'd held her head high and finished out the last hand of poker, but Cal's reprimand, being written up, and her dad being furious with her—all that at once was almost more than she could stand. She couldn't think what to do about Cal. One thing was sure, it was time to move forward and find a one-story place for her dad. Lost in thought, she worked behind the bar, slicing lemons and limes and performing other miscellaneous duties mechanically.

A wedge of light broadened on the floor and Apple opened the door to enter the bar, Norman hopping in behind her.

Izzy squirted the bar with some disinfectant and ran a cloth over it. "Didn't expect to see you today, you're scheduled off."

Apple shoved her glasses up on her nose. "I am,

but you need a friend."

Izzy tossed her hair back with a shake of her head and put on what she thought was a pretty brave face. A tear gave her away, however, and slowly trickled down her cheek.

"Put the dishtowel down and sit here by me," Apple said patting the barstool next to her.

Izzy looked at her wild-haired friend and then at the clock. The bar wouldn't see its first customer for at least fifteen minutes, so she gave in. She put the tea towel down next to the sinks, and went around the bar to sit next to Apple.

Apple patted Izzy's hand. "Spill, girlfriend."

Her best friend's touch was all it took. Sloppy tears rolled down Izzy's cheeks and splashed on the bar. Apple gave her a hug and Izzy said, "I'm just completely humiliated by Cal's drastic response to my getting that realtor's listing. Why couldn't he have dressed me down privately?"

Apple nodded. "It stinks."

"I thought I'd had such a great idea getting that list to cross-reference," Izzy protested. "I didn't follow protocol, but sometimes the others break with protocol too."

"I'm sure they do," Apple said. "But they're not rookies."

Izzy stiffened.

"Don't get all defensive," Apple said. "I'm on your team, remember?"

Izzy nodded.

"The truth is those guys get a little latitude because they have the experience to handle it. Besides, if everything isn't done by the book, they could lose this perp, and everybody wants to take him down."

Izzy sniffed and nodded again.

"More truth is, Cal wouldn't have been so mad at you if he didn't care about you so much."

"I know, I know. I thought of that too. But he should have talked to me in private."

Apple nodded this time. "Yes. And I'm sorry you're so hurt. But we both know it is what it is and Cal is unlikely to apologize. So, what are you going to do?"

Izzy puffed an ever-so-small laugh. "You mean the pity party is over?"

Apple smiled at her and patted her hand.

"I guess I'm going to do the only thing I can do. I'll march in there on Monday, shoulders squared and prove to them that I'm not a flunky."

"And Moreno?"

"If he's my shadow, he'll have to square his shoulders, too, I guess. I'm sure he doesn't want to be on babysitting duty."

"Don't look at it that way. Look at it like you have a personal, professional tutor at your disposal at all times."

"You're always the spin doctor, Apple."

"Maybe playing doctor with Moreno wouldn't be so bad…" Apple trailed off.

"You're incorrigible."

"Just teasing," she said.

Izzy looked at Apple and turned serious.

"I had another dream last night. You know, the one with the crowd around the fire and the boy stoking it?"

"Yeah. And?"

"I saw things in more detail," Izzy said. "The crowd was made up of men, women and children.

There was one guy who seemed to be the leader. He carried a bundle over to a funeral pyre and threw it on. I saw what the bundle was."

"What was it?"

Izzy shuddered. "A woman. And her throat had been slit."

"That's horrible," Apple said. "Then what?"

"That's where the boy stoking the fire comes in," Izzy said. "In my dream, some of the onlookers went to a woodpile and picked up small logs. They walked over to the pyre and added their kindling to fuel the fire."

"Oh, Izzy, are you thinking what I'm thinking?"

"I think so. I believe there may be more victims out there. I think this killer has been killing for a long time—I have a hunch that this is possibly part of a cult ritual—if that's what the crowd I'm seeing is."

"What are you going to do?"

"I'm going to do some research."

"How are you going to manage that? Cal will never let you follow up on a hunch you got from a dream. And what about your new shadow, Moreno?"

"They don't need to know I'm doing the research. I can do a lot of that from home—and Moreno doesn't need to stand next to me while I'm typing. If this amounts to anything, when I have evidence to support it, I'll tell Cal and Moreno. I'm not planning to get written up twice."

The door to the bar opened and the first two customers walked in. Izzy smiled at them and thought she recognized the man, but she couldn't be sure. She rose to greet them and heard a scream.

"A rat! It's a huge rat!" said the woman who had just entered.

Izzy rushed toward the woman. "What? Where? We don't have any rats here."

The woman was standing on a chair quivering and pointing to the corner under the stairs.

"There!"

Norman poked his head out from the dark corner.

Izzy ran over to him and picked him up.

"Ma'am, I'm so sorry he scared you. This is just Norman. He's a very friendly bunny. He, um, must have gotten out of his cage."

Apple approached and said, "I'll put him back." She made a show of walking upstairs with him, as if to imply that's where he lived.

Izzy smiled at the customers and apologized again. When her gaze fell on the man, she suddenly realized where she'd seen him before.

He reached into his pocket and took out a calling card.

"You're Ms. O'Donnell, right?"

Izzy gulped. "Yes, sir."

"Perhaps you remember me. I'm the health inspector, and this establishment is closed for 24 hours for inspection—starting right now."

Izzy deflated.

"Ms. O'Donnell, I'd better not find so much as one bunny marble, not one crumb on the floor, not even one ant leg on the premises. Do I make myself completely clear?"

"Crystal."

She walked to the entrance, switched off the OPEN sign, and locked the door. It was going to be another long day. At the end she might just kill Apple and serve *hasenpfeffer* for dinner.

Chapter Twenty-One

Dear Brother Hamor,

You will be pleased to know that I have once again continued your teachings by performing another cleansing ritual.

As you taught me, I watched this woman over time to be certain not to make a hasty decision prior to performing the deed. There is a fine line between helping people by cleansing them and hurting them for pleasure. I would never want to inflict pain for pleasure. That would be wrong.

This woman did not exhibit temperance. She got drunk with wine and other spirits. She had most certainly been led astray by strong drink. I have witnessed her debauchery as early as 10:00 a.m.

She was cleansed in the prescribed manner. As always, I took measures to keep myself pure and away from the unclean blood.

The authorities are still confused, however. They seem to think that someone meant to do her harm rather than save her. The story of her cleansing, and that of the others, is being broadcast on the television and in the newspapers as a serial murder. How can I make them understand?

My fervent prayer is that she is free of her debauchery and now leading an eternally temperate life in the arms of her Holy Father.

I am blessed to know that you understand me.
Your Hevite Brother,
Seth

Chapter Twenty-Two

Izzy took a bite of her foot-long chilidog. She'd had another of her headaches, and Moreno dragged her off to lunch, maintaining that if she were to eat more regularly, she'd probably quit having them. *Whatever*...But, hey, if Moreno was paying, she'd eat a dog and enjoy his cologne while she was at it.

Izzy's phone chirped. She pulled it from her waistband and saw it was Lt. Boggs. She tossed the phone to Moreno and pointed to her chipmunk cheeks full of food.

"O'Donnell's phone. Moreno," he said.

Izzy chewed and waited.

Moreno hung up the phone and Izzy swallowed her bite.

"Well," she said. "What's up?"

"We got another murder," Moreno said. "And you're not going to believe this."

"What?"

"The victim is Lupita Vazquez," Moreno said.

"What? The store manager at Rico's Electronics?"

"That's her. I wonder if God decided to smite her," Moreno said.

"Well, somebody decided to smite her," Izzy said. "Fat chance it was God."

They drove to the address Lt. Boggs had given Moreno. The Vazquez residence was located in a nice neighborhood. The house stood on the corner of two streets. The red clay tiles on the roof were a few shades darker than the house paint. Yucca plants and flowers adorned the beds framing the front of the house.

Dr. Dan was already at the scene. Uniformed officers had cordoned off the property with yellow police tape to hold back the onlookers.

Izzy and Moreno got out of the car and walked into the house. The husband, a distraught Jaime Vazquez, sat crying on a leather couch, head in hands. His full head of black hair shook with his sobbing. A Pekingese dog wanting in scratched and yipped at the sliding door between the living room and the outside.

One of the uniformed officers indicated to Izzy and Moreno that the victim was down the hall to the right.

Moreno rounded the corner to the bedroom first. Izzy lagged behind, readying her plastic just-in-case bag.

"What have we got, Doc?" Moreno said.

"Looks like the same scumbag," Dr. Dan said.

Izzy rounded the corner to find Lupita Vazquez staring at the ceiling with dark brown, unseeing eyes. Her throat was slit and blood pooled and soaked into the blue plaid comforter where she lay. The blood was still moist and the room smelled like copper. She hadn't been dead long. Blood spattered on the white wicker nightstand and chest of drawers on the side of the bed where she lay. Arterial spray, thought Izzy. Lupita's blouse was torn open, displaying her chest cavity. Her heart lay on the bed next to her with a large wall cross on top.

Izzy coughed hard, choking down bile. Moreno looked at her and pointed to the bag she carried. Izzy shook her head. She was okay for now.

Dr. Dan pulled a stainless steel thermometer probe from the woman's liver. He read the dial. "This woman has been dead only about an hour and a half. I place her time of death between 11:45 a.m. and 12:15 p.m."

Izzy opened her forensics kit and donned a pair of gloves, still too big, but she'd be careful.

"I see her heart there on the bed," she said. "What else have you found?"

Moreno dropped to his knees and looked under the bed. "No paper with Bible verses here."

"Right," said Dr. Dan. "No verses anywhere."

Izzy shuddered. At least they had the heart

"Wait a minute," she said. "Why isn't she burned? All the other victims have been burned."

"I wondered about that myself," Dr. Dan said. "Maybe because this house doesn't have a fire place. The only fire-burning structure is the *chiminea* on the back porch. No body would fit in there."

"So the perp switched things up again?" Moreno asked.

"I don't like this," Izzy said. "Something's not right."

"We need to get the body to the lab for an autopsy," he said. "If anything extraordinary turns up, I'll let you know."

Chapter Twenty-Three

On Monday morning Izzy sat at her desk at the cop shop. She rubbed lotion into hands that were still red from all the scrubbing and chemicals she'd used the other day to clean the bar. The health inspector came back later to check the premises again. He hadn't found any marbles or ant legs, but he did find a few pretzel crumbs and a fly wing. The fly wing was nestled on a windowsill. It was brittle—proving that it had been there "for quite some time," or so the inspector said. Izzy decided he needed a new hobby and wondered if he inspected his own family home.

Apple had written the check for the citation. In an effort to save Norman from the stew pot, she'd stayed to help scrub corners with a toothbrush.

The lotion's citrus scent filled the air around Izzy and she took a moment to relax. Moreno interrupted her by plopping a small paper bag on her desk.

She indicated the bag. "What's this?"

"Open it," he said.

She complied and inside the bag were the two most perfectly glazed maple cake donuts she had ever seen. "Thanks." She snatched one out. "What's the occasion? Are you proposing?"

He gave her a sideways smirk. "Not exactly," he said.

She took a not-so-dainty bite.

"I just figured you could use a donut this morning—Cal was pretty rough on you the other night. You're not the only rookie to ever get a written reprimand, but he didn't need to tell you about it in front of everyone. It was hell on you and uncomfortable for us."

Izzy felt all warm inside. "Thanks, Moreno. Thanks for saying that." She didn't really want to, but she offered him the second donut as a sign of gratitude.

"No thanks," he said. "They're both for you."

"You really *do* love me, don't you, Moreno?"

He laughed and slapped her on the back.

"Yeah, whatever," he said.

He indicated the stack of papers on her desk. "What's all that?"

"An effort to redeem myself."

"Oh?"

She licked the last of the maple off of her fingers. "Remember I told you I've been having dreams with a kid stoking a fire?"

He perked up a bit. "Yeah?"

She told him about her dream and her theory that a cult or ritual killing might be involved.

"I hesitated to say anything to Cal, because he thinks I'm nuts when it comes to this, but I wanted to check it out anyway."

"I thought Cal's orders were clear, Izzy. You and I are attached at the hip."

"I know, I know. I didn't violate any orders. I just searched the Interwebs a bit at home and came up with a few interesting tidbits."

"Such as?"

"Well, Marcus Wesson was convicted of killing his

146

family in Fresno back in 2004," Izzy said. "Six females and three males, ages one to twenty-five were all shot and found in a pile in a bedroom. The guy twisted religious beliefs to justify his conduct. The crazy religious thing fits, but there were no post mortem mutilations or fire, and this was a family not a huge cult."

"Sicko," Moreno said.

"Yeah, and there's plenty of them out there who twist God's word into a reason for killing." Izzy shuffled some papers and pulled out another stack. "Jeffrey Don Lundgren killed five people in 1989 because God spoke to him. Then he said since he was a prophet of God, he didn't deserve the death penalty. To top it off, Fox news said he told the jury that the 'spiritually unclean had to be dealt with' and referred to the killings as 'pruning the vineyard.'"

Moreno shook his head. "Sheesh. Then of course there's David Koresh and Charles Manson."

"Yup," Izzy said. She indicated a large pile of paper. "I found all this. All of it is about cult killings. I found a fundamentalist cult located in Kansas—they called themselves the Hevites. This cult operated about twenty years ago. They kept to themselves mostly until their leader started to perform ritualistic burnings of women members living in the compound. He burned three women to death. A Josie Peters escaped from the cult and contacted the feds. Said she left after the leader burned his own daughter. Josie was the daughter's best friend. Anyway the feds raided the compound about eighteen years ago. Busted them up. A few members of the cult escaped when the Feds stormed the castle, but they were never heard from again."

"Who was the leader?"

Izzy shuffled through some papers and pulled out a page with a sticky note on it. "Looks like his followers called him Brother Hamor. His real name is Russell Flatt. He's incarcerated in the maximum security United States Penitentiary at Terre Haute, Indiana. The last news article I dug up was right after they incarcerated him. Says they were keeping him on a short leash back then until they determined how dangerous he was on the inside. He got life without parole. The whole thing pretty much blew over after the trial."

"Good work," Moreno said. "We have to tell Cal."

"If you think so." She hesitated and added, "But we don't know if there's any connection. Until we know for sure, we don't want to blow a Federal whistle."

Moreno stood in deep thought. His dark eyes stared at the wall, his ever-present toothpick twirling. He focused on her again and began to speak. "I think we should get the results of that fingerprint you got us from Traesk's calling card stapled to the housing list and see what we learn. We may already have our guy."

"Or not," she said.

"Or not," he agreed.

"You know Cal's going to go ape if he learns I got this from a dream."

"That's why we'll cross that bridge when we come to it,"

Chapter Twenty-Four

After calling the lab and being told they were still running the Traesk print, Moreno and Izzy grabbed a cup of coffee.

"What's our next step with Lupita Vazquez?" Moreno said. "The lab report won't be in for a while."

"I think we need to go visit Paul Winters. He did warn us that someone would smite her." Izzy made quote marks with her fingers.

Moreno nodded. They drank the last of their coffee and headed for the car. Twenty minutes later, they arrived at Heaven's Gate Sanctuary. They walked in and found a buzz of activity in the foyer. People were filing into the theatre-church.

Izzy walked to the left and approached a short, thin woman holding a clipboard; a pencil perched over her right ear. Izzy couldn't tell if her hair was brown with blond streaks or blond with brown streaks and when she turned toward them, her green eyes didn't give away any hairdressing secrets. Izzy flashed her badge. "I'm Detective O'Donnell and this is Detective Moreno. What's going on here?" Izzy said.

"We're almost ready to go on the air," the woman said. "I'm Lydia, Production Manager. How can I help you?"

"We need to talk to Brother Gideon," Izzy said.

"I'm sorry, that's not possible. He's in makeup."

Lydia glanced at her watch and in a loud voice, shouted, "Camera in ten."

People in the hallway beyond the woman scattered like cockroaches and replied in unison, "Thank you, ten."

For a fleeting moment, Izzy thought she was back in high-school drama class. "I know time is short—with only ten minutes before air time, but we just have a couple of quick questions for Brother Gideon," she insisted.

Moreno stepped forward. "Two minutes, tops."

The woman hesitated. "He's in makeup and he's not going to like this. Come with me."

She led the way through the door and down the hall to the right. A door with Brother Gideon emblazoned on it stood cracked open.

Lydia knocked lightly. "Brother Gideon, there are two detectives here to see you."

"Sister Lydia, please ask them to come back later. We're about to go to church," he said.

Izzy pushed past Lydia and through the door. Twelve bright lights framing a large mirror overheated the room. Brother Gideon sat perched in a reclining barber chair. He wore a terry-cloth bib and a very attractive, tall redhead was applying makeup to his face. She dabbed a shiny spot and it disappeared.

"We just need to ask a couple of quick questions," Izzy said.

Brother Gideon sat up in his chair. His gaze shot to her. "I don't mean to be rude, but as you can see detective, I'm busy. Come to church and we can talk afterward," he said.

The redheaded makeup artist chased him around as

he spoke. She filled in eyebrows with a pencil.

"All we ask is two minutes of your time," Moreno said.

Brother Gideon glanced at Lydia. She held up seven fingers. He looked at Izzy and Moreno.

"Two minutes. No more. Lydia will keep track of the time," he said.

"Are you aware that Lupita Vazquez was murdered today?"

"I'm sorry to hear that," he said. "I'm confident that whoever this poor woman was, she has gone to meet her maker in heaven."

Moreno took a step toward Brother Gideon. "Lupita Vazquez is the manager at Rico's Electronics. Perhaps you remember, when we visited the other day, Paul Winters mentioning that he felt God would smite her."

"I do recall that. Yes. Because she was impatient with him."

Izzy nodded. "We'd like to talk to Paul. Do you know where we can find him?"

"Camera in five," Lydia shouted practically in Izzy's ear.

Izzy scowled.

A chorus of, "Thank you, five," sounded up and down the hallway.

"Time's up," Brother Gideon said. "I must go backstage now."

Brother Gideon unhooked the terry cloth bib and smiled as he handed it to the redhead. "Thank you, Andrea," he said.

Andrea tipped her head to him and he headed toward the door.

Moreno reached his palm out and placed it on Brother Gideon's chest. "Not so fast," he said. "My partner asked where we could find Paul Winters. Surely that answer won't take five minutes."

Brother Gideon looked at his shoes. Izzy wondered if he was mad. Perhaps he was collecting himself so he didn't deck Moreno.

Brother Gideon looked at Moreno. "I'm sorry to tell you that Brother Paul Winters is in the intensive care unit at Kendall Regional Hospital." He pushed past Moreno, smoothing his tie and suit coat. "Now if you'll excuse me, I have a worship to lead."

Chapter Twenty-Five

"Hospital?" Izzy said.

"That's what the man said," Moreno answered.

They drove to Kendall Regional on SW 40th Street and found a place to park. The candy striper at the information desk directed them to ICU.

A large RN with a face like a bulldog sat at the nurse's station. She wore chartreuse scrubs and looked up at them from behind gold-rimmed bi-focal glasses. Her nametag read "Julie Williams."

"May I help you?"

Izzy and Moreno flashed their badges. "We understand you have Paul Winters here," Izzy said.

Nurse Williams eyed them suspiciously. "That's right."

"We need to talk to him," Moreno said. "He may have some information about a murder investigation we're working on."

Nurse Williams adjusted her glasses with a pudgy hand. "He may not be able to tell you much. He's in bad shape. He fades in and out of consciousness. They beat him up pretty bad."

"Is that why he's here?" Izzy said. "Somebody beat him up?"

"That's right," Nurse Williams said. "We're supposed to call the police when he regains consciousness so they can send someone over to take a statement. I was getting ready to call—not that he's awake, but I'm not sure he's going to make it. If you are going to talk to him, you'd better wait around and talk when he comes to next time. I don't know how much you'll get, though."

She escorted Izzy and Moreno to Paul's room and opened the sliding glass door. She indicated two chairs for them.

"Please, be quiet and don't wake him. If he wakes on his own, you can talk to him, but don't upset him. He doesn't need the stress," she said.

Izzy and Moreno nodded and took their seats. The heart monitor beeped and drew green mountains and valleys, the oxygen tank hissed and IV lines snaked from a bag suspended overhead into his veins.

Paul's head was wrapped in several layers of gauze. His left leg was splinted and suspended in the air by traction. Both arms were in casts, both bent at the elbow.

The scene took Izzy back to the hospital where her dad spent weeks recovering from the subdural hematoma and broken bones he suffered when he fell from a tall fence while chasing a perp. She'd spent hours sitting at the hospital with him, hoping and praying he'd recover. She couldn't count the number of nights she'd spent sleeping in a reclining chair next to his bed. She talked to him, read to him, told him old jokes—anything to let him know she was there for him. Cal would spell her on weekends so she could go home and get some rest. He had to work, and it was hard for him to be without his partner. Apple kept the bar running and Dr. Dan even came to visit in his fishing vest, hoping it would cheer his buddy up, but he never woke up to see him. Finally, Spencer regained consciousness and eventually got well enough to be moved to a rehab hospital where they taught him to walk with his new hip and knee. Not to mention the many daily living skills he had to brush up on since he'd lain in the hospital so long, his muscles atrophied.

"Izzy?" Moreno said. "Are you listening?"

"Um, sorry, no. I was just thinking. What's up?"

"I think Paul's waking up," Moreno said. "Let's call the nurse."

Izzy nodded and pushed the call button. Nurse Williams bustled in.

"We think he's waking up," Izzy said.

Nurse Williams walked over to her patient and checked his pupils. "Mr. Winters, how are you?" she said in a somewhat louder than normal voice.

Paul's eyes drifted around then focused on her.

"Where am I?" he said.

"You're in the hospital," she said. "Some college kids beat you up pretty badly, but we're taking care of you now."

Moreno looked at the nurse, his face a question mark.

She nodded to him.

"A couple of police officers are here to see you. Think you can talk to them for a minute?"

Paul nodded.

Nurse Williams stepped toward the door, but waited in the room. "Keep it short," she said.

Izzy nodded. "Paul what happened to you?"

"I was preaching outside a bistro," he said. His words came in breathy snippets. "These college kids and their girlfriends were eating lunch. The girls were

155

wearing little sundresses. They were too skimpy. I told them they needed to cover up, that they were causing men to lust after them. I told them the body is the temple of the Lord. They wouldn't listen. Then their boyfriends jumped me and started to hit me. That's all I remember."

Paul closed his eyes, obviously exhausted.

"A bystander saw the kids jump him and they called the police and an ambulance," Nurse Williams said. "That's how we got him here. The police told me they were rounding up the kids who did it."

"Paul, can you describe these kids?" Moreno asked.

"Tired. Ask Brother Gideon."

"Brother Gideon?" Izzy said. "What's he got to do with this?"

"He sent me out to do his work. I have to get back to help him finish... save those sinners..." Paul said.

"What work?" Moreno asked.

Paul didn't open his eyes or answer. The heart monitor made a long, shrill tone. Izzy looked at it. The green lines that were making peaks and valleys now made a flat line.

Nurse Williams sprang into action. She picked up the telephone and dialed. Over the intercom, her voice called a code blue.

"Out. Now," she ordered.

Izzy and Moreno left the room but stood on the far side of the hallway. A flurry of doctors, nurses and attendants flew from every direction to Paul's room. Someone pushed the crash cart.

Izzy was swept back in time to when she lived this scene with her father. She put her hand on her cheek.

Moreno put his hand on her shoulder.

They stood and watched in silence. Muffled calls of "clear" intermingled with the hissing of oxygen and voices shouting orders and responses. The heart monitor that, mere moments ago, chimed a long, steady tone started to beep, beep, beep while drawing weak hills and valleys again. Paul Winters was on the edge and if he didn't make it, Izzy knew they hadn't learned much.

Chapter Twenty-Six

Izzy followed Moreno to the forensics lab and morgue. Dr. Dan was at his desk when they walked in.

He looked up at them over his glasses. "Detectives," he said.

Still self-conscious about being dressed down in front of everyone the other night, she gave a timid wave. "Hi, Doc."

Moreno nodded.

Dr. Dan swiveled in his chair and picked up a box of latex gloves, size small, and handed them to Izzy.

"These are for you," he said. "I claimed a box of small ones.. Thought you might like to put them in your field kit."

Izzy took them. "Thanks," she said.

She looked at him. There was a soft kindness behind his eyes. But, being one of her dad's contemporaries, she knew he'd never reveal his true feelings behind his little gift to her. Obviously the team felt bad about the way Cal had ripped into her. Donuts and gloves were their "hang in there" messages, she knew.

Moreno cut the awkward moment with a question.

"So, what's the scoop on the realtor's finger print? Any news?"

"We ran it through AFIS and came up with nothing," Dr. Dan said.

"Wasn't there enough to match?" Moreno asked.

"There was plenty. Got a full index and thumb. Just no match," Dr. Dan said.

"So that leaves us nowhere," said Izzy.

"No, not really," Dr. Dan said. "It just means that Mark Traesk isn't our guy."

Izzy rolled the stress out of her shoulders. *Another dead end.*

Moreno looked at Izzy. "It's time to take your theory to Cal," he said.

"Theory?" Dr. Dan asked.

"Izzy's been looking into cults," Moreno said.

"I think there might be a connection," Izzy said.

"Speaking of connections, I've finished the autopsy on Lupita Vazquez and I found something very interesting," Dr. Dan said.

"Oh?" Moreno said. "What's that?"

"Well, as you recall, the body wasn't burned. That was different than the usual M.O., but then I noticed something else. I noticed her scalp was intact."

"What? The killer didn't take his trophy this time?" Izzy asked.

"Exactly," Dr. Dan said.

Moreno shrugged. "So what are we talkin'?"

"I don't think it's the same killer," Dr. Dan said. "Think about it. It has been in the press that these killings have a religious flair to them—but we haven't said what that is."

Izzy nodded. "Yeah, usually it's Bible verses, but we never found any at Lupita's—just that cross on top of her heart."

"Right," Dr. Dan said.

"And," Moreno added, "We've never found a

murder weapon at any of the scenes, except for Lupita's."

"We've mentioned that body parts are cut out or severed. We've also stated that the bodies are burned. But, we never told the press our killer was taking a bit of scalp and hair as a trophy."

Izzy perked up. "You're right," she said.

"So who wanted Lupita Vazquez dead?" Moreno said.

"Well, not Paul Winters," Izzy said. "He was busy getting beaten half to death when Lupita was murdered."

"Who then?" Moreno said.

Dr. Dan's glasses flashed in the light. "That, detectives, is for you to detect," he said. "As for me, I've got a young man on my table in there, and he has one last story to tell."

Izzy and Moreno turned to leave. Moreno's phone chirped. He picked it up. Izzy watched as his toothpick twirled in his mouth then stopped.

"On our way," he said, and hung up. He looked at the others. "We got another one. They want you there, Doc. Let's roll. "

Moreno rattled off the address and Izzy wrote it down for Dr. Dan. He'd be along after he put his storyteller back in the cooler. Izzy and Moreno stopped to grab their forensic kits. Izzy made sure to put some of the new gloves in hers. They made their way to their unmarked Avalon and pulled out of the parking lot. Izzy's mind buzzed with all the new information.

They drove to the seedy side of town, and cruised down Biscayne Boulevard toward North East 69th Street. The corners were dotted with scantily clad working girls. Breasts of all sizes real or imagined were barely covered by cloth. Long, lanky legs perched atop high heels and each face was overly made up. Hooking was definitely profitable. Izzy should know, she'd spent enough time working vice. She was glad those days were behind her.

Moreno pulled the car to the curb a few doors down from the building where they'd been called. Izzy grabbed her kit and Moreno followed suit. When they exited the Avalon, some of the working girls scattered and yelled, "Run, Marie!"

A tall, slender woman with sharp features stayed put.

"Where you goin', girls?" the woman hollered to her scrambling companions. "These two ain't vice. They're worse. They carryin' kits. Somebody dead."

Izzy walked along the sidewalk, sticking fairly close to Moreno. When they approached the woman, she spoke again. "Where you two headed? Who dead?"

Moreno snapped his gaze to the woman and said, "Move along, Marie. This doesn't concern you."

Relieved that Moreno had stepped in, Izzy looked the woman up and down. She stared back.

"What's the matter, Cher? You never see a New Orleans chick with a dick?"

Surprised, Izzy swallowed hard. She'd worked vice, but this was a new one on her. This solicitor was a man and Izzy hadn't even clued in. He obviously knew that because he started to laugh and punched Izzy on the shoulder.

Moreno instinctively palmed him in the chest and backed him into a telephone pole. "I said, move along, Marie."

Looking annoyed and arranging his bosom, Marie said, "Watch it. You're messin' up my breastage. I was just havin' little fun, Cher."

"Have it somewhere else," Moreno threatened. He let loose of the man and walked down the street.

Izzy fell into step. "What was that all about?"

"Marie, oh, he's a regular. And he's harmless," said Moreno. "These folks really aren't out to hurt anybody. They're just society's sadness trying to make a buck. But I hate it when anybody touches a cop. Especially you."

"Thanks, but I can handle myself. I worked vice, remember?"

"Yeah, I know," he said.

"It's that machismo thing, huh?"

"Call it what you want. Where I come from, we take care of our own."

Izzy had to smile a bit at that. Sometimes she couldn't tell if Moreno was going to assume the role of unstoppable flirt or big brother. Today it was big brother.

They arrived at a door with peeling green paint and Moreno opened it. They walked in and found a small landing with mailboxes imbedded in the wall to the right. A short flight of stairs led to a landing where a uniformed cop stood outside a door.

They walked up the stairs, flashed their badges and nodded to him.

A techie just inside the door met them and said, "Get ready for this one."

Izzy put her kit on the ground, opened it and pulled out a plastic grocery bag.

"What's that?" Moreno asked.

She brushed through the door past the uniform and turned to Moreno. "It's a bag."

"I can see that. What's it for?"

"Just in case."

"Of?"

"In case I don't have the stomach for this," she said.

Moreno shook his head and blew a long breath at her.

"Look, Toots," she said. "Maybe I don't have the world's strongest stomach. And maybe I puked at a scene. And maybe I even fainted, but I'm not going to compromise evidence. I do my job well. On an empty stomach."

The corners of Moreno's mouth twitched into a smile. He pulled out the toothpick and said, "You got this all figured out, don't cha, Izzy O?"

Izzy started to protest when one of the CSI techs called them.

"Detectives. Over here."

Izzy led the way, bag in hand, in the direction of the voice and she found herself over a female corpse. The body had been mutilated. The woman's breasts lay beside her on the floor and she had been slit from sternum to pubis. Blood pooled everywhere and soaked into the cheap, dirty carpet. Ropes of intestines spilled out of a gaping wound in her abdomen. It was obvious that some of the woman's viscera were missing because there was a cavity where something ought to have been.

Izzy took a good hard look. Nausea pounded relentlessly. She swallowed hard against it but in the end, jammed the bag up to her face and relieved herself of breakfast. She tied a knot in the bag and set it on the floor. Without skipping a beat, she looked up at Moreno and said matter-of-factly, "You ready to do this?"

He looked at her dumbfounded and eventually said, "Yeah."

They busied themselves helping the CSI crew dust for prints, and look for clues. They found condoms in the bedroom. Someone had cooked breakfast and left the dishes in the sink. Eggshells with fingerprints were bagged. Hair that didn't match the victim's was categorized. Izzy wondered how much use some of these items would be. If this was a flop for prostitutes, there was no telling how many people could have deposited hair, earrings, clothing, and DNA. Izzy scoured the place looking for a note with Bible verses on it. There was none.

Dr. Dan arrived and took possession of the body. There were marks around the woman's throat and defensive wounds on her hands.

"Moreno," Dr. Dan said. "Look at this." He pointed to the marks around her neck. "This woman was strangled like the others."

"And mutilated," Moreno added.

"But there's no note," Izzy said. "And no body part to find. The breasts are placed next to the body, like trophies. They're not wrapped up like a package for us to find. And the viscera are nowhere to be found."

"Not just viscera," Dr. Dan said. "This woman is specifically missing her uterus and ovaries." He turned her head and looked at the nape of her neck. There was a small piece of scalp and hair missing. "It's him. He took the same trophy."

"Which means we haven't looked hard enough for the note and those body parts," Izzy said. She took a quick look around the room then barked an order. "Okay, everyone," she said. "We've got to look again. There's a note here somewhere, and probably a uterus. Let's go over this one more time."

She heard one of the uniforms mumble and snigger, "O'Donnell lost her uterus."

Izzy stiffened and addressed him. "Excuse me, do you have something to share with the class?"

Everyone in the room stopped what they were doing and looked at her.

"Do you really think it's amusing to have a mutilated woman here and a killer on the loose?" she said.

The uniform looked down. "Detective, I, uh...I was just—"

"I know what you were doing. Just get back to work. Gentlemen, a uterus, ovaries, and a note, please," she said.

Moreno leaned over her shoulder. "I think you might be growing a set, newbie."

Izzy cocked her head. "Steel ones, Moreno."

She gazed out over the room. Everyone renewed the effort to find the missing items. She could tell the uniforms were not pleased. According to Dr. Dan, the victim had been dead for about twenty-four hours and the pungent smell hanging in the air said Miami's heat had already started to claim it. The uniforms were definitely ready to move on to other duties. Any other duties.

Izzy looked under the couch for the third time, as if a uterus might suddenly appear. While scooting around on the ground, she found a small clump of mud dotted with blades of grass. She picked it up with a gloved hand and put it in an evidence bag.

"Hey, Moreno," she said. "Look at this."

Moreno turned to her and she handed him the bag. He studied it and looked somewhat bumfuzzled. "It's dirt, Izzy O. Dirt."

"Ah, but not just any dirt," Izzy said. "There's grass in it."

"Point?"

"No grass around here. This had to have been transferred."

Moreno raised an eyebrow. "We'll have the lab check it out. Did you find any other samples like this on the victim's shoes?"

"Nope. Just this one tiny clump right here next to the blood on the carpet."

Moreno opened his mouth to say something, but was interrupted by the chirping of his phone. "Moreno," he barked into the mouthpiece. "Okay, just a sec." He turned to Izzy and said, "Cal wants this on speaker. Said to get Dr. Dan and you."

Izzy got up off the floor and Dr. Dan walked to where Moreno stood. Moreno hit the speaker button and said, "Okay, Cal, we're all here."

"Moreno, we just had a delivery addressed specifically to Izzy here at the station," Cal said.

"To me?" Izzy said.

Cal's voice from the phone said. "It's a box. It looks suspicious. No return address and it looks blood stained. I'm gonna open it."

Izzy heard him cut cardboard and tape. Dr. Dan's face filled with concern. Izzy reached into her kit and pulled out another grocery bag, just in case. Moreno nodded his consent.

The trio stood and stared at the phone while rustling sounds came through the receiver.

"Oh my God!" said Cal. "I was afraid of that. It's blood, all right, and an organ, I think."

"Is it sort of triangular?" asked Dr. Dan.

"Yes."

Moreno rubbed the back of his neck. "Folks, I think we just found that missing uterus."

Chapter Twenty-Seven

"Skankalicious." What kind of a word was that? It was the word Apple used when Izzy told her about the bloody package that had been addressed to her and delivered to the cop shop. Izzy was lost in thought while sifting through mail in the mailroom, mulling over recent strange events. After Cal opened the bloody box, he'd put a freeze on the mailroom until Izzy had a chance to look for any notes containing Bible verses. She'd been sifting through mail for an hour and found nothing.

What bothered her was that the killer knew her and where she worked. The mailroom lady had gone to lunch. Moreno had left her there with strict orders to stay put while he walked the two blocks to grab a couple of take-out delicacies from the burrito man.

Izzy picked up an envelope that didn't have a return address and looked at it. Without warning, her vision blurred and her head started to swim. She sat down quickly in a nearby chair and leaned against a mailbag to steady herself. Her mind's eye saw fire again. But this time there was no corpse burning on a funeral pyre. This time she saw a small, contained fire. A man stood on one side of the fire and two young boys stood on the other. One of the boys was the one from her earlier dreams. The other, she'd never seen before. The man wore a fire glove and pulled a long, metal poker out of the fire. It glowed red-hot. At the end of the poker, a V was hammered from the metal. The man gave some instruction, but in the silence of her vision Izzy couldn't tell what he'd said. The boy Izzy had seen before came forward and lowered the collar on his shirt. The man took the poker and seared the boy's collarbone, branding him with the V. The boy recoiled in pain and tears shone in his eyes, but he didn't cry out. He looked up at the man who nodded in response. The boy took his place again on the other side of the fire.

The man then indicated that the second boy should come forward. The second boy moved tentatively. When he took his place in front of the man, he trembled with fear. The man took the poker and moved the boy's shirt collar himself. When the poker touched the boy's skin, the boy screamed in pain. He took a step backward, away from the poker. The man grabbed at him and the red-hot poker seared a swath across his chest and the cloth of the boy's shirt was singed. The boy stumbled and fell. The man lost his grip on him. The boy hit his head against a stone on the ground and didn't move. Blood flowed from a gash on his head. The first boy watched from his place by the fire. His expression said that he didn't dare move. The man went to the fallen boy and said something to the first boy. Then the man left. The first boy ran to the second boy and leaned over him. He took off his shirt and placed it over the boy's bleeding wound. Izzy saw the fresh brand on the first boy's collarbone. It was raised and the skin already bubbled from the burn. Then, the vision faded and Izzy came around slowly.

She still held the envelope with no return address

in her hand. She stared at it and blinked. Why would she have such a reaction when she touched this envelope? It was somewhat suspicious that it didn't have a return address. Izzy opened the envelope and took out a single sheet of paper. It read:

"'Flee from sexual immorality. Every other sin a person commits is outside the body, but the sexually immoral person sins against his own body.
1 Corinthians 6:18"

"'For this is the will of God, your sanctification: that you abstain from sexual immorality.'
1 Thessalonians 4:3"

"'Let us walk in the daytime, not in orgies and drunkenness, not in sexual immorality and sensuality, not in quarreling and jealousy.' Romans 13:13"

"The Book says, 'To preserve you from the evil woman, from the smooth tongue of the adulteress.' Proverbs 6:24 "

At the bottom, there was another note: *"These women need to be cleansed of sexual immorality so they can see the Lord."*

A shiver ran up Izzy's spine. This killer thought he was doing these women a *favor.* She whipped out her cell to call Moreno. Before she could press the send button, the door to the mailroom opened.

"Hope you're hungry," Moreno said. "I got your favorite, the shredded beef burrito with green chili sauce."

Izzy nodded her thanks and took the bag. "I was just trying to call you. You're not going to believe what I just found."

Over lunch, Izzy showed Moreno the Bible verses and told him about her vision of the boys being branded. "We're dealing with some kind of a cult and the killer thinks he's helping clean up society.

"The weird thing is," she said between bites, "that in those Internet searches I did, there were lots of references about killing in the name of God, but there was only one reference to a cult that killed sinful women."

"Really?" Moreno said.

"Yeah," Izzy said. "Remember I told you about a cult in Kansas that was busted up by the Feds? It's that one. Those guys started out burning unconscious women but ended up killing them left and right."

"Yeah, like you, I did a little extra-curricular checking on that," Moreno said. "That raid went down just before Cal left the FBI."

"Really?" Izzy said. "You think he might know something about this?"

"Dunno," Moreno said. "I also found something else out."

"What?"

"Remember Marie, the Cajun hooker?"

"Yeah?"

"Turns out she and the dead hooker used to inform for Cal when he was a vice cop. Cal knew the dead woman."

"Why didn't he say anything?" Izzy said.

"Good question." Moreno paused. "Plus it gets better. You know that Polly Fullerton? The dead woman where we found the ear? Cal's wife used to work with her. And Alma Ruiz whose liver we found? Cal arrested her for public intox a few years back."

"No way!" Izzy blurted out. "That's a lot to have uncovered with a little extra-curricular snooping. Do you think Cal's connected somehow?"

"I don't know, but I think it's pretty strange that we're three for three on that deal. I think we need to circumvent Cal on this letter you found. We need to go to Lieutenant Boggs and tell him everything we know before we proceed. Nobody ever wants to wonder about a partner, but what if he's involved? What if he's cranky for some other reason than what he told you? Maybe he's covering something up. We need to know."

Chapter Twenty-Eight

When the mailroom lady returned from lunch, Izzy asked her to look for and report any suspicious mail. She showed her the envelope she'd found. When everyone was on the same page, Izzy and Moreno picked up the leavings from their lunch and made it to Lieutenant Boggs's office.

Izzy knocked on the door.

"Lieutenant? Got a minute?" she said.

Boggs looked up from a pile of paper on his desk, removed his glasses and rubbed his eyes. "Sure, come on it. What is it?"

Moreno weaved his way past a stack of files on the floor and took a seat. He turned the second chair in front of Boggs's desk a little so Izzy could sit down without having to dodge another teetering pile.

"Lieutenant," Moreno said, "O'Donnell found something interesting in the mail room." He turned to Izzy, who produced the letter she'd found.

"Take a look," Izzy said, handing the letter to Boggs.

Boggs put his glasses back on and Izzy and Moreno sat quietly while he read the letter.

"That's a definite connection to this killer. Sick bastard thinks he's doing his victims a favor," Boggs said. He paused and added, "I don't like it that he knows where you work. Just another reason for you and

Moreno to stick close."

"Yes, Sir," Izzy said, glancing sideways at Moreno. "But there's more."

Boggs raised a questioning eyebrow in her direction.

Moreno chimed in. "Sir, O'Donnell and I have been doing some research, and we learned a few things we want to bring to your attention."

The questioning eyebrow turned to Moreno and Izzy felt a warm spot growing inside for Moreno that he hadn't finked on her about her search over the weekend.

"Tell him, Izzy," Moreno prodded.

Izzy recapped her search about the Hevite cult in Kansas that the FBI busted up for killing women.

Boggs leaned back in his chair and took in the tale.

"But that's not all, sir," Moreno said when Izzy had finished. "This is where it gets sticky. In my research, I learned that Cal has a connection to the dead hooker, the mom who had her ear cut off, and the vic whose liver was removed."

Boggs straightened in his chair and leaned over his desk.

"O'Donnell, close the door," Boggs said, then to Moreno, "What are you saying?"

"We just think it's a little too coincidental that Cal has these connections," Moreno said.

Boggs' brow knit into a tight line. "Hmm," was all he mustered.

"We all know Cal was with the FBI years ago," Izzy said. "Nobody wants to believe there's a connection between Cal and all of this. Moreno and I just want some direction before we proceed."

Boggs sat, thinking. Izzy and Moreno exchanged

glances, but didn't say anything. Finally, Boggs took his glasses off again and rubbed his forehead.

"Thank you for bringing this to my attention, detectives," Boggs said. "I can't believe that Calahan has anything to do with this, but protocol states that we can assume nothing. We must check it out. I'll call Internal Affairs immediately."

"Wait," Izzy said, a little too abruptly.

Boggs and Moreno looked at her.

"I mean, isn't there another way? Reporting someone to Internal Affairs always stirs things up and people get jumpy and defensive. Can't we check it out ourselves?"

"And just how do you propose to do that, O'Donnell?" Boggs said.

Moreno looked at her and his face had *yeah, how?* written all over it.

"Let us talk to him, feel him out," Izzy said. "We could talk to him today. Please give us a chance to report back to you before you call IA in on this."

Boggs looked at the two of them. "Moreno, what's your take on this?"

"It's worth a try," Moreno said. "If we're discreet, maybe we can learn something."

Boggs looked from one to the other. Izzy knew she was on the lieutenant's radar screen and could almost hear a little beep, beep, beep when he looked at her.

"Okay," Boggs said, finally. "Let's not jump to any conclusions. You can question Cal while you're briefing him on the latest findings in the mailroom. But be discreet. He's a seasoned officer; he's not stupid. Tread gently. I'll call a contact at the FBI and see if I can find out if Cal was somehow involved with the raid on that Kansas cult. You have my word I won't call IA until after I hear back from them and you."

Izzy smiled slightly, "Thanks, Lieutenant." She nodded to Moreno and the pair rose to leave.

"One more thing," Boggs said. "O'Donnell, if this one is too close to home, I'll understand if you want to put in for a transfer to another case or team."

Izzy gulped. "Sir, thank you, but I'm fine."

Boggs looked at her over his glasses, but didn't say anything before returning to his stack of papers.

Moreno reached to open the door and without looking up, Boggs added, "Good work, detectives."

Izzy looked at Moreno who said, "Thanks."

By the time they hit the hallway, Izzy felt awful, like she'd just ratted on her uncle. She took heart in the lieutenant's words that they shouldn't jump to any conclusions just yet. Surely there would be no connection. Surely a strange set of coincidences had just been put in motion.

The knot forming in the pit of her stomach was doubling in bulk like dough. How was she going to take part in telling Cal about the new developments while watching Cal's every tic and, quietly, ever so subtly, interrogating him at the same time?

If that wasn't enough, she was concerned that Boggs had asked if she wanted to be transferred. She was glad that he recognized how hard this was on her, but she wanted to stay on the case. Suspecting Cal was harder than hard. He was like family. If he was involved in some way, it would destroy her dad. Not to mention how she would feel. She herself couldn't believe it.

Izzy and Moreno walked silently along the hallway

to their desks. She opened her locked drawer and pulled out all the information she'd researched on the computer.

Izzy handed half of the stack to Moreno. "Let's go through this and pull out the stuff that doesn't seem to fit," she said. "We won't toss it, but we can at least narrow the field."

Moreno took his stack, and together, they read historical references to cult killings. They weeded through stacks of paper and came up with a few leads to follow. In particular, they found a reference to branding boys and men in the Hevite cult from Kansas. Brother Hamor again, thought Izzy. She put the rest of the files in her drawer and tucked this particular file under her arm. Izzy had a sense of dread. But she knew she had to pretend that nothing was wrong. She squared her shoulders and walked next to Moreno.

"Guess we should go find Cal and show him the Bible verses I found in the mail room," she said.

Moreno nodded.

They walked through the bullpen toward Cal's office and somebody yelled to them.

"Hey, O'Donnell, Moreno, you got a fax coming in."

They made a detour over to the machine that was spewing a document from the Federal Penitentiary in Terre Haute. The warden, Dean Rodman, had written a letter.

Detectives:

We have been following the news of the serial killer you're tracking in Miami. We recently intercepted these letters that were mailed to one of our inmates, Russell Flatt. On reading them, it looks like they might be significant to your case and we wanted to alert you immediately.

Let us know if we can assist you in any way in this matter.

Sincerely,
Dean Rodman
Warden

Izzy held the fax and flipped to the letters attached. They were addressed to Brother Hamor and they were a play-by-play description of the murders she and Moreno were investigating.

Izzy was elated.

"This is great," Izzy said to Moreno. "What a break." What she didn't say was how happy she was that she had nailed it. The folder describing the cult in Kansas she held under her arm referred to Brother Hamor.

"Yeah, this is good," Moreno said. "Only problem is that if Cal's involved, he'll find a way to weasel out of this. We have to be very careful how we approach this. We don't want to send him underground."

Izzy knew Moreno was right, and deep down, trepidation grew. How was she supposed to interrogate her favorite uncle?

Chapter Twenty-Nine

Izzy and Moreno left the fax machine and the din in the bullpen and walked silently toward Cal's office. Not looking forward to the next few minutes of acting normal while she had so many questions whirling through her head, Izzy stopped before they got there and turned to Moreno.

"Moreno, I've got a favor to ask," Izzy said.

"What's that, Izzy O?"

"I want to do this alone."

"That's not what Boggs said."

"He said to bring Cal up to speed and to feel him out. I want to talk to him. I need this."

Moreno regarded her. "I don't like it. We should do this together."

"Look, I'm not up for male head butting. Let me do the good cop thing. Subtle. You could pretend to take a phone call and just listen from outside the door."

Moreno's eyes went soft and she could tell he was considering it.

"Like I said, I don't like it, but I'll do it," Moreno said. "But know this, Izzy, if anything sounds like it's going south in there, that pretend phone call is going to end. Got it?"

Izzy smiled. "Got it. Thanks, Moreno."

They walked the rest of the way to Cal's office. Izzy took a deep breath then walked through the door.

"Hey, Cal," she said.

He looked up and, through a mouthful of sandwich, he said, "Where have you two been?"

"Just got a bite," Izzy said.

Cal looked up at Moreno who held up his index finger in a "just a second" gesture and he stepped outside Cal's office to take his pretend call.

"I found something interesting in the mail room," Izzy said.

Cal dabbed at the corners of his mouth with a napkin and tossed the remaining crust from his sub sandwich into the trash next to his desk. "What was it?"

Izzy handed him the letter with the Bible verses on it, now encased in a plastic evidence bag. Cal took it and read the verses about chastity. Then he read aloud from the letter, "These women need to be cleansed of sexual immorality so they can see the Lord? Wow. Another nut case who thinks he's doing God's work."

"I'm worried," Izzy said.

"Yeah, we're all worried. We gotta stop this guy, and soon."

"It's more than that," Izzy said, her heart racing like a rabbit.

"What?"

"I'm worried about you."

"Don't start that again. I'm fine," Cal said. "Lillian has a lead for a job."

"Not what I mean, Cal. We've uncovered a connection between you and three of the victims. Polly Fullerton knew your wife, you arrested Alma Ruiz for public intox, and Marie the hooker used to inform for you."

"So?" Cal said. "When you've been a cop as long

as I have, sometimes there are connections."

Izzy handed Cal the fax from the prison warden. "This just came in."

Cal took the fax and read it. His face went suddenly ashen and Izzy was filled with a sense of foreboding.

"What is it, Cal?" Izzy said.

"Oh, um, n-nothing," he stammered.

"Seriously, Cal, what is it?"

"Uh, I just remember hearing about this Brother Hamor back when it all went down. But that was years ago. It was ugly, that's all."

Izzy gave a nonchalant shrug. "What do you make of the warden in Terre Haute saying that this Brother Hamor is really Russell Flatt?" Izzy pressed on.

"Everybody has to be somebody," Cal said. "So what? So the guy used a different name as leader of a whacko cult."

"Do you remember anything about this guy?"

"Yeah, like I said, it was a nasty when it all went down," Cal said. "The leader was sent away for life, his followers were debriefed. Some were put in prison, others were sent for psychiatric help. The whole thing was a mess."

"Cal," Izzy said as gently as she could muster, "We have to pull the file and look into this. With the three other connections, it looks like somebody might be trying to implicate you in these murders. When we look into the Hevite file, will we find someone who might want to involve you? I want to know what to look for so I can clear your name."

Izzy wondered if he could hear her heart beating. Cal shuffled paper and put two pens away in a drawer.

"Look, this may look bad, but I don't have anything to hide. Who would want to drag me in on these murders? I can save you a lot of looking. Don't. There's nothing pertinent there to find."

"Did you know anyone in the FBI who was there when they busted up the colony?"

"Yeah, sure," Cal said, shuffling papers on his desk. "So?"

"So, who?"

"There was a whole team involved in that raid. The perp is in prison. Great. I'm telling you, leave it alone where it is with the Feds."

Moreno ended his call and walked in. "I heard the last part of that. What about the raid?"

Cal's eyes flashed. "Look, Hamor or Flatt or whatever the hell his name is, is in jail. Case closed."

"Cal, we're trying to help," Moreno said. "What if one of his followers is still out there and has become active again after all these years?"

Cal slammed his fist into his desk, scattering paper clips. "That's impossible!"

Izzy stepped in and gently nudged Moreno out of the way. Good cop, bad cop.

"Why is that impossible?" she asked.

Cal's gaze shot around the room. "Because it is."

"Cal," Moreno asked, "Does this have something to do with when you were in the FBI?"

Cal's eyes flashed, beads of sweat were forming on his brow. "Leave. It. Alone."

"It's just a question, not an accusation. We're your partners, your friends who want to help," Izzy said.

Cal regarded both of them for an instant. He picked up the fax they'd brought in, crumpled it into a ball and hurled it at them. They dodged in unison.

He picked up and slammed a pile of folders on his desk. "Get out!"

Chapter Thirty

Izzy and Moreno left Cal's office. Cal slammed his door behind them. The other cops in the bullpen stared at them as they headed to their desks.

"What was all that about?" she said.

"Izzy O, that's a man who is hot about something," Moreno said.

"Yeah. What's he hiding?"

"Dunno, but I still can't believe he's involved in any way."

"I agree." She paused and stopped.

He turned to her. "What is it?"

"This is just weird for me. I mean I grew up around Cal. He was my dad's partner. We do have to treat him like a person of interest, don't we? I mean, just like Mark Traesk and Brother Gideon?"

"For now, yes," Moreno said. "I'm betting after we report Cal's reaction to the Lieutenant, he'll have no choice but to take it up the chain of command, and Cal will get suspended."

Izzy shook her head in despair. "And it'll be my fault," she said. "He's gonna hate me."

Moreno put a hand on her shoulder. "Izzy, if he gets suspended it's not your fault. If something's up with a member of Miami's finest, don't look at uncovering it as being anyone's fault. Look at it like you're doing your job." He stopped walking and turned to look at her. "We both know Cal's no killer. We'll just have to figure out what's up and clear his name. That's all."

She looked him in the eyes and nodded slightly. "You're right, I suppose," she said.

He patted her shoulder and turned to continue the walk to Izzy's desk. "Yeah, that's me, Mr. Right." He grinned and glanced at her sideways.

Izzy was glad that he was trying to bring the mood up. But her heart was dragging the floor. It wasn't easy to suspect Cal. How was Cal feeling about all of this? What would her dad say when he found out?

They walked in silence to Izzy's desk. They locked their documents in her file drawer for safekeeping and stopped by Boggs' office. He listened with a somber face. Izzy and Moreno knew what would be coming down the pike for Cal soon.

****

After a long day dealing with the mailroom, faxes, meetings and phone calls, Izzy was exhausted. She really just wanted to go home and put her feet up, but she had made an appointment to meet Mark Traesk to see a house on her way home. She knew she had to tell Moreno, and he'd have to come along. She hated to ask him, but mostly she hoped he wouldn't give her any grief about it.

She peered up over her computer monitor and saw Moreno at his desk sifting through paperwork.

"Hey, Moreno," she said.

Moreno shifted his gaze. "Wuzzup, Izzy O?"

"I've got a favor to ask," she said. "I'm supposed to meet Mark Traesk and see a house on my way home, and that means you need to be my guard dog. You in?

Or should I cancel?"

Moreno took a second before he answered. Here it comes, thought Izzy.

"Do you really think it's a good idea?" he said.

"Yes, I do," she said with deliberate defiance in her voice. "Dad can't make the stairs anymore and I think he needs to move to a one-story place."

Moreno's face flushed with exasperation. "Not *that*, Izzy, we all know that's a good idea. I meant using a possible suspect for a realtor."

Izzy was a little embarrassed that she'd jumped to a conclusion. "Oh, sorry," she said. "We cleared him, remember?"

"I still think it's fishy that he's the common denominator with two victims. He's not off my list of interest."

"Well, look at it this way, it gives us a chance to keep an eye on him," Izzy said.

A smile tugged at the corners of Moreno's mouth. "We've both had a hard day. What's in it for me?"

Izzy pursed her lips in thought. "Well, two things."

Moreno raised an eyebrow at her. "Two things?"

"Yup. One, you'll know that you're following orders by protecting me—"

"And two? That's the one I'm more interested in," he said.

"Two, I'll buy you a couple beers at the bar afterward."

Moreno stood up, grabbed his blazer, put it on over his shoulder holster and said, "You're on. Let's go look at a house."

Izzy grinned. It was comforting to know she could count on Moreno. He was a flirtatious twit sometimes, but she couldn't help liking him.

The pair drove across town and dropped Moreno's car in the parking lot of the bar. They decided to take Izzy's car to meet Mark. It would look better if they were in one car, since they wouldn't have to conjure an excuse for Moreno being along.

They drove a few short miles to a small, apartment complex. Mark was already there waiting.

He approached Izzy's car and opened the door for her.

"Good afternoon, Izzy," Mark said. He noticed Moreno sitting in the passenger's seat and a question flashed in his eyes.

"Hi, Mark," Izzy said. "I'd like you to meet a co-worker. This is Pete Moreno. We're carpooling."

"The more the merrier. I was just surprised to see someone with you," Mark said.

Izzy thought that was a strange remark.

Moreno caught her eye when he got out of the car and walked over to shake Mark's hand. He flashed her a smile then turned to Traesk.

"Pleased to meet you," Moreno said.

"Likewise," Traesk said.

Traesk looked at Izzy and smiled. He extended his hand in a welcoming gesture toward the door. "Shall we?"

Izzy smiled. "Yes, thank you," she said. She took a few steps toward the main entrance to the apartment complex. She looked back to check on Moreno. He was right behind her, and Traesk was pulling up the rear. He was looking Moreno over top to bottom, and he had a slight scowl on his face. When he noticed Izzy looking at him, he said, "We'll just take the elevator to the left.

I'm right behind you. "

Izzy smiled at him, but she didn't buy his jovial act. Something was bugging Traesk.

When they arrived at the elevator, Moreno put his hand on the small of Izzy's back and guided her to the side. Izzy sensed Traesk's gaze on her. Was he jealous? Moreno pushed the up button and turned to the realtor.

"What floor are we headed to?" Moreno asked.

"The seventh."

"Oh," Izzy said.

"Is that a problem?" Traesk asked.

"Well, just in case of a fire or other emergency. I'm not sure my dad would be able to make seven flights of stairs," she said.

"It's so nice you take such things into consideration for your dad," Traesk said. "But I assure you, this building is very safe."

Izzy smiled uncomfortably. Why wouldn't she take such things into account? Spencer was her dad after all, and it didn't matter how safe a building was, if the elevators went out, Spencer couldn't manage seven flights of stairs.

Traesk seemed to pick up on her thoughts. "This building is very popular and rarely has any vacancies. But from time to time an apartment will come open. It's a much sought-after complex. If you're not happy with an apartment on the seventh floor, perhaps you can look at this one to see if you like it since all the layouts are similar in this building. Then, if an apartment on a lower floor comes up, you'll already know the floor plan."

Izzy said, "That works."

The elevator stopped smoothly and the trio walked

out. Traesk fiddled in his pocket and produced a key to open the door.

They walked inside and the view from the sliding glass doors overlooking the city was stunning. Palm trees danced in the breeze in the parking lot below. Izzy hugged herself and sighed. This would be nice. No maintenance at all—that would be someone else's problem. Up until this moment, she hadn't considered an apartment for Spencer. She looked around. There was a nice-sized kitchen and dining area that butted up to the balcony where there were two chaise lounge chairs. Izzy looked around the apartment. Yes, an apartment might be nice.

Traesk chatted about the monthly rent, average cost of utilities and maintenance fees. It all sounded do-able. The two men watched her as she looked around. She overheard Traesk making small talk with Moreno. They were talking about her. She eavesdropped while pretending to interest herself in the kitchen.

"How long have you worked together?" Traesk asked.

"We've known each other for a while, but we've just recently been assigned to the same team," Moreno hedged.

"She's very nice, I think."

Moreno nodded his agreement.

"She and her dad own that bar, but I've never seen her drunk. I like that. I had a client once who drank like a fish and I found it to be very disconcerting to have to show her a house when she was inebriated," Traesk said. "I don't have her as a client anymore."

"I can only imagine how frustrating that would be," Moreno said.

"You know, Izzy and I stopped for a cup of coffee once, and I saw her put her change in the charity jar at the counter."

Moreno laughed. "That sounds like her. Always got her heart into something."

Puh-lease. Didn't *everyone* put change in the charity jar when buying a cup of coffee at the convenience store? She looked through the cupboards and then went in to see the bedrooms and bathroom. Yes, this would suit Spencer just fine.

When she was done, she walked back out to the living room where Traesk and Moreno waited.

"Well, I have to admit that I like the floor plan," she said. "It's cozy and roomy at the same time."

Mark smiled. "I thought you might approve," he said. "And they allow pets. Didn't you say you thought your dad might like to have a dog?"

"Yes, I think so," Izzy said. "But I really don't like the seventh floor arrangement."

Traesk led them out of the apartment and back downstairs. "If something comes open in this building, I'll let you know."

Izzy was grateful. "Thanks for showing me this place, Mark. I hadn't considered an apartment, but it might be a good solution."

"No problem. I'll call you when I have some more properties to show." He shook Izzy's hand then turned to Moreno.

"It was nice to meet you, Traesk said, extending his hand.

Moreno shook his hand. "Likewise."

Moreno led Izzy to the car and opened her door for her.

"Wow, Moreno, you opened a door for me? What's up? Got a fever?"

Moreno walked around to his side of the car and got in. "I guess Mr. Smooth just rubbed off on me. Don't get used to it."

Izzy scoffed. "Believe me, I won't."

Moreno looked wounded. "Maybe I should be nicer to you and your fellow womenfolk. That guy is frothy smooth, and I think he has a crush on you."

Izzy tossed her head back and laughed. "What?"

"I'm not joking, Izzy. I think that guy has a crush on you. He was asking me all kinds of questions like do you have a boyfriend, and do you go to church. The best part was that he said how humble and virtuous you are because you don't flaunt your cute figure." Moreno laughed out loud.

"What's so funny?" Izzy said. "I work hard to keep my figure."

Moreno stopped laughing. "Sorry, Izzy. Not laughing at that. Never." He looked her up and down. "You're cute, Izzy. I like what I see."

Exasperated, Izzy snapped her fingers in his face. "Moreno, hello? Focus, buddy, focus," she said. "Let's stick to task, here. Don't you think it's weird that he used the word virtuous?"

Moreno shrugged, "No. Not particularly."

"Moreno, don't get all caught up in the smooth act. He's a high-end realtor. He practices smooth. He makes money with smooth."

"Yeah, rookie, I know. I remember the conversation about how you thought he was so nice and didn't want to believe he could be involved in this," Moreno said.

"Okay, if we're supposed to acknowledge his connection to this case, then we should consider everything. And I'm telling you, there's more to this guy than meets the eye. What if virtuous Mr. Smooth might be asking you questions about me for other reasons? Remember the uterus that was addressed to me? Some killer knows who I am. Nobody's interested in *me*, Moreno. I just hope you didn't tell him where I live."

"Izzy, he already knows where you live. You told me the first time he met you it was at the bar. He *absolutely* knows where you live."

Chapter Thirty-One

Izzy and Moreno rang the doorbell at the Vazquez residence. Jaime answered the door.

"May we come in?" Moreno said.

Jaime hesitated, then opened the door. "Please do," he said.

Izzy walked into the living room where a week ago, a distraught Jaime had sat on the couch weeping over his lost wife. This afternoon, there was a very attractive Latina sitting on the couch. Her wide brown eyes searched Izzy's face. Lips with smeared lipstick curled into a smile.

Jaime indicated the woman. "This is Esmeralda Marichal. A friend of the family," he said.

"Looks like a very good friend," Moreno said.

Izzy knew what he was thinking. That lipstick and low cut blouse. Izzy elbowed him.

"Mr. Vazquez, we have a few questions for you. Perhaps your guest would like to continue her visit another time?" Izzy said.

Jaime and Esmeralda exchanged glances.

"No. She's a close friend. Anything you have to ask me, you can ask in front of her," he said.

Izzy shrugged mentally. *Okay, if you say so.*

"Mr. Vazquez," Moreno said. "Did your wife have any enemies?"

"What, like someone she wouldn't give credit to at

193

the store? No. No enemies. Everyone loved Lupita."

"Everyone?" Izzy said. "Including you?"

Esmeralda shifted uneasily on the couch, but didn't say anything.

Jaime's face looked a little pinched.

"We were married twenty years. Of course I loved her. She was my wife," he said.

Izzy sensed he was lying. She glanced at Moreno. He showed no reaction.

"Your wife was killed in a similar manner to the way other women have been murdered recently," Izzy said. "But we know it wasn't the same killer."

Jaime looked suddenly stricken and Esmeralda picked nervously at her cuticles.

"But how do you know?" Jaime said. "Everything was the same, just like in the newspapers. The slit throat, the heart removed, the cross on top of the heart—for the religious aspect. Everything. The only difference was that the body wasn't burned. There's no place to burn her here. That's the only thing he did differently."

"You have this all figured out, don't you?" Moreno said.

"Dios mio," Esmeralda said. "I told you, you should have just asked for a divorce, Jaime."

"Cállate," Jaime said. "Quiet, *chica.*"

"No, I think she hasn't said quite enough," Moreno said.

"I'm just a friend," Esmeralda said.

"Honey," Izzy said. "You're more than just a friend. Your lipstick is smeared all over your face and your panties are under the coffee table."

"Tell ya what," Moreno said, indicating the coffee

table, "why don't you take a minute to put those panties back on, and we'll all go downtown and have a little chat."

Chapter Thirty-Two

The next day, Izzy and Moreno sat at their desks, accomplishing nothing. The lieutenant had made an announcement. Cal was taking leave and any details of his cases, phone messages, faxes, or anything of that sort should be directed to Moreno. Then he walked into his office and closed the door without another word of explanation.

The rest of the detectives all looked at Izzy and Moreno with questioning gazes. Moreno madly twirled his toothpick in his mouth. Izzy could tell he was uncomfortable. Probably for the same reason she was. People were going to ask questions. Izzy was about to confer with Moreno about what their line should be. The phone between their desks interrupted. They both dove for it, but with his long arms, Moreno reached it first.

"Moreno," he said into the receiver. He listened and didn't say anything more than, "We'll be right there." Then he hung up.

"We're needed in the morgue," he said. "Dr. Dan has something to show us."

Izzy picked up her blazer and put it on. Moreno took a last swig of his coffee and grabbed his blazer, too. They headed for the door. Izzy was glad to get out of the bullpen and away from all the staring eyes.

They walked quickly along the corridor and made

their way downstairs to the morgue where they found Dr. Dan in the lab hunched over a microscope.

"Hey, Doc," Moreno said.

Dr. Dan didn't look up. "Good morning, detectives," he said. He looked up at Izzy who waved at him with a pair of plastic gloves in her hand.

"Don't worry, Izzy, you won't be needing those today. I've got something to show you."

Izzy and Moreno waited silently.

"Remember that clump of dirt you found on the carpet at the hooker's place?"

Izzy nodded.

"I have the results of the analysis back. In fact, if you come over here, you can look under the microscope and see what I'm looking at."

Izzy and Moreno filed around to the other side of the table. Dr. Dan relinquished the lab stool he was sitting on and gestured for Izzy to take a seat.

Izzy put her eye to the microscope. "What am I looking at?" she asked. "Besides a clump of dirt?"

"Do you see those spikey looking balls?" Dr. Dan said.

"Yes."

"That my dear detectives, is pollen."

Izzy moved over so Moreno could take a look. "So what?" Moreno said. "There's pollen all over Miami and all over Miami's soil."

Dr. Dan seemed to be enjoying this. He had his hands clasped behind him, and he rocked back and forth on his shoes. It seemed to Izzy that he looked like a large professor-shaped punching bag bobbing in the corner.

"Pollen, yes. There is pollen, but this is not just any

pollen, and it isn't just any soil," Dr. Dan said.

He looked at Izzy and Moreno, then continued. "What is really interesting is that this soil is topsoil like you would buy in a bag. This isn't regular soil from around here. And the pollen is *definitely* not from around here."

"Okay, Doc," said Moreno. "Enough with the science lesson. What have we got here?"

"What we have here is pollen from a sunflower," Dr. Dan said.

"A sunflower?" Izzy said.

"So what? People feed birds all the time," Moreno said.

"Ah," Dr. Dan said, "But *this* sunflower is actually growing and it's from a giant sunflower. Those aren't the kind of seeds found in bird mix."

Izzy furrowed her brow. "Nobody grows giant sunflowers in Miami."

Dr. Dan shrugged. "Well, apparently somebody does, and that somebody was at your crime scene."

Chapter Thirty-Three

Two days had gone by since Dr. Dan had shown Izzy and Moreno the pollen. Everywhere they happened to drive, they looked in yards and over fences for any sign of giant sunflowers. They saw none. But, Miami was a big place, so canvassing the streets probably wasn't a great way to find a perp growing sunflowers.

It was lonesome without Cal at the office. As predicted, Lt. Boggs had suspended him with pay, pending the investigation. Izzy knew Cal would be relieved about the monetary part of it.

She and Moreno were holding the fort down, but it didn't feel the same. She was busy on the phone, calling greenhouses and gardening supply companies to see if she could get a line on people who were growing sunflowers.

She had just hung up after calling the twentieth gardening lead in the phone book when Lt. Boggs stopped by her desk.

"Moreno, O'Donnell, in my office," was all he said.

Izzy glanced at Moreno and they both followed Boggs. He indicated that Moreno should close the door. Izzy took a seat and Moreno followed suit.

"Detectives," he said. "I have news about Cal."

Izzy shifted uneasily in her seat and waited for him to continue.

"As you might know, Cal was in the FBI for a time when he first entered law enforcement."

Izzy and Moreno both nodded.

"He was a young man and it seems he was part of the team that raided the Hevite cult compound."

Inside, Izzy was giving herself a mental high five. Outwardly, she tried not to grin. She was right. There not only was a cult connection, but Cal had been involved.

Moreno smiled and kicked her sideways under the cover of Boggs' desk.

Izzy straightened a bit and said, "Go on, Lieutenant."

"Well, it went down like this. The FBI got word that the Hevites, as they called themselves, were performing ritualistic killings and mutilations of women. After they killed the women, they'd burn their bodies. When the FBI raided the compound, they rounded up the leader, one Russell Flatt, who was known as Brother Hamor. Izzy, I believe you found a letter addressed to Hamor in the mail room," the Lieutenant said.

"Yes, I did," Izzy said.

"Good work," he said.

Izzy beamed. "Thank you, Sir."

"What's this got to do with Cal?" Moreno asked.

"Orders were to round up each and every member of the Hevite colony. They were all to be questioned, and in turn, any women and children being held at the compound against their will would be released after processing and making a statement if they were cleared," Boggs said.

"Why not the men?" Moreno asked.

"It was a patriarchal society, so all the men served as father figures to all children. The men had absolute power in the community, and Hamor had supreme power," he explained.

"I still don't get how this involves Cal, though," Izzy said.

"I told you that to get to this," Boggs said. "According to the report, Cal saw a young woman who had two boys with her. They were about twelve years old. One was badly burned and had a bandaged head. The woman pleaded with Cal to let her and the boys go, and Cal turned a blind eye while they escaped through a hole in a fence surrounding the compound. Problem is, there was a roster of all the Hevites, and three of them came up missing. Cal's three. Up until that point Cal had a spotless record, but he was written up and told he wouldn't advance because he disobeyed a direct order."

Izzy shook her head. "That explains his reaction to the fax we showed him about the Brother Hamor letters the warden at Terre Haute found," Izzy said.

"And why he went nuts when I pressed him," Moreno said.

"Look, you were just doing your jobs," Boggs said. "Don't worry about Cal. He left the FBI to start over, he moved here and joined the Miami PD, started in vice. You know the rest. He's got an exemplary record," Boggs said.

"Wow," Izzy said. "No wonder he never talks about his FBI days. So is he cleared to come back to duty?"

"Not quite yet," Boggs said. "There's still the little bit about his connection to the victims."

Moreno sat up. "Actually, I did some digging into

that," he said.

Izzy raised an eyebrow. Why hadn't he shared this with her?

"What did you learn?" Boggs said.

"Cal's wife worked with Polly Fullerton years ago before Polly got married and quit to raise a family. According to Cal, it had been years since he'd seen her and she changed her name when she got married, so there was no reason for him to make a connection," Moreno said.

"As for Alma Ruiz, Cal and his wife were out on the town one evening and this really drunk woman was lying on the sidewalk outside a bar. Cal wasn't on duty, but he stopped to see if she was okay. He sat the woman up and she puked all over him. He ended up arresting her for public intox," said Moreno.

"What about the hooker whose uterus was addressed to me?" Izzy said.

"We've all worked vice," Moreno said. "She was one of Cal's informants. Sometimes hookers, especially informants, die."

Izzy smiled. "Well, there you have it, then," she said. "Cal's clear. When will he come back to work?"

Boggs looked very grave. "Not so fast, O'Donnell. I know you and Cal are close, but I'm the bearer of more bad news."

Izzy sat on the edge of her chair and Moreno leaned forward. "What bad news?"

Boggs shoved a file folder over his desk toward Izzy and Moreno. "Somebody in Fraud downstairs brought me this yesterday," he said.

Izzy opened the file folder. Inside there were two life insurance policies each for $100,000. One was for

Polly Fullerton, and the other was for Alma Ruiz. The named beneficiary was Cory P. "Cal" Callaghan. And it was signed by Cal himself.

Chapter Thirty-Four

After the meeting with Boggs, Izzy wanted to rush to the phone and call Cal. But she decided to wait. By Thursday, it was time. She needed to talk to him, to know how he felt about everything and especially how he felt about her and all of this. Besides, tomorrow was poker night and she figured it would be better to clear the air before the game.

She found a moment on her way home from work to stop by his house. She rang the bell and Cal opened the door.

"What do you want?" he said.

Great. He's in a stellar mood. "I just wanted to come and check on you. How's it going?"

"How do you think it's going? I'm friggin' suspended. Thanks to you," Cal said. He didn't invite her in.

The sheer weight of his statement knocked Izzy back.

"I didn't set out to get you suspended. I just reported evidence I found."

"You brought up the one event in my career I thought I had put in the past. But no, you had to dig it up."

Caught between blame and duty, Izzy chose to defend herself.

"Look Cal, yeah, I found a connection, but Boggs

was the one who pulled your FBI skeleton out of the closet, not me. And so what? That's past. You started over and you've made a name for yourself with the Miami PD. You're the best. Do you think it was easy for me to take this to Boggs? You're family to me. C'mon. We can either argue about who's to blame for what, or we can figure a way to fix it. What's it gonna be?"

Izzy's chest swelled. She nailed that speech—and off the cuff, too.

He opened the door.

"Come in," he said.

She walked into the home she knew almost as well as her own. Julius, the family dachshund, scampered up to meet her. She scratched him behind the ears and made her way into the living room. Sun shone brightly through the plate glass window onto the tile. She took a seat on one of the two beige sofas adorned with a tropical bamboo and flower motif.

"You know I just hate it when you're right," he said.

"Right about what?" Izzy said.

"About having to figure this out. I want to blame you, but I know I should only blame myself," he said.

"Whatever," she said in an effort to save his pride. "How are we gonna fix this? What about those insurance policies?"

Cal blew out a sigh and rubbed his bald spot.

"I didn't take those policies out, Izzy. You've gotta believe me."

"Cal, nobody thinks you're committing insurance fraud, but that sure looks like your signature, so we have to figure that one out."

"I'm stumped," Cal said. "Been thinking. How would somebody get my signature to forge?"

"I've been wondering about that too," Izzy said. "How could somebody get hold of your signature? Come to poker tomorrow and we'll bat it around," she said.

Cal paused and then with the edge back in his voice, he said, "No. No poker."

"You'll be among friends," Izzy said.

"Don't push it. I said no."

With that, Izzy knew the conversation was over. She bade Cal goodbye and saw herself out the door.

****

Friday evening rolled around, and Izzy was downstairs in the storeroom under the stairs at the bar setting up for poker night. What a week.

Dr. Dan burst through the door wearing his fishing vest, lapél pins winking in the light. Izzy had to smile despite herself. She wondered if she would recognize this man at a poker table without it. The vest was nothing more than a placeholder for the many pins it displayed, and Izzy wondered if the backs of them ever poked him when he wore it.

"What can I do to help?" Dr. Dan asked.

"Grab the other end of this table?"

He set his sock filled with bottle caps on a chair and moved over to the table to help her slide it to the center of the room.

"Thanks," she said.

"No problem. "Where's Spencer?"

"Moreno went upstairs to get him. They'll be along in a minute."

Dr. Dan looked at Izzy, his face pensive. "Cal isn't

coming tonight, is he?" he said.

Izzy sighed. "I asked him. He said no."

"I think he's embarrassed," Dr. Dan said.

"Yeah, I can see that. But he'd be around friends," she added.

"Yeah, but friends who *want* to believe in his innocence and would want to talk about it all."

Izzy nodded. "He probably just needs some space."

"It's just as well. Then he won't feel awkward and neither will we," Dr. Dan said.

Izzy had to agree, but she didn't say it out loud. They were saved from further conversation when Moreno and Spencer came into the room with the deck of cards.

They settled themselves around the table. Apple brought a round of drinks and some nibbles she had set out on a plate. One of the other employees was on duty that night, so Apple pulled up a chair next to Izzy to enjoy the camaraderie. Norman sat perched on her lap. There was a large sign on the door displaying a circle. Inside the circle, in big, bold letters, was the word NORMAN with a line through it—just to remind everyone that Norman was to stay in the storeroom lest Izzy get slapped with another citation from the health department.

Just as Izzy knew it would, the conversation eventually rolled around to Cal.

"So what's this business with Cal and the insurance policies?" said Dr. Dan.

Izzy and Moreno looked at each other. Moreno gestured at Izzy.

"Go ahead."

Izzy explained how a member of the fraud

department had given the Lieutenant some insurance policies on women who had been murdered recently. Cal was the beneficiary.

"It looks bad," Moreno said.

Spencer put his cards down on the table and rubbed his forehead.

"I don't believe it for a minute," he said. "In Ireland, when I was growing up, we had an expression, 'A friend's eye is a good mirror.' I'm here to tell you that there's another explanation."

Moreno piped in. "There's gotta be."

"That may be true, Dad, and I know Cal's been a good friend for many years, but I have something to tell you that doesn't bode well for him," Izzy said.

Everyone put their cards down and looked at Izzy.

"A few weeks ago, he confided something to me, and I feel really bad not keeping that confidence. However, I think under the circumstances, I should tell you."

All eyes were on Izzy.

"What is it?" Moreno said.

"Cal's wife lost her job and money is really tight right now. Jeremy's in college and Heather is on her way next year. They're having difficulties and may even have to move," Izzy said. "Cal told me they were going to put their house on the market."

Dr. Dan blew out his cheeks. "Wow," he said.

Apple patted Norman and didn't say anything.

"That's rough," Spencer said. "But it's no reason for you to throw my best friend and your partner to the wolves."

"What? I didn't throw Cal to the wolves," Izzy said.

"Then why is he suspended?"

"Look, Spence, Izzy was just doing her job. She found some evidence and she brought it to light." Moreno said. "It was Boggs who suspended him pending investigation. It's all routine. You know that."

"When a man has a terrible secret that doesn't hurt anyone but himself to keep, you don't dig it up for him," Spencer said.

"You knew about him letting those people go from the cult?" Izzy said.

All eyes were on Spencer.

"Of course I knew," he said. "He was my partner for twenty-five years. I know everything about him. I know how loud he snores. I know how he takes his coffee. I know that he has a mole under his left arm. I know *everything*."

"Why didn't you say anything?" Dr. Dan said.

"What's there to say? He let those people go and got smacked because of it. What's that got to do with this case? And it doesn't have anything to do with how his signature ended up on insurance documents," Spencer said.

Izzy set her cards down. "Don't you get it?"

Moreno twirled his toothpick. "Get what?"

Izzy looked around the table at her friends. "That kind of windfall money could defray college costs for Cal and get him and his family out of financial trouble."

"So now you're trying to find ways to implicate Cal?" Spencer said in a huff.

"No, Dad. That's not it at all."

Moreno took the toothpick out of his mouth. "I think Izzy's just trying to point out that if Cal had some sort of prior knowledge of who was going to be killed, he could really clean up."

Dr. Dan slumped back in his chair, and his "I climbed the Great Wall of China" pin glinted in the light. "This looks rotten."

"There must be a logical explanation," Spencer said. "I just can't accept that Cal would be involved in something like this." He turned to Izzy and shook a finger at her. "And I'm shocked you would even think he could be involved."

Exasperated, Izzy set her cards face down on the table. "Look, guys, I'm just stating the obvious. I thought we were all supposed to think like cops. I'm not saying Cal's guilty. I *am* saying, from an outside perspective, it could be construed that he has motive and that really looks bad for him. We need to find a way to clear his name."

Dr. Dan thought a moment. "We can do a forensic analysis on the signature on the insurance policy."

Spencer fiddled with his cards. "What other facts have come in this week?"

Izzy and Moreno took turns filling him in. There was the sunflower pollen and the results of the blood found at the Polly Fullerton crime scene. Most of the blood was Polly's, but there was another woman's blood there, too. There was no match for it in the system.

"Well, if there was blood at the crime scene, it had to have gotten there somehow," Dr. Dan said. He tapped a gold caduceus pin on his hat. "I should know. I am the doctor after all. We learn about blood in school."

Izzy couldn't help but smile.

"If your perp is a woman, wouldn't she have to be

pretty big in order to be strong enough to take her victims down?" Apple asked.

Everyone agreed that the suspect would have to be a good-sized woman to subdue and kill these victims, and it was more plausible that the perp was a man.

Apple, who had sat silently and listened, perked up. "Are you sure there isn't a wounded witness out there?" she said.

Chapter Thirty-Five

Izzy and Moreno pulled into the parking lot of *La Parilla*, a Latin restaurant known for its grilled seafood. They were meeting Mark to question him, but they had told him they wanted to talk about houses. Izzy hated to mislead him, but it was the only way to hook up with him without being conspicuous, and if he was culpable, the last thing they needed was for him to bolt.

The *maître d'* showed them to a table in the corner. Moreno held Izzy's chair for her.

She looked at him and raised an eyebrow.

"What?" he said. "I told you I know how to be polite. Quit looking so surprised."

"I'm just not used to it from you, Moreno," she said.

"Yeah, well don't get used to it, either," he said. "I'm just trying to show you I can be as well-mannered as Mr. Smooth."

Just then, the door opened and Mark Traesk walked in.

"Here he comes now," Izzy said. She rose from her seat and gave a little wave in Traesk's direction.

He walked over and they exchanged greetings. Moreno shook his hand and indicated a chair. "Have a seat."

The table was covered with a white tablecloth set with goblets of ice water and a dish with swirled butter.

The waitress came by and handed each of them a menu. After some deliberation Izzy ordered a shrimp and pineapple curry dish, Moreno chose the blackened mahi-mahi, and Traesk selected the red snapper. They handed their menus to the waitress and sat back sipping their water.

"So," Mark said. "Have you made a decision on a place for your father?"

Izzy glanced at Moreno then turned to Traesk. "No, not yet. But I'm narrowing it down. Actually, I'd like to ask you some questions."

Mark reached inside his jacket pocket and retrieved a small notepad and a pen. Poised to take notes, he said, "Okay, I'm ready. Fire away."

Moreno leaned in a bit. "It's not about houses."

Traesk looked a little confused.

"Mark," Izzy said. "We do work for the city, and Moreno here is my partner. We're cops."

Traesk stiffened slightly.

"We just want to ask you a few questions," she said.

"About what? I haven't done anything wrong," Traesk said.

"We've discovered a strange coincidence," Moreno said.

Izzy put her hand on Moreno's arm. "Let's start at the beginning," she said. "Mark, you know about those killings around town, right?"

"Ah," he said, relaxing a bit. "I know what this is about. A couple of those women were clients of mine."

"Yes," Izzy said. "What can you tell us about them?"

"First of all, it's really unfortunate that they died.

And it was bad for business. Their families called after their deaths and said they no longer needed my services—they had put house hunting on hold."

"Mark, she means do you have an alibi for your whereabouts when those women were killed?" Moreno said.

"Well, of course I do," Traesk said. He looked at Izzy. "Remember I told you that, like you take care of your dad, I help my mom?"

Izzy nodded.

"I was with her," Traesk said. "That's pretty simple, really. When I'm not at work, I'm usually with her."

Izzy understood how that worked. Nonetheless, they'd have to corroborate his alibi.

"Great," she said.

Moreno butted in. "But we'll have to talk to her anyway."

Traesk smiled. "My mother raised me in a Godly home. I can assure you we always try to do the right thing. When would you like to meet her?"

His willingness to help was commendable. If he was going to bolt, he'd do it after she laid her next question on him.

"Soon. We'd like to talk to her soon. Mark, we need a DNA sample from you," she said.

"Whatever for?" he said.

"Routine," Moreno said. "We're asking everyone who has been around the victims to submit a DNA sample. Even family. Even cops."

Nice, thought Izzy. She'd have to remember that line.

"Well, you won't find my DNA at your crime

scene, so I have no reason not to comply," he said cordially. "How do we do this? Is it like on TV where you swab my cheek?"

Izzy laughed. "Yes, in fact it's exactly like that."

Moreno took over again. "Look, Mark, this is a nice restaurant. You're being very helpful. Let's not embarrass you by doing this at the table. If we take a moment in the men's room, I can collect a cheek swab there and then we can enjoy our lunch and talk about houses. Will that work?"

"Of course," Mark said. "Thanks. Anything I can do to help. Need finger prints or anything else?"

Izzy didn't blink. "I think that's all we'll need for now."

Moreno and Traesk rose and headed to the men's room. This would take all of thirty seconds, Izzy knew. But she had to wonder about Mark. For someone who was closely associated with murdered people, he seemed very compliant. Maybe he didn't have anything to hide. But, he also didn't seem very ruffled about having two of his clients murdered. Wouldn't that affect a guy? He hardly flinched, and his explanation about the families no longer needing his services was reasonable, but he'd said it so smoothly, without emotion.

Either he was innocent or he truly was Mr. Smooth.

Chapter Thirty-Six

Later that evening, after Spencer had gone upstairs to get ready for bed, Izzy and Apple stood behind the bar doing dishes. Izzy washed and rinsed, handed the glasses to Apple who dried and put them away. They'd done this together so many times, they worked like a finely tuned machine.

"So what's new about your murder case?" Apple said.

"Well, we've been taking DNA samples from various people," Izzy said.

"And that's notable for what reason?" Apple said.

"It just feels weird to take Cal's."

"I thought it was routine to compare DNA with the cops handling the case," Apple said.

"Well, it is. We all have DNA samples on file. It's just that this time, comparing Cal's is not simply for the usual reasons of elimination. He's actually implicated in the case. I feel awful that he is in the spotlight when nobody believes he's culpable, but evidence does point toward him with this whole insurance policy business."

"Have you talked to him recently?" Apple said.

"Yeah, I went over there with Moreno the Shadow, yesterday."

Apple laughed. "Togetherness is a good thing. To-partness is also a good thing. I bet you're getting pretty tired of Moreno."

"Having him shadow me isn't as bad as I thought it would be," Izzy said.

Apple wiggled her eyebrows at Izzy. "Oh?"

"Not like *that*, you goofball!"

"There's always hope," Apple said. "So, how was Cal?"

Izzy paused with her hands still in the soapy water. "He's grumpy—"

"And that's new because…?"

Izzy shot her a glance. "Just because you two don't get along is no reason to be like that."

"Sorry," Apple said.

Izzy continued. "Well the other day when I called him, he accused me of causing his suspension. Mostly he doesn't want his past debacle at the FBI brought to light. His pride took a hit on that one."

"He's had years to prove he's a good cop," Apple said.

"Did you just say your rival is a good cop?" Izzy asked.

"Izzy, just because I can't stand the old coot doesn't mean I think he's a bad cop."

Izzy smiled. "Well, he's grumpy, but when Moreno and I were over there yesterday, he seems to be taking the suspension in stride. At least on the surface, that is."

"Well, what's he saying?" Apple said.

"He flatly denies taking out insurance policies on those victims," Izzy said. "He's trying to hold his head high."

"Well, what did he want you to do?" Apple said.

"He wanted me to get him an Italian sandwich from Vinnie's deli," Izzy said.

They both laughed.

Turning quiet, Izzy looked at Apple. "I had another dream."

"Oh? When?"

"The other night. I didn't want to say anything until we had a quiet moment. I'm afraid people are going to start to think I'm crazy," Izzy said. "I'm not, though. I mean, anyone could have dreams if they're working on a case. Especially if it's gruesome like this one."

"Right," Apple said, but she didn't sound convinced. "So what was this dream about?"

Izzy picked up a towel and dried her hands off. "I saw two boys and a man. That's not so different. I've seen them before. But they called the man Brother Hamor and he called one of the boys Seth. Then my alarm clock went off, and that's all I got. It's probably nothing. We got those letters addressed to Brother Hamor—from the warden in Terre Haute, they were signed Seth. I'm sure it's all related to this dream."

Izzy looked at Apple. Apple shuddered.

"What?" Izzy said.

"I just had a cold chill," Apple said.

"Want me to turn the air down?"

"Not *that* kind of a cold chill. A real cold chill."

Izzy was a little confused. "What are you talking about?"

Apple pushed her glasses up on her nose. "I mean, the name Seth."

"What about it?"

"The name Seth means 'Anointed One'."

Izzy looked at Apple. "Have you gone loopy on me?"

There was no expression of frivolity on Apple's

face. She was dead serious.

"Be careful, Izzy. If this Seth is a religious freak thinking he's anointed and doing God's work, he's very dangerous."

Izzy pooh-poohed Apple's warning. She was just reaching now, Izzy was sure. All names meant something.

"The only thing I'm afraid of right now is that this sick-o is stalking a new victim," she said.

Apple took Izzy's damp hands in hers. "Izzy, my friend, mark my words. Mark them."

Chapter Thirty-Seven

Izzy and Moreno ate a late lunch retrieved from the burrito man.

"I hope you're not going to have a fainting spell like the last time you ate one of these," Moreno said.

"How about if I feel like I'm going to faint, I promise to pull over first?" Izzy said.

"Fair enough," Moreno said, stuffing an enormous bite into his mouth.

The light turned green and Izzy put her burrito on her lap so she could drive. "Tell me again why we couldn't eat at the burrito stand before we started out across town?"

"Because we need to get over to Brother Gideon's before he starts getting ready for his daily gig," Moreno said.

Izzy took a bite. "Oh yeah," she munched out.

"I'm done eating. You want me to drive?" he said.

They stopped at another red light.

"Naw, I'm good. I can finish at this light."

She stuffed an overly big bite into her face.

Moreno looked at her. "Nice and dainty," he said. "You might not faint, but you're gonna give yourself indigestion."

"Cork it, Mom," she said.

Five stoplights and a Diet Coke later, they arrived at Heaven's Gate Sanctuary. Izzy wondered how the vast grounds always looked so beautiful when she'd never seen anyone tending them. Must be a miracle, she joked to herself.

They walked in, found the lobby empty, and headed toward the theatre. There on stage stood Brother Gideon. He was talking to a nicely clad man holding a pad of paper in one hand and pointing a pen with his other.

The pair had obviously not seen Izzy and Moreno arrive, so Izzy cleared her throat. The men looked up.

"Brother Gideon," she said. "May we have a word?"

"Detective," Brother Gideon said. "How may I help you today?"

The second man quickly put his pad in the briefcase that stood at his feet.

Izzy followed Moreno down the long staircase toward the stage.

"We'd like to talk to you. Is this a good time?" Moreno said.

"I was just finishing up with Jeff Parks, my accountant," he said. "We can talk now. Have a seat and I'll join you."

Brother Gideon walked down the stairs at stage right and Jeff followed him. Polite introductions were made, the accountant left, and everyone else settled in.

"Brother Gideon, did you get the news that Paul Winters had a heart attack?" Izzy said.

Brother Gideon shook his head. "Yes, sadly, I did. Such a tragedy for such a faithful man to be beaten for his beliefs."

"Where were you at approximately noon on the twenty-second?" Izzy asked.

"You mean the day Lupita Vazquez died?" Brother Gideon said.

"Yes," Moreno said.

"I don't remember," Brother Gideon said.

"Do you have a calendar you can check?" Izzy asked.

Brother Gideon pulled a pocket calendar out of his coat pocket. He turned the pages until he found the day in question. A fleeting expression of worry crossed his face, but then he recovered.

"It seems you'll just have to take my word for it that I was here at work. You know I'm here every day. You've found me here every time you've come calling."

Izzy didn't trust him. He was hiding something, she was sure. "May I see your calendar, please?"

He handed it to her. There was nothing written on the day in question. The only thing present was a red line under the 12:00 p.m. indicator on his day timer. She flipped through the pages. There were few appointments present. One for the dentist and a few others for luncheons. Nothing stuck out. The only thing out of the ordinary was the occasional red mark under a time indicator. The rough pattern seemed to be that they showed up mid-morning or around the lunch hour.

"What do these marks indicate?" she asked.

Brother Gideon gulped. "Those? I take medication and those are marks to remind me when I took it. So I stay on track. I have a busy schedule, and it can be confusing," he said.

Izzy looked at him. She didn't believe him, but she couldn't get a good read, either.

"I see." She turned to Moreno. "You have any

other questions?"

"No, I think that about covers it for now," he said. "But, Brother Gideon, stick around. Don't leave town on any business trips or anything. Got it?"

Brother Gideon's mouth twitched. "I have no travel plans. Let me know if there's anything I can do to help you."

"Don't worry, Brother Gideon, we will," Izzy said.

Chapter Thirty-Eight

The next day, Izzy and Moreno were driving back from the hospital after checking on Paul Winters. He was still in ICU and in no shape to be questioned for long. A uniform had been placed at his door with orders to call if there were any drastic change in his condition.

"I'm starving," Moreno said. "My belly button is yanking on my spinal cord."

"Don't be such a drama queen, already." Izzy glanced in her side mirror and changed lanes. "Where do you want to eat?"

"Someplace quick. We need to pay a visit to Mark's mom today."

"Okay," Izzy said, pointing. "There's a *Pollo Tropical* up ahead. Will that work?"

"Sounds *delicioso*," Moreno said, with a perfect accent.

"Whatever, Stud."

They pulled in and got out of the car. Moreno didn't wait and hold the door for Izzy this time. She smiled to herself. Curious how Moreno was more of a gentleman when Traesk was around. Maybe he was jealous. Or maybe she shouldn't tease him so much when he did something right—like pull a chair out for her. She entered the restaurant and the scent of grilled chicken filled the air. They ordered and found a booth where they sat and waited for their order.

"Hello, Izzy, Pete," a familiar voice said.

Izzy looked up. It was Traesk holding a tray of food. A blonde bombshell stood beside him. Her hair was poofed and held in place with an abundance of hairspray, Izzy was sure. Three shades of eye shadow expertly blended adorned her lids. Mascara-laden lashes framed the eyelids *à la Monet.* Izzy made a mental note to buy stock in makeup because this woman alone could push it up. Her tight red, zippered spandex top screamed for mercy as it barely covered the woman's bountiful bosom. From her dainty waist hung a skirt so short that Izzy wondered why the woman bothered at all. Legs went on for days until they met her perfectly French-manicured toes that were adorned by strappy little red sandals the exact hue of her spandex top.

Izzy blinked hard and then turned to Traesk. "Hi."

Moreno nodded, his mouth stuffed with *arroz* and *habichuelas.*

"Who's this?" the bombshell said, looking Moreno up and down.

"I'm sorry, Lolly. Permit me to introduce you to another one of my clients, Izzy O'Donnell," Traesk indicated Izzy. "And Pete Moreno."

She shook their hands. "I'm Lolly Glad," she said. "Pleased to make your acquaintance."

They stood there for an uncomfortable moment. Izzy looked at Moreno. He responded with an almost imperceptible shrug and said, "Care to join us?"

Lolly shoved past Traesk and slipped into the booth next to Moreno. She smiled seductively and said. "I'll sit next to Pete." She put her tray down and leaned over toward Moreno, her conspicuous cleavage strategically pointed in his direction. "You're cute," she said.

Moreno tried to move away from Lolly, but he was already up against the side of the booth and there was nowhere to escape. He gave a little smile—one Izzy had seen before. The one she knew had "help" written all over it.

Mark took his seat next to Izzy, maintaining a respectable distance. She felt compelled to mount a rescue attempt for Moreno, but Traesk beat her to it.

"Moreno," Traesk said, "help me get some salsa for everyone?"

Moreno looked relieved and said, "Excuse me," to Lolly so he could get out of the booth. "Our order will be ready in a second."

Lolly turned sideways to let him out, but she didn't move completely out of the way, so Moreno was forced to brush up against her as he got out of the booth. Once out of the booth and standing behind Lolly, he gave Izzy an *is she for real* look. She stifled a grin and watched Moreno and Traesk go on their way. She turned back to Lolly.

"So, what do you do?" Izzy said.

Lolly turned to her and primped her hair. She swaggered that bosom a little and said quite matter-of-factly, "My husband is a plastic surgeon and I help him by being his showcase. I host parties and he provides information and can deliver the goods."

Izzy nearly spat her food. "Sorry," she said. "Choked. Um, Really?" she managed. "His showcase? How interesting."

Lolly grinned. "Yes. Don't meet many people like me, do you?"

That's an understatement, sprang to Izzy's mind,

but she didn't say it. "No. Never met a showcase first hand. So, um, how's business?"

Lolly was finishing a dainty bite of food. She put her fork down and made a sunshiny gesture with her hands. Looking heavenward, she said, "Business is *great*."

Izzy held her fork in the air. Her bite of food was getting cold, she knew, but she was positively mesmerized. She wondered if there were any original parts left on this babe.

"Business is great. Glad to hear it," Izzy managed. Then in an attempt to change the subject, she asked, "So are you two out looking at houses?"

"Yes, yes," Lolly said. "I've worn poor Mark down to the nubbins, I believe. He's shown me about forty houses. But I want the *perfect* house. My husband has set me on a quest to find it."

Izzy was afraid to ask, so she just smiled and took a bite of food. Lolly got up suddenly and went around the table to sit next to Izzy. She dug in her purse for a card and handed it to her.

Izzy took it and looked up at Lolly, certain that her expression looked as confused as she felt.

Lolly stared deeply at Izzy. Her gaze roved all over Izzy's face. "You should come to one of my parties. No offense, honey, but you could use a little help."

Stunned, Izzy glanced down at the card and said, "No offense taken." But she had to admit the comment took her aback.

Traesk and Moreno returned to their seats with a couple of containers of salsa and Moreno and Izzy's order. Once again, Moreno looked relieved when he noticed Lolly on the opposite side of the table. He sat down and Traesk sat next to him.

Lolly stared at Izzy while the others finished their food. Izzy tried to ignore it, but she felt uglier by the second. She wondered if her eyebrows were properly tweezed, if her mascara had smudged from the tropical heat, or if Lolly could somehow tell that she hadn't shaved her legs this morning. She gave herself a mental head slap. Why was she letting this plastic person intimidate her? She might not have a size DD bust line, but her Cs were all hers, baby. She smiled at herself.

"Izzy?" Moreno said. "Earth to Izzy. "Yoo hoo…""

Izzy jerked. "Sorry. Dreaming."

"We need to wrap it up, don't you think?" Moreno said, tapping his watch.

Izzy nodded.

Mark said, "Lolly, I think we need to let these folks get on with their day."

She frowned and said. "Oh? That's too bad. I like them, Mark."

"Well, I hate to break up the party, but we have police work to do," Moreno said. "You go ahead and finish your lunch. We're done. Aren't we, Izzy?"

"Done." She scooped the last of her rice into her mouth and took a swig of her water.

"I like cops." Lolly pouted at Moreno. "Too bad you're not in uniform, sugar."

Izzy stepped in. "Actually, not all cops wear uniforms."

She ran a pink tongue across her teeth. "I know that," she said. "I just like a man in a uniform."

Izzy could tell Moreno was starting to squirm again. "We need to go."

Moreno nodded and excused himself. Traesk got

up to let him out of the booth.

"Well, you guys go catch a criminal, okay?" Lolly said as she took a mirror out of her purse and refreshed the already perfect, bright red lipstick. "I just don't feel complete without having my lips on," she said to Izzy. "You know what I mean." She paused and looked at Izzy. "Well, then again, maybe you don't." She winked at Izzy, then made way for her to get out of the booth. "You've got my card. Call me, honey. Seriously."

Izzy grinned broadly. "Nice to meet you, Lolly. Great seeing you, Mark."

"I'll be in touch," Traesk said.

Izzy and Moreno took their leave. She looked back at Traesk who mouthed "I'm sorry" to them. Izzy just kept grinning. She couldn't help herself. How in the world did straight-laced Mark Traesk ever end up with a client like Lolly Glad?

Moreno walked through the door to the parking lot. On the way to the car, he said, "Wow. She's somethin' else."

"Yeah. She exudes sex, that's for sure," Izzy said. "You think she's one of those women who just looks at houses to get the realtor in the sack?"

"What?" Moreno said.

Izzy snapped her fingers at him. "C'mon Moreno, if you can't keep up, go home. Do you think Lolly's one of those women who flaunts it to get laid?"

"Dunno. But she's all about flaunting it," he said, shaking his head. "What do you think?"

"I think she's a harmless and incorrigible tease," Izzy said. "She'd probably run and hide if some man made a move. Works herself up with other men then takes it home to her husband. "I bet Lolly's truly on a quest to find the perfect house. That's what she told me when you guys were off getting salsa and food."

"Hmph," Moreno said. "What she really wants is to be noticed. She's so plastic it makes me cringe." He shuddered. "I suppose it's good advertising for her plastic surgeon husband."

"Yeah, and for her parties," Izzy said dejectedly.

"For the record," Moreno said. "You don't need to call her."

Izzy smiled and felt herself blush. "Thanks, Moreno."

"Yeah, yeah, yeah," he said. "Don't let a compliment go to your head. Sheesh. Let's get out of here."

Izzy smiled inwardly but didn't say anything. They buckled up and headed out of the parking lot to the street.

Forty-five minutes later, they were at Mark's mother's door. Moreno rang the bell.

A female voice inside demanded, "Luke, get the door."

A few moments went by, and the same voice grumbled, "Never mind. Christmas will come before you do. I'll get it."

A slight, old woman with gray hair pulled into a bun opened the door. A screen stood between them. She wore a modest blue dress with a daisy print that brought out the blue in her eyes. At 5'4" she didn't look like she could possibly overpower women and kill them, Izzy thought.

"May I help you?"

Izzy and Moreno flashed their badges.

"Sarah Traesk?" Izzy said.

"Maybe. Who wants to know?"

"I'm Detective O'Donnell and this is my partner, Detective Moreno—"

"I gave at the office," Sarah said. She started to close the door on them.

"We'd like to ask you a few questions," Izzy said. "May we come in please?"

Sarah looked a little nervous. She didn't open the door any wider and she didn't move. "Well, what's this about? I haven't done anything wrong."

"Just routine, Ma'am," Moreno said.

"Just routine about what? If you haven't done anything wrong, the police don't come to your door," Sarah said.

"It's about your son," Moreno said.

Sarah's eyes flickered. "He hasn't done anything wrong, either," she said. "He's a sweet boy. Does everything I ask of him. I'm not as young as I used to be. He helps me out and does whatever I ask him to do."

The screen door was still firmly latched between Sarah Traesk and the detectives. Izzy decided to take a chance. If she made a wrong move, the front door would close in her face, she thought.

"Sarah, I can tell you're very close to your son. Right?" Izzy asked.

"Yes," Sarah said. "What's that got to do with anything?"

"Well, we know your son is a realtor, and we'd like to ask you a few questions that will help him," she said.

"Help him sell a house? I don't understand," Sarah said.

"No ma'am," Moreno chimed in. "Have you heard

on the news that there have been some women murdered?"

Sarah's eyes narrowed. "Yes, and…"

Moreno glanced at Izzy. She knew it was her cue to take over.

"So, your son knew a couple of these women. He was showing houses to them," Izzy said.

"Are you trying to say my son killed them?"

"We've talked to Mark already," Izzy said.

"We just want to verify his whereabouts during the times that those women were killed. Only because he knew them," Moreno said. "Routine."

"We're asking the same questions to everyone who knew them," Izzy added.

Sarah fiddled with the latch. "Well, I suppose it will be all right for you to come in for a minute," she said. "If it will help Mark. He's good to me, you know."

Izzy smiled at her and Sarah opened the door. She showed them to a comfortable sitting room just inside the door and to the left. The room was painted taupe with white woodwork. Hanging on the walls were a couple of watercolor prints. There was a piano along one wall. On it sat a photo of a younger Sarah standing in a group of people. It must have been taken at a church function of some sort, because a preacher stood in the center of the picture surrounded by food set out as if for a potluck. A bookcase was positioned opposite the window facing the street. It held the usual assortment of best-selling novels, a dictionary, a Bible, and two crossword puzzle dictionaries. Interspersed among the books were knick-knacks, a bell, a horsehair key fob and some photos of Sarah. In one, she was receiving an award of some kind. In another, she was dressed in scrubs and holding a dog. It looked pretty much like every living room in Miami. A card table sat under the window. There were newspapers in a trashcan under it, and scrapbooking materials, glue and scissors on it. A small, yellow and blue plaid loveseat sat across from two rattan chairs with coordinating cushions. A wicker coffee table served as the centerpiece in the sitting area. A flower arrangement adorned it. A couple of magazines lay on the table. One was opened to a crossword puzzle and a pencil lay in the crease.

"Somebody likes crossword puzzles," Izzy said.

"Yes, I find them relaxing," Sarah said. She indicated to them to sit down. They took their seats in the rattan chairs facing the kitchen.

"May I get you something to drink?" Sarah offered.

They both declined.

"So, what's this all about?" Sarah said, sitting on the couch. "Realtors meet lots of people."

"Yes they do," Moreno said. "But it's pretty unusual for someone's client to get murdered. Much less, multiple clients."

Sarah showed little reaction. "But what does that have to do with Mark? Killing clients would be bad for business."

"We just need to verify his whereabouts on the dates and during the times that these women were killed."

Izzy pulled out a notepad and read out the chronological details of the killings.

Sarah Traesk sat calmly and very matter-of-factly said, "Mark was with me at those times."

"Do you have anyone who can corroborate that?"

Moreno said.

"Yes, I do," she said. "Luke was with us."

"And who is Luke?" Izzy said.

"He's a good friend who lives with us. He's like family to us, so they're like brothers."

"I see," Moreno said. "Is he here? Can we speak with him, too?"

"Yes, he's here," Sarah said. She turned her head and called out. "Luke? Come in here."

Such a feisty one for such a little old lady, Izzy thought.

Sarah turned again and smiled at Izzy and Moreno. "He'll be along in a moment," she said.

"What does Luke do for a living?" Moreno asked.

"He does a little bit of everything to help Mark prepare houses for sale." Sarah glanced over her shoulder toward the door. "Our Luke is slightly disabled," she said in a hushed tone.

Izzy nodded and wondered what Sarah meant by that. She heard footsteps heading in their direction and decided not to ask. A tall man, Izzy guessed about six feet, four inches, emerged in the doorway. He had blond hair, blue eyes, a square jaw with a dimple in the middle and a sturdy frame. He was nicely dressed, wearing khaki pants and a pale green polo shirt. A pair of boat shoes completed his ensemble. To Izzy he seemed like a past-his-prime football player in khakis. With a deep-set dimple.

"Luke," Sarah said. "These are detectives. They're asking a few questions about where we were on a couple of occasions."

"We have just a couple of routine questions to ask," said Izzy. "Can you please tell us where you were on July 28 at 2:30 p.m.?"

Luke looked at Sarah. "I can't remember, but I can get a calendar." His words were thick with a speech impediment.

"Thanks. That'd be great," Moreno said.

Luke walked to the kitchen and took a calendar off a nail in the wall. When he reached for it, he accidentally knocked over a glass of iced tea sitting on the counter. At the sound of it, Sarah turned toward the kitchen and glared at him. His expression became suddenly stricken. He looked into the living room at Sarah and lunged for a tea towel. Sarah made a tsk tsk sound and Luke mopped at the spill with speed and expertise.

"I'm so sorry," he said. "Please forgive me."

Sarah turned away from Luke and back to Izzy and Moreno. "Clumsy," was all she said.

"It looked like an accident to me," Izzy said. Then to Luke, "Need any help?"

"Just sit," Sarah ordered in the most formal voice Izzy had ever heard.

"I didn't mean to offend," Izzy said. "Just trying to help."

"You can help by not interfering," Sarah said.

Moreno tapped Izzy's foot with his. She sat back, not knowing what to think about this old woman.

They waited in an awkward silence as Luke cleaned up the rest of the spill. When he had collected his towels, he put them in the sink and returned to the calendar. He removed it from its resting place on the nail, flipped to the appropriate month, and walked back to the doorway.

"What date?"

Izzy repeated the dates she was curious about and Luke ran his finger down the calendar. "The calendar says "Clean up" on those days. Yes, I remember now, Mark and Sarah and I were cleaning up on those days. We put it on the calendar to schedule a time when we can all help."

"What were you cleaning up?" Izzy asked.

"We cleaned up the house," Luke said.

"All three of you together?" Moreno asked.

Sarah nodded and smiled ever so sweetly. "Yes. We always do that together. I need help."

Moreno glanced at Izzy. "Well, okay then. Anyone else see or help you?"

Luke looked a little confused by the question. Sarah smiled at Luke. Then she turned to Moreno and Izzy.

"It doesn't take more than the three of us to clean. So, no, just the three of us."

Izzy nodded. "We appreciate your cooperation."

Moreno stood to leave and Izzy followed suit. Sarah walked them to the door.

"Thanks again for your time," Izzy said. She handed Sarah a calling card. "Here's how to reach me in case you want to get hold of me for anything."

Sarah thanked them and they made their way back to the car. Izzy tossed the keys to Moreno.

"You drive, okay?"

He shrugged and caught the keys.

Once inside, Izzy turned the air conditioner on full blast to combat the heat that had accumulated in the vehicle. Palm trees didn't offer much shade. She buckled up. Moreno settled himself and when he was ready, he pulled out into the street.

"So?" Moreno said. "What do you think?"

"Well, Traesk's alibi holds up," she said. "And I feel kinda sorry for him."

"What? How?"

"Moreno, he's working, he's helping take care of his mom, *and* their family friend, Luke. There was something else not quite right with him—besides the speech impediment."

"Yeah, Sarah said he was disabled. Guess she didn't want to elaborate and hurt his feelings knowing he'd be right there any second." Moreno changed lanes and added, "You think he's mentally challenged?"

"Most likely," she said. "But, like my dad, he probably does his share to help out." She touched Moreno's arm. "Moreno?"

"What is it, Izzy O?"

"I can really identify with Traesk, ya know?"

He glanced at her.

"I have a job, I help out at the bar and take care of my dad. That takes a lot of time. I don't ever go anywhere or do anything social besides play poker with you guys."

"What are you saying, Izzy?"

"It's like this. I go to work, then I come home, fix dinner, help around the bar, take care of Dad—and that can mean many things. Sometimes, when he's having a good day, he's fine and doesn't need much attention. Other times, when he's not doing so well, I have to help out a lot. When he's confused, sometimes he can't even find his slippers. Other times, like when he doesn't realize that he's repeating himself, I have to answer the same question over and over again and try to be patient while I'm doing it. It's exhausting. And when that's all done, I get to help close the bar for the night. Then it starts all over the next day. I'm not complaining about taking care of Dad, I'm just explaining the life of someone who cares for another adult."

"Point?"

"My point is this guy is busy."

"You like him," Moreno said. "I can tell."

"It's not like that," she said, but inwardly she longed to have an ally who fully understood her job plus caretaker roles. "Look, he has two people he's looking out after. I don't see him having *time* to kill people on the side."

"I see your point. Besides, they gave him a rock solid alibi," Moreno said.

"Apparently so," she said. "So, what now?"

"I think we have to really clear him," Moreno said.

"I agree," she said. "That leaves us with Cal as our major suspect."

"Yup," said Moreno as he pulled into the station. "And *that's* a problem."

Chapter Thirty-Nine

"Hey, Moreno," Izzy said. "I've been thinking about those little lines in Brother Gideon's day timer."

"And?"

"And it doesn't add up," she said. "If he were taking medication, he'd want to make a mark to remind himself when to take it, not to remind himself when he *had* taken it. That's silly. Most medications are supposed to be taken on a schedule. Did you believe Brother Gideon's story about the lines in his day timer?"

"Nope. Not for a minute," Moreno said. "He's lying about something. I just can't figure what."

"That's what I think, too," Izzy said.

She picked up her phone, put it on speaker and dialed.

"What are you doing?" Moreno said.

Izzy wiggled her eyebrows at him. "Listen and learn."

The phone rang. "Heaven's Gate Sanctuary," a female voice said.

"Yes, I'd like to speak with Lydia Reynolds, please," Izzy said.

"One moment," the voice on the other end of the phone said.

A few moments later, another voice came on the line. Izzy recognized it as Lydia's voice. She recalled the production manager's blond and brown dye job.

"Lydia? This is Detective Izzy O'Donnell. How are you today?"

"Fine thank you, Detective. How can I help?" Lydia said.

"I was just wondering if Brother Gideon was available?" Izzy said.

"No, I'm sorry, he's not in at the moment."

"Oh, that's right," Izzy said. "He mentioned he had to run an errand to get his medicine from the pharmacy. Sorry, I forgot."

Lydia laughed. "You must be mistaken, Ms. O'Donnell. Brother Gideon doesn't take any medication. Perhaps you've confused him with someone else. May I take a message for him?"

Izzy grinned. "No thanks, I'll catch him later."

Chapter Forty

Izzy was exhausted. It had been a busy night at the bar after a busy day at the office. Monday night football on the big screen always brought the crowd in. Spencer had tried to be helpful during the rush, but she could tell he was tired, too.

Toward the end of the evening, he had started to ask Izzy and some of the customers the same questions over and over. She could tell the customers were getting annoyed, so she tried to give him a job away from everyone. She sent him to the stock room to load beer on the dolly for tomorrow. But when he got there, he came right back out to tell her what he was going to do. He went through three iterations of this before Izzy finally went to the stock room to get him started.

Izzy and Apple had gone nuts trying to keep up during the game. Afterward, the crowd had thinned. Now the last few stragglers were packing it in. It was time to clean up.

"Need any help?" Moreno asked.

"You still here? I thought you left after the game ended."

"Yeah, I was going to, but Apple told me she had to run home to feed Norman, so I decided to stay and see if you needed anything. I know it's been a long day."

Izzy brushed an auburn strand out of her face with

the back of her hand. "Thanks Moreno. But, I think we've got it. Dad's in the back room readying beer for the coolers tomorrow. I'll give you a beer if you want to just hang and visit with me while I do the dishes, though."

"That's a deal," he said.

She reached into the stainless steel cooler and dug through the ice for his favorite brand. She wiped it off with a towel and handed it to him. "You want a mug?"

"Nah, I'm good. Thanks," he said.

He popped the top off and took a swig.

Izzy put her towel down and rubbed her temples.

"Headache?" Moreno asked.

"Yeah," she said absently.

She staggered a little and steadied herself on the edge of the bar. *Not again. Not another headache now.*

Moreno hopped off his stool and hurried around the bar to help her.

"You sure you're all right?" he said.

She weaved a bit. "I'm okay."

"You feel faint?"

"Not really. Just a headache. No fainting spells. No dreams."

"How often do you get these?"

"It's pretty random."

"Is it, Izzy? It seems like the last few times you've had one of these headaches, you've been around Mark Traesk or his family."

"Maybe so, Moreno, but what of it? I'm under a lot of pressure with these grisly murders, finding a place for my dad to live, and taking care of him when he needs it. Mark's the realtor and the case is the case. There's no connection."

He raised an eyebrow at her.

"Okay, so maybe there is a connection between the case and these episodes, but certainly not to Traesk. He alibied out. Remember? And, if there is a connection to the case, what am I supposed to tell Lt. Boggs? 'I have headaches and these weird dreams where I see fire and boys' like that's supposed to mean something concrete that we can take to court? It's probably just all the drama surrounding the case. No big whoop."

"Maybe you're right," he said skeptically. "But I'm worried about these headaches and stuff. You should get some rest."

"I will. Right after I finish cleaning up."

Moreno stepped around to the other side of the bar. "I'll put the chairs up before I leave," he said.

"Thanks, Moreno, but you don't have to do that."

"I'll be done with it before you're done with the dishes," he said. "Consider it a thank you for the beer."

She grinned. A true friend, she thought.

He moved from table to table and stacked chairs upside down on them. He finished quickly and returned to the bar where Izzy was rubbing a streak off of it with window cleaner.

"That's done," he said. "Guess you're ready to sweep. Want to hand me the broom?"

"You've done enough. I'm almost finished back here, and Dad likes to sweep. He considers it his nightly job, so I save it for him."

"Well, okay then. I'll see you in the morning."

"See ya. Thanks again."

Izzy walked Moreno to the door and watched him drive off. After he left, she turned the blinking neon shamrock off and locked the door.

All that was left was to count the register and sweep. She emptied the register onto the counter and began to count.

Spencer rolled the dolly out of the storeroom and stacked the cases of beer behind the bar. He took up his broom. His nightly ritual.

"You stacked the chairs for me, daughter?"

"No, Dad, Moreno did that. Nice of him."

"It was indeed," Spencer said, seemingly back to his normal self.

Izzy sorted bills and counted change. She separated the money to go to the bank in one pile and reloaded the cash register drawer for the next day. She reached under the counter and picked up the bank bag. Under it she found some papers.

Curious, she thumbed through them. They were from Mark Traesk. He had promised to drop off some properties for her to preview. He must have stopped by when she was busy and hadn't noticed him. She perused the properties and found a couple to be interesting. She'd call him and let him know which ones appealed to her so she could go see them.

On the back of the stack there was a picture and a description of a 5,000 square foot house with a pool and a large deck. Five bedrooms and a kitchen to die for. Izzy frowned at the paper. Why was this here? There was a handwritten note up in the corner by the staple. It said, "Glad." Written next to it was a date and time.

Izzy connected the dots. This must be a house that Traesk was planning to show Lolly Glad. Izzy chuckled to herself. Obviously, her paperwork had inadvertently been stapled to Izzy's. She didn't think any more of it, and set the paperwork back down.

Izzy swept the room with a glance looking for any leftover glasses. In the corner on a bus tray, she saw a bin filled with glasses and trash. Overwhelmed with exhaustion and a crushing sense of self-pity, she walked over to pick it up.

"Why did Apple leave this here?" she said aloud to no one in particular.

"I thought I was *done*." The glasses clinked in the bin as she walked over to the bar. She set it down and filled the sink with soapy water yet again.

"Daughter? What's wrong?" Spencer said from across the room.

Izzy had momentarily forgotten that he was there. She looked up.

"I'm just exasperated that Apple didn't bring this tray of glasses over to the bar to be washed before she left for the evening."

"Maybe she forgot them. We were very busy tonight," he said.

"It's her *job* to collect dishes before she leaves," Izzy said, listening to the irritation in her voice. Deep down she knew her father was right, Apple probably simply forgot and she shouldn't be so upset with her, but Izzy was just *that* tired tonight. Irritated, she slung soap around and spat out a cuss word.

Spencer shuffled over to the bar and stood watching her. She looked at him but did not speak. He reached across the bar and touched her damp arms.

"Patience is a virtue," he said.

Izzy stopped what she was doing and looked at him. Eyes moist with tears of fatigue and despair.

"What did you say?"

"I said, patience is a virtue. What I meant was—"

"That's *it*," she said. "A virtue."

Spencer looked at her confused. "Did I say something wrong, daughter?"

"No, Dad. You said something exactly right."

Izzy drained the sink and washed the bubbles off her hands. She dried them in a towel and walked around the bar to sit next to her father.

"Don't you see?" she said.

Spencer shrugged. "See what?"

"The seven heavenly virtues."

"Seven heavenly virtues?" Spencer echoed.

"Yes," Izzy said excitedly. "You know, chastity, faith, charity, temperance, patience, humility and kindness. That's *it*. The killer is killing people who are not virtuous."

Spencer stared at her and blinked. "Are you sure?"

"Yes! And Apple was right. This guy thinks he's doing God's work. I have to call Moreno. Now."

Chapter Forty-One

Izzy tossed and turned. She fluffed her pillow and lay there watching the minutes tick by on her clock. Her body was tired, but her mind pulsated with thoughts.

Initially, when Izzy called Moreno, he thought she'd gone loopy. Eventually, though, he had to admit that she might be onto something. But only after she recalled Traesk's reference to a client who wanted to drink while seeing houses and how he "doesn't have her any more" did Moreno come around to her way of thinking. He still wasn't completely convinced, though. He kept repeating that they didn't have "any solid evidence, newbie." How she hated being called newbie.

But her rookie guts were telling her that this killer, whoever he was, was using the Seven Heavenly Virtues as a yardstick to measure who lived and who died.

Nobody was perfect, so everyone in Miami was in danger.

With a very sober sense of impending disaster, she thought about Cal. How could it be that Cal would take out an insurance policy on someone who got murdered in short order after the policy was written? She felt bad that he had been suspended, and she knew she had to redouble her efforts to clear his name. There had to be a logical explanation.

Even Mark Traesk chafed her mind. He was clearly not implicated in the murders. He had an alibi corroborated by two other people. You can't be cleaning house with your mom and a friend and simultaneously be across town committing murder. It wasn't him.

So who was it? What did she have to go on?

Murdered women, body parts and organs, Cal's signature on an insurance policy, and giant sunflower pollen.

Panicky, she flashed the message to herself in neon. I have to figure out these steps, the pollen conundrum, and clear Cal's name. Then in her spare time, she'd help run the bar and find a place for her father to live. She sighed heavily.

The thought of it all so exhausted her weary body and mind that she stared, unseeing, at the ceiling and waited for sleep to take her.

****

Izzy woke with a start and sat upright in bed. Her T-shirt was in a wad around her from all her tossing and turning. In a daze, she realized her cell phone was ringing. She reached for it on the nightstand and in the process, sent the ammunition clip to her gun skittering across the floor.

Her phone rang again. Izzy fumbled and picked it up.

"O'Donnell," she said trying to sound more awake than she felt.

"Izzy, it's Apple," a familiar voice said on the other end of the line.

Izzy glanced at the clock.

"Apple? What's wrong? It's 4:00 a.m."

"I know. I'm sorry to call you at this hour, but I had a dream and telling you about it couldn't wait."

Izzy pushed hair that was pressed to her face back to its rightful place and sat up against the headboard.

"Dream? Um, okay. Tell me about it."

Apple's voice was strained with panic as she spoke. "It was dark and there were people running all around through a town square of some sort. There was shooting and men in S.W.A.T. gear wearing vests that had FBI printed on them in large white letters." Apple paused to take a breath.

"And then what, Apple?" Izzy said.

"Then, like in a movie or something, I saw a panicked woman talking to two boys off behind a building. The woman was wearing nightclothes and the boys wore shorts but no shirts. It looked like they had been burned. No, not burned, branded. Each had a deep "V" scar on their collarbone. One of the boys had more deep burns across his torso. Weird burns. Like lines. And his head was bandaged.

"There was a man—an FBI agent—whose face was really blurry. He opened a fence panel and helped the woman and two boys through it. Just as he closed the fence panel after them, the woman stuck her face back through and said, 'Thanks.'" Apple paused again. "This is where it gets weird."

"Go on," Izzy said.

"When the FBI agent turned away from the fence, his face came into focus," Apple said. "It was Cal."

"What?" said Izzy.

"It was clearly Cal," Apple said.

A chill snaked down Izzy's spine. "Lt. Boggs said that when Cal was in the FBI, he was part of a raid on a Hevite colony and he let a woman and two boys go," Izzy said.

"That wasn't everything in my dream," Apple said. "What more could there be?"

"I saw the woman again. She was talking to the boys. She said they should pray for Brother Hamor who was taken away in the raid. And for this man who did a kind thing by letting them go."

"Apple, I know that you had an upsetting dream. I understand that. You've read the newspapers and listened to the news like the rest of us. It's no wonder you're having dreams about all of this—especially because you hang out with the cops on the case. Your imagination is inventing details, running away with you. Try to forget it," Izzy said.

"Don't you dare pooh-pooh this," Apple said. "This is not to be pooh-poohed."

Confused at Apple's reaction, Izzy backed off a little. "Okay, so what am I missing? How could your dream possibly relate to the case?"

"Izzy, even if it was just a dream, my imagination playing tricks, don't you see?"

"See *what*, Apple?"

"Maybe my subconscious has sorted out something obvious that we've all missed."

"Like what?"

Apple sighed into the phone. "Like maybe someone feels like they owe Cal a debt."

"What's that supposed to mean?"

"I don't know. You're the detective. You figure it out."

Chapter Forty-Two

Izzy and Moreno sat across the table from Brother Gideon in the interrogation room. Catching him in a lie was the last bit of information they needed to get an arrest warrant from the DA.

Brother Gideon's face was ashen. He could have used some of that makeup he wore every night to keep the stage lights from sucking the color out of his face.

"You lied to us. You lied when you said those lines in your date book were medication reminders. What are they really?" Izay said.

His head sank. "I don't remember," he said.

"Cut the crap," Moreno said. "You know what they are. You remember. We all know that."

Brother Gideon looked up at them. "I can't say."

Izzy stared him down. "You do realize you'll be charged for multiple murders?"

He didn't answer. He didn't look up or acknowledge that she had said anything.

"And that your only alibi is a bunch of little lines in a date book?" she said.

He looked at her now, but said nothing.

"To top it all off, your alibi about medicine is completely bogus," she said.

Izzy looked at Moreno. It was his turn.

"Brother Gideon, how is it that you use the Bible to justify killing?" Moreno said.

"I didn't kill those women," Brother Gideon said.

"You're a preacher, aren't you?" Moreno said.

"Yes, but—"

"You can quote scripture chapter and verse, can't you?" Izzy said.

"Yes, but—"

"So how long did you watch those women before you killed them? Was it a week? A month? Three months?" Moreno said.

Brother Gideon's lip quivered. "I didn't kill them. I didn't."

Izzy shrugged. "Convince me."

"Tell us where you were," Moreno said.

Brother Gideon started to cry. He brought his hands to his face and sobbed.

Izzy looked at Moreno.

"Where were you?" Izzy said.

Brother Gideon looked at Izzy. Big sloppy tears ran down his face. "I can't tell you. If I tell you it will destroy me."

"Destroy you more than spending the rest of your life in prison?" Moreno said.

"Unless you can prove to us that you have a rock solid alibi, you're going down for these murders," Izzy said.

"I was with Andrea," he said.

"Andrea? The redheaded makeup artist?" Izzy said.

Brother Gideon nodded. He wiped his tears with his sleeve.

"Can you prove that?" Moreno said.

"Yes. She'll tell you," Brother Gideon said. "And her day timer will have the same marks as mine. That's how we made appointments to meet with each other.

Sometimes in the dressing room. Sometimes at her house. I didn't kill anybody. Please believe me."

He looked at Izzy with pleading eyes.

"Don't tell my wife. It will destroy her," he said. "It will destroy my ministry. Please."

"Perhaps you should have thought of that before you started screwing around," Izzy said.

Chapter Forty-Three

The next day, Izzy sat at her desk. She was trying to jiggle her leg and move around a bit, because every time she sat still for very long she started to nod off. She really needed some sleep.

Moreno arrived about forty-five minutes after her. He walked in bearing two cups of coffee and a donut box. Izzy looked at him and put on her best puppy face.

"Is one of those cups of coffee for me?" she asked.

"Yes, as a matter of fact, it is," Moreno said.

"Does it contain caffeine?"

"As a matter of fact, it does," he said. "And I have donuts." He wagged the box in front of her. "They're maple cake," he added.

"Moreno," Izzy said cocking her head to one side.

"Yes?"

"If I get down on one knee and ask nicely, will you marry me?"

Moreno tossed the box of donuts on Izzy's desk and handed her one of the cups of coffee. "Not a chance in the world," he said. "But I'll bring you donuts in bed if you'll sleep on your desk here at the office."

"Ha, ha," she said. "There's one in every crowd."

He winked at her and took his seat at his desk opposite hers.

"I'll be here all week," he said.

Izzy chose to ignore that one and opened the box.

The choices were endless. The maple cakes caught her eye immediately, of course. She snagged one of them. Then she scrutinized the rest. The lemon filled one looked like it didn't have much lemon in it. Izzy decided that if she was going to spend the calories on a donut, she wanted it to be worth her while. In the end, she selected a chocolate long john filled with Bavarian cream. She passed the box to Moreno.

"Thanks for breakfast," she said.

"You're welcome," he said. "Thanks for leaving me the other maple cake donut."

She gave him a sticky grin.

The phone between their desks rang. Moreno pointed to it and then to his mouth stuffed with donuts. He looked like a hamster. Izzy reached for the phone.

It was Dr. Dan's voice on the other end. She reached for a pad of paper and a pen.

"I have the results from the DNA that came back from your last crime scene," he said.

"Already? A two-week turn around?" Izzy said.

"Yeah, but the lab had orders to rush this along. This killer isn't slowing down. I don't want to find out who got bumped to do this one—they're gonna be steamed," he said.

"Whatcha got for us?" Izzy said.

"I cannot put Mark Treask at the scene," he said.

"That doesn't surprise me," Izzy said. "Turns out he has an alibi corroborated by two witnesses."

"Well, in this case, prepare to be blown away."

"In that case, let me put you on speaker," Izzy said. "Moreno's sitting right here."

"Traesk wasn't at the scene, but a female relative was," Dr. Dan said.

"A female relative?" Izzy said.

"Yup, you heard me right.

"Okay, well that throws a loop back in the equation," Moreno said.

"What about any of the trace evidence?" Izzy asked.

"Some of that has come back, too" Dr. Dan said. "Everything from the hooker scene has been cataloged. There's so much there, that it's hard to know if hair was from people who were turning tricks in that apartment or if it's from the killer. The best we can do is hang onto it and then when we have something else solid, we can use what we already have and cross-reference it."

"Thanks, Doc," Moreno said. "We'll get back to you if we need anything else."

"No problem," Dr. Dan said. "Let me know if I can help." And he was gone.

"What does all that mean?" Izzy said.

"It means that either Mark and his mother and their friend are all lying to us, or they failed to tell us about another person in the equation. I think we need to talk to Traesk. And while we're at it, let's see if his gardener is available. Ask him about sunflowers. He might know something about those."

"Okay." Izzy pulled on her jacket. "Let's go."

Chapter Forty-Four

On the way to Mark's office, Izzy told Moreno about Apple's dream.

"Ya know, Apple's heard bits and pieces about this case from us and in the newspapers," Moreno said. "It's hard to know if she's having a psychic moment or if her subconscious mind is filling in the blanks."

Izzy nodded absently, but didn't answer. She was looking out the window.

"What are you so deep in thought about?" Moreno said.

"I'm looking for sunflowers," Izzy said.

"What if that was just pollen from some bird seed that sprouted?"

"Could be, but that usually isn't the giant sunflower variety," she said. "I searched on the Internet. Bird seed usually contains those black oil sunflower seeds."

"Who knew? You're just the Interweb-searching Queen aren't you?" Moreno said. "Hey, didn't Traesk take you to see a house around here someplace?"

"Yeah, about three streets west. Why?"

"Let's take a detour and see if his gardener is there."

Izzy agreed and directed Moreno to the house.

They turned the corner and drove down the street. The houses were all made of stucco and painted in pastel colors. The yards were neat as a pin. Some had grass and others had rock gardens. The ever-present king palm trees lined the streets and some of the shorter sago palm varieties had been planted in gardens.

This early in the day, there wasn't much activity in the neighborhood. Izzy figured things would look significantly different when school let out and kids started to play along the block.

She indicated the house. No car sat in the driveway when they approached, but Mark's gardener was there. He was bent over trimming a hedge and there were a few small piles of weeds neatly placed alongside the beds. The back of his blue chambray shirt was streaked with sweat and it hung unbuttoned around his torso. His hat was pulled down over his head. A fringe of blond hair showed beneath. Earphone cords dangled from his ears attached to an mp3 player that was apparently in his pocket.

"That's him," Izzy said. "I remember him now. I saw him at one of the properties Mark showed me. Same hat, same build, same piles of weeds."

Moreno pulled over to the curb. "Okay, so let's do it."

They got out of the car, but the gardener didn't seem to notice. He must have had a good tune playing because his head bobbed slightly to the beat. Their approach startled him.

The gardener ripped the earphones out of his ears and whirled around. Izzy gasped. Hideous scars scored all across his stomach and chest.

The man grabbed at his shirt and closed it. He hurriedly buttoned it up, missing the first hole and causing the shirt to hang askew on his chest.

"You won't tell her will you, Miss Izzy?"

Izzy was startled to hear her name. She looked under the hat and saw Luke peering timidly at her.

"Luke?"

"Yes, Miss Izzy. You won't tell her, will you? She'll be mad."

"Tell who?"

"Mama. You won't say anything. Right?"

Izzy glanced at Moreno. "What are you so worried that we'll tell Sarah?" she said.

He clutched at his shirt and buttoned another button. "That I had my shirt undone. I just got hot when I was working. That's all. Mark says it's okay if she's not around." He looked nervously from Izzy to Moreno. "I wasn't trying to be immodest. Don't tell her, please, mister."

Luke looked like a puppy afraid of being kicked. Izzy stepped between him and Moreno.

"It's okay." She reached out and gently touched his arm. "Why don't you tell us what this is all about? We can go talk over here in the shade by this bench."

Luke pulled his hat down farther over his ears.

"I'm not supposed to leave my gardening tools. I don't want her to get mad," he said.

"What happens when she gets mad?" Moreno asked.

"She makes sure I learn from my mistakes," he said. "It's for my own good."

Izzy's heart sank. This man had the mind of a child and it was clear that Sarah Traesk had abused him.

Izzy opened her mouth to ask a question, but Moreno beat her to it.

"Did she whip you? Is that what those scars on

your chest are?" he asked.

Luke began fiddling with the buttons on his shirt again. His thick fingers were matching buttons with their proper buttonholes. Intent on his task, he didn't answer.

"Luke?" Izzy said. "How did you get those scars on your chest?"

This time, Luke looked up. "I fell during the marking ceremony. He dropped the hot stick on me."

"Marking ceremony? Tell us about that," Moreno said.

"During the ceremony, Brother Hamor marked us with a hot stick, but I was bad. I had fear in my heart and I moved away and tripped and fell. The hot stick burned me. But I still got the mark. See?" He pointed to a V on his collarbone.

"That must have hurt," Izzy said. She shot Moreno a glance and thought fast.

"Tell you what, Luke. I bet you're thirsty after doing all this yard work in the heat. Want to come to our office and cool off a little? Have something to drink?"

Luke nodded. "I'm thirsty, but I can't leave."

"You can't leave because you don't want to get in trouble, right?" Izzy said.

Luke nodded again.

"Yeah, I kinda know what you're up against," she said. "My sister was always the favorite. No matter what happened, I'd be the one who got in trouble and my sister didn't. Is it that way with you and Mark? Do you get in trouble more than he does?"

Luke furrowed his brow at her. "How did you know?" he said.

"Just a lucky guess," Izzy said. "What if Moreno and I helped you put your tools away? Would that make it easier to come with us?"

"That would be good, but if they come to pick me up and I'm not here, she'll make me learn from my mistake of leaving early," Luke said.

Izzy took her cell phone off her belt and held it up for Luke to see.

"What if we called to tell them that you're safe and with us and we'll bring you home? That way they won't worry about where you are."

Luke thought a moment and then said, "Okay. But I have to pick up my tools first. And put the weeds away in the trash. I don't want Mark to be disappointed that I left a mess. He lets me help him. My job is to help him keep the yards mowed so he can sell the houses. And I help Mama clean them when they're real dirty."

Izzy picked up a hefty branch that lay on the ground. "Okay Luke, we'll help you. Where does this go?"

Luke looked stricken and quickly took the branch from Izzy. "You shouldn't do that. That's men's work. The men do the heavy work," he said. "*Not* women."

Confused, but wanting to roll with the punches, she handed Luke the branch. "Okay. Can I help put your tools away?"

Luke nodded. "They go in the garage, then we lock it," he said.

Moreno stooped and picked up a pile of weeds. "I can carry these."

Luke led them to the garage. Izzy put the tools away. Luke put the branch out by the curb and Moreno deposited the weeds in the trashcan.

"I can't stay with you for very long," Luke said. "I have to help Mark and Sarah clean a house later. I promised."

"Will they come get you?" Moreno asked.

"Yes. Later," Luke said.

"Okay, Luke," Izzy said. "We'll call them and make sure everything works out."

Luke smiled at her and he looked relieved.

Moreno led the way back to the car and got in. Izzy and Luke weren't far behind. Izzy was talking to Luke and he seemed to be warming to her. This was a good thing, she thought. If Sarah Traesk was abusing Luke, why wasn't Mark Traesk stepping in? Something didn't make sense.

"Luke, how long have you been helping Mark with the gardens?" Izzy asked.

"Since he started selling houses," Mark said. "I like working with the plants and making the yards look pretty."

Moreno glanced in the rearview mirror at Luke. "You're good at it."

Luke smiled. "Thanks."

"Do you have any favorite flowers?" Izzy said.

"I like them all, but I really like the ones that I grew from seeds," he said.

"What kind are those?" Izzy said.

"Giant sunflowers," he said. "I have some in the back at Mama Sarah's house. They're really tall."

"Really? Giant sunflowers? In Miami? How interesting," Izzy said.

"You don't see them very much here," Luke said. "That's why I like to grow them."

"Where have you seen them before?" Moreno said.

"In Kansas. There were lots of them in Kansas. I brought seeds when we moved here. And I grow them."

"Tell me how you do that, Luke. I've never grown a plant from a seed before," said Izzy.

"I have some pots," he said. "I put some soil from a bag at the store in the pots. Then I put the seeds down in the soil, but not too far, or they won't grow. I have to water them a little bit a couple times a week. At first you have to make sure the seed stays wet. It's not hard Miss Izzy. I could show you how."

"Thanks, Luke. It sounds like fun," Izzy said.

"What do you do with the plants when they outgrow their pots?" Moreno asked.

"I transplant them. In the yard. Do you know when the sunflowers get big you have to put a net over them so the birds don't eat the seeds? Then you can dry the flowers and save the seeds for later. I like to eat them," Luke said.

"They are pretty tasty," Izzy said. So, Luke, when were you in Kansas?"

"We lived there when I was little—after my mom and brother died," he said. "I lived with Mark and Mama Sarah. Are we almost there? I don't want to be late for cleaning the house."

"Almost there," Moreno said.

Izzy shot him a glance. If the sunflower pollen had come from Luke's shoes, then that could place him at the crime scene. Why would a simpleton like this be downtown in a hooker's apartment? That didn't make sense. Surely straight-laced Mark wouldn't take Luke downtown to visit hookers. And with his mental capacity, Luke certainly didn't drive. It would be hard for him to maneuver the bus system. They could follow up on it, but there had to be another explanation.

When they arrived at the station, Moreno tried to call Traesk, but couldn't reach him on the phone. He told Izzy to interview Luke. He was going to try and track Mark or Sarah down in person. He wanted to bring them in so they could figure out what was going on. At Izzy's request, a uniformed officer brought some lemonade for Luke.

Luke got agitated. He stared at the uniformed officer and pulled at his ear. They walked through the station and Luke wiped his palms against his shirt. When they stopped in the hallway, he shifted his weight from side to side and his gaze darted quickly from uniformed officer to uniformed officer. Izzy was relieved when they reached an interrogation room and she showed Luke a chair. He seemed to calm down slightly but he continued to rock back and forth, wringing his hands. She asked Luke if she could ask him some questions and he said "yes," but reminded her he needed to be done in time to help Mark and Mama Sarah clean.

"I'll do my best," she said.

Izzy looked at Luke and then into the one-way mirror. She knew other detectives were watching. Now she really did feel like a rookie. But she could do this without Moreno. He had gone to track down Mark. She'd done many interviews before, but none with a man twice her size, alone in the room with the tape rolling and the observers watching her like a fish in a bowl. She tried to shake it off.

"Luke, are you okay?" Izzy said. "What seems to be the trouble?"

"I don't like those men," Luke said.

"The police officers?" Izzy said.

"Yes. The ones in uniforms."

"Why is that, Luke?"

Luke rocked harder in his chair and wouldn't meet Izzy's gaze.

"I want my Mama Sarah and Mark," he said. "Tell them to come get me now."

"Why do you want them to come get you now?" Izzy asked.

"Police people killed my mom and brother," he said.

"I don't understand," Izzy said. "Sarah and Mark are just fine."

"No," Luke said with an edge in his voice. "My *real* mama and brother. Mama Sarah and Mark are my Hevite family. I want my *real* mama, but the police people killed her dead that day."

Izzy's heart leapt. "Tell me about that day. What happened with the police?"

Luke looked at her. His blue eyes seemed to look back to another time. Another world.

"They had black vests on and they had big guns. They wanted Brother Hamor," Seth said.

"Where was Brother Hamor?" Izzy asked.

"He was preparing for a cleansing."

"Cleansing?" Izzy asked.

"Yes. To cleanse an unvirtuous woman from her sins. She had taken more than one man unto her," Luke said.

"So what happened?" Izzy said.

"All of the Hevites—except for Brother Hamor— were having supper when the police people came. Their guns were black and shiny. When they saw that Brother

265

Hamor wasn't in the great hall with us, some of them went off to find him. They said we all had to stay there and wait. But one of the elders distracted one of the police people and another elder shouted to us to leave. There was lots of running and shouting and the police people said, "stop" but nobody did.

My mother and brother and I were eating with Mama Sarah and Mark. My mother said that the police people were not here to do God's work. She took a knife and stabbed one of them in the leg. My brother tried to do the same and the police people shot them dead."

Luke's eyes filled with tears and he swiped at them with his sleeve.

"I'm so sorry, Luke. Where was your dad?" Izzy asked.

"I told you. All the dads were eating dinner."

"All of the dads?" Izzy asked.

"All men were fathers. Nobody had just one. And Brother Hamor was the leader. The main father," Luke explained.

Nasty-sounding cult. "What happened next, Luke?"

"Mama Sarah grabbed Mark by the arm and told him to bring me. I was still sore where the hot stick hit me during the marking ceremony the day before, and my head was really hurting with all the noise. It was bandaged because when I fell during the ceremony, I hit it on a rock on the ground and my head bled and bled."

Izzy wondered if this was what had caused Luke's intellectual disability. When she was a kid, she remembered Grandma Keyna telling her to walk at Halloween because a kid in the neighborhood had tripped over his costume and hit his head on the curb, rendering him mentally challenged for the rest of his years.

Luke blew his nose in a tissue. Izzy jerked back to the present. She had to stay focused. She couldn't lose Luke now.

"So, you and Mark and Sarah ran away?" she said.

"We went out back and we were going through a hole in the fence when a police person stopped us. Mama Sarah begged him to let us go. He said he was supposed to make sure everyone stayed. She showed him my head and my stomach. She showed him our marks from the marking ceremony. She said it would show kindness if he would let us go."

"And so you got away then?" Izzy said. "What happened to the others?"

"The TV said the police people took everyone. Brother Hamor had started the cleansing and they took him away to jail. The police people thought he murdered the unvirtuous woman, but he was *helping* her. Unclean people don't understand. He took out the bad part of her that was making her sinful so she could go to God. They even took the people who clean up to jail. They took everyone but us because the nice police person let us go."

Izzy blinked hard. "Who was the nice police person? Do you know?"

Luke shook his head. "No, but Mama Sarah said we should always be thankful for his help. Mama Sarah has cut out his picture from the paper for a long time. Mark gets money from people he shows houses to."

"When he sells them a house?" Izzy said, trying to prompt him to explain.

"Uh huh. But lately, Mama Sarah says the nice

man who saved us needs the money, so they're going to give him some the next time Mark gets money," Luke said.

Izzy paused and turned to Luke again. "Did you say you had to help Mark clean up?"

"Yes," Luke said. He started to rock back and forth again. "I need to go help Mark. Is he here yet?"

The cold truth clicked. "Does cleaning up mean cleaning up after a cleansing ritual?"

"Yes," Luke said.

"And those key fobs at your house—they're made out of hair Mark collected at the cleansings, right?"

Luke nodded.

The back of Izzy's neck prickled. She had to reach Moreno. She left Luke in the interrogation room and tried to call Moreno. Once, twice. His phone went to voice mail again. She slammed the cover on her phone. If someone at Mark's office gave him a list of properties he was showing, he could be in grave danger. Why wasn't he answering her calls? Izzy left instructions with an officer to keep Luke comfortable, but at the station. He was not to be let go under any circumstances. Moreno went after Traesk and he could be walking in on something so much bigger than he knew.

Chapter Forty-Five

She hurried to her desk and grabbed the keys to the car. While she was buckling up, she tried Moreno again.

"Damn!" she said. "Why aren't you answering?"

She turned to look over her shoulder before pulling out and saw a stack of papers stapled and tossed on the back seat. She put the car back in park, unbuckled to lean over the back seat. She grabbed the papers and frantically sifted through them until she found what she was looking for—the misplaced address for the high-end property on the southwest side of Miami Traesk was going to show Lolly Glad.

She grabbed her phone and texted Moreno. "Mark is the killer. He's showing Lolly Glad a home on SW 110th Street. Meet me there."

She pushed send. She picked the magnetic cherry light off the seat, rolled down her window and attached it to the roof of the car, called HQ for backup.

Lights blazing and siren wailing, she roared southwest. Weaving through traffic, she knew it must be Mark who was following Cal's life. A blue Subaru cut her off and she swerved. *Damn! Get out of my way.* Cal had let Mark and his family escape during the raid of the Hevite colony along with his mother and his friend. She slowed for an intersection so she wouldn't get clipped by a red runner. Mark could easily follow

Cal's police career through the crime reports in the newspapers. Being a realtor, any new listings would pop up on his computer, so he would know Cal's house was on the market and might figure Cal was in trouble for dollars. Drivers pulled out of her way along the boulevard and she picked up speed. Finally, she was making time.

Clever. Mark had found a way to watch Cal and now that Cal was seeing some hard times, he wanted to repay the debt he felt he owed him. Siren still screeching, she tried to dial Moreno again, no dice. *Shit! Answer already.*

She dodged a Ford F-150. Money. After supporting himself, Sarah, and Luke, how would Mark have enough time and energy to find more for Cal? Izzy slapped the steering wheel when it came to her. Insurance money.

Izzy flew through intersections slowing at each one. *Blasted radios. People always had them on so loud they couldn't hear a siren.* Mark had to know his victims. He could know them through the real estate business. An attractive man——women would want to talk to him, to know him. Women hadn't been afraid of Bundy, had they?

Once he identified their flaws, how they were falling short of the Seven Heavenly Virtues, he could take out an insurance policy on them before killing them. She slammed on the brakes when someone in front of her pulled out. *What? Were drivers deaf?* Once victims were dead, he'd cash in. But it wasn't that easy. You couldn't just randomly take an insurance policy out on someone for no reason. What was the angle?

Izzy sped down the street. She passed cars and

palm trees, her mind buzzing. For him to be able to take a policy out on someone, he'd have to show the person was an insurable commodity to him. Getting a policy application to forge wouldn't be that hard. She was getting close now. Time to watch for cross streets. She went around a red Toyota... They would have to work for him, a key employee or related to him. Or, if not, it would have to be a black market deal. Possible. Not probable.

She turned off the main road into be a neighborhood, cut her siren. Right now she needed to find Moreno and get to the house that Traesk was showing Lolly. If she was right, Lolly could be his next victim.

Chapter Forty-Six

Izzy cut the siren a few blocks from her destination. She glanced at her cell phone again and checked it for the hundredth time. No calls or messages from Moreno. She put the phone in its holder on her waist clip and turned another corner. When she entered the neighborhood, she exercised caution and slowed down.

The neighborhood touted high-end residences, $750,000 and up. Manicured yards framed pastel-colored houses with crisp white paint accenting balconies and guttering. Everything looked perfect. This could be the sort of place that would end Lolly Glad's quest for the perfect home. In more ways than one.

Two more turns and Izzy found the street. Half way down the block, she spotted Traesk's car in a driveway. Amazed to have found him, it had been so easy, she pulled in behind his car. Still no sign of Moreno, or the backup she'd called for, though. She checked her phone, and he still hadn't made contact.

She looked around, thought about her rookie orders from Cal. Moreno was to be her shadow. The neighborhood was deserted. There would be no one to call for help if she ran into trouble. She took out her phone again and called in to check on backup.

"On the way," said the watch captain. "Be advised

to wait for it," he said.

Just in case Moreno hadn't gotten her text, she texted him, *I'm going in. Backup is on its way. Hurry.*

Second thought. She put down her cell phone and thought about her dad. If she went in now, things could get dicey. She slumped back in her seat. She'd better wait for backup. *Damn!*

She unrolled her window, thought she heard a scream. Horror crawled over her body. She pulled her service revolver and went into the courtyard by the front door. She stood by the door, back against the wall, weapon ready, and listened. She heard it again. Muffled, but a definite scream. Sweat rivered down the nape of her neck.

Surely backup wouldn't be long. Someone had screamed. It was time for action. She felt the gnaw of fear, but knew she had to go. She turned the knob of the door and let herself in.

"Hello?" she called, "Miami PD."

She heard footsteps, then a familiar voice before anyone came into sight.

"Hello? May I... Izzy?" Traesk said.

She saw his reflection in a mirror now. He was alone and unarmed, walking toward her down the hall. She dropped her gun to her side and behind her hip. Ready. She adjusted her grip.

Mark turned the corner. A fleeting expression of shock crossed his face and vanished quickly. He approached her, arms spread in a welcoming gesture. Palms up and open.

"What are you doing here?" he asked.

Thinking quickly, Izzy said, "When you dropped the paperwork off at the bar the other night, this address and appointment time were attached to it with the name Glad. I just thought it might be fun to see this house with Lolly. She's so nice. She even invited me to one of her parties. I just really wanted to see this house. I probably should have called first—"

"Izzy, you and I don't have an appointment, and I'm showing a house." A cold front blew across Traesk's tone. He indicated the door. "Perhaps I can call you later. This isn't a good time."

A moan came from down the hall where Traesk had emerged.

An apprehensive shiver chased down Izzy's back. "What was that?"

Traesk again indicated the door. "I didn't hear anything." With an even stronger edge in his voice, "I'm afraid I'm going to have to ask you to leave."

Izzy felt her back stiffen. She cocked her head at Traesk. "Where's Lolly?"

Before Traesk could answer, Izzy's phone chirped with a text message. *Moreno* she thought. She had to know if he was on his way. Her gun was still concealed in her right hand. She reached across her body to get the phone with her left. Traesk lunged at her and she came down on his shoulder with the butt of her gun. He swaggered, recovered and grabbed her phone.

She trained her gun on him. "Drop the phone," she said.

He pressed a button and read the screen. "On my way with backup," he read to her. His eyes narrowed. "I don't think so."

"I *said* drop it," she shouted. Her voice was a growl. An animal.

He tossed the phone down. It skittered across the

floor and disappeared under the couch.

"Hands in the air," she said.

He complied. Put them up.

She held the gun on him. Dread quickened. "What's going on here?" she asked.

"I thought you were virtuous," he said. "But you have become unkind and unvirtuous."

She fumbled for the handcuffs in her waistband with her free hand.

Traesk rambled on. "I spoke with your dad when I dropped those papers off. He said you just want to put him away. He said you were the one responsible for having Officer Callahan suspended."

"Save it," she said. She reached above his head, took one of his hands and cuffed it.

"You are not kind," he said. "Not virtuous."

"I said *save* it."

She reached for his other hand and when she brought it down to cuff it, he swung around on her and grabbed her by the arm, hard. She jerked but before she could squeeze off a shot, he wrenched her gun from her hand and threw it across the great room.

"Guns are no use to me," he said. "Cleansing requires a blade."

He grabbed her other wrist and held so tightly that she thought he might break it. She raised her knee to kick him in the groin and he dodged her. He held her even tighter and twisted her around so her back was against his chest. Being held like that gave her the sense of being surrounded by the purest evil left in the world. Fight or wait? She chose wait. She'd wait for an opportunity to make a move. To escape.

"Why, Izzy?" he said.

"Why what?" she said, heart pounding, belly tightening with cold, sick fear. She struggled to stay calm. She'd have to wait for the right moment to make her move. Where the *hell* was that backup?

"Why are you discarding your father when he needs you most?"

"Shut up, Traesk."

He squeezed her arm even tighter. She could barely feel her hand. He'd cut off the blood flow. She was living an unfolding nightmare. She raged against him.

He squeezed her arm even tighter.

Another moan.

Obviously distracted, Traesk loosened his grip ever so slightly. Izzy could feel blood starting to flow back into her fingers.

Shouting from down the hall.

Traesk was definitely distracted now. *Just keep him talking*, Izzy thought.

"But how did you get Cal to sign for the insurance?"

"Real estate closing documents are kept on file as public record. I have a good scanner," he said. "I lifted his signature."

As he bragged, Traesk's grip on Izzy's arm lessened again. She slammed her heel hard into his instep. For a split second, he let go of her arm. In one move, she reeled around on him and elbowed him in the solar plexus. He recoiled from the blow. She got away from him and dove for her weapon. He was after her in an instant. She grabbed at the gun. Before she knew it, he was on top of her wrenching her arm behind her. Her shoulder popped and pain flooded the joint in a wave of heat.

"You impertinent woman. You must be cleansed quickly," he hissed.

"I already had a bath, Traesk. I don't need cleansing."

A solitary handcuff dangled from his wrist. All Izzy had to do was immobilize him. Somehow. She struggled toward the gun on the floor. He twisted her shoulder and she winced in pain.

"No guns," he said, mad eyes darting. "There isn't time for the ritual, but you must be stopped."

He moved her away from the gun and toward a wall where a large iron cross hung. He backed her up against the wall and let go of her. If she could only reach that cross…

"There is no time for the ritual, but you need to hear the words so you can repent. The cleansing, the cleansing…"

She continued to scooch toward the cross. He grabbed her again, pushed her against the wall. "Stop moving," he said. "Be still and pay attention."

"Proverbs 19:22 What is desirable in a person is kindness, and it is better to be poor than a liar."

Izzy watched his eyes glaze over as if he were in a trance.

"You're Seth," Izzy said, half knowing and half as a distraction.

"*We* are Seth," Traesk said, eyes focusing on her again.

Izzy froze. *We?*

Traesk pulled a knife with a long blade out of his sports jacket. The blade already had blood on it.

Where was Moreno? She had to buy time. "What about Deuteronomy? What about thou shalt not kill?"

Izzy said.

Traesk looked addled, then said, "Exodus: An eye for an eye."

He looked at his blade.

In that instant, Izzy reached behind her and grabbed the large iron cross off the wall and clubbed him on the head. He went down to his knees. She grabbed the loose handcuff and quickly attached it to a spindle of the wrought iron banister. He yanked wildly at the cuffs. Blood bubbled up through his hair where the corner of the cross hit him.

"You must be cleansed," he roared, yanking at the cuffs. "It's for your own good. Set me free so I can help you."

"Not bloody likely," she said.

She ran to her gun, picked it up and headed down the hallway.

"Stop!" Traesk shouted. "You'll interrupt the cleansing ceremony. Don't go down there. You're not pure."

The handcuffs rattled loudly.

Izzy raised her gun and started to clear each room as she made her way down the hallway. Where the goddamn hell was backup? Moreno?

Izzy heard a moan come from behind the door at the end of the hallway. She rushed to it. The door was unlocked. Filled with a terrible foreboding, Izzy opened the door. Her heart pounded an unfamiliar rhythm. She peeked around the corner, gun leading the way.

Just inside the door, Lolly Glad was tied to a chair in front of a three-way mirror. Her face was bleeding from several cuts. An array of surgical instruments was laid out on a small table next to her.

Izzy took a step inside the door and someone hit her hard from behind.

She crumpled to the floor, rolled over and looked up. A woman with gray hair stood holding a scalpel in her hand. It was Sarah Traesk.

Izzy shook off the pain and trained her gun on Sarah. "Drop the knife," Izzy said.

Sarah looked at Izzy. "What are you doing here? What have you done with my son?"

"He's in the other room. Drop the knife, Sarah. It's all over."

Sarah held the scalpel in front of Lolly's face.

Lolly moaned and said, "No, please no."

Izzy edged closer to Sarah and the tray of knives.

"Sarah, put the knife down. I don't want to hurt you," Izzy said.

"I already told you once not to interfere," Sarah said.

Izzy's mind raced back to when Luke spilled the drink in the kitchen and how icy Sarah had been.

"I'm not here to interfere," Izzy said. "I want to help this woman. You're hurting her."

Sarah looked at Izzy and then down at Lolly. In a fluid arc, she moved toward Lolly's face with the knife. "Stop!" Izzy shouted, squeezing off a round that grazed Sarah's hand. Sarah spun, dropped the knife and clambered to the instruments, tried to grab another. Izzy popped off another shot. It missed Sarah and hit the leg of the table.

The weapon recoiled in Izzy's hand. Pain shot through the arm that Traesk had injured and she knew she wouldn't be able to get another shot off. Her arm was too damaged, and, left-handed she couldn't hit a thing. But Sarah didn't know that. Izzy changed hands, kept the gun trained on her, hoping that Sarah wouldn't see the gun shaking.

"I said, drop it," Izzy demanded.

Sarah held the knife over Lolly's face again. Izzy lunged at Sarah, knocking her and the tray of knives to the floor. Sarah stabbed at Izzy with the scalpel. She dodged. Sarah kept after her. Izzy dropped and rolled to get away, but Sarah landed on top of Izzy. She held the scalpel firmly in her hand and thrust it at Izzy's arm. Izzy dodged the blade but Sarah found flesh and slashed the knife hard at Izzy's collar bone, down and back up in a perfect V shape.

Izzy shrieked in pain. Sarah writhed and kicked on the ground, but Izzy's body slammed her flat and pinned her. She wrenched the knife free and tossed it out of the reach of the crazed woman. The red stain under Izzy's collarbone mushroomed.

Without thinking, Izzy reached for her cuffs, but they weren't there. Damn, they're on Traesk, she remembered. She listened and heard the cuffs scraping and Mark kicking against the banister. Goosebumps rashed her arms. She was no match for Traesk if he got—

Running footsteps in the hall. He'd broken free from the banister. She grabbed her gun, jerked her head around toward the door and took aim.

Moreno blasted through the doorway, gun drawn, gaze sharp.

Izzy stopped and dropped her gun, wild with feelings.

"It's me," he said. "It's all over."

"I almost…"

"Almost doesn't count."

Izzy eyed him from across the room, curiously, furtively, dangerously. "It's about time you got here," Izzy said.

He walked over to her. "You okay?" Moreno said, holstering his gun.

A strand of auburn hair dangled down her forehead and stuck to her nose. "Let's see," she said. "I'm covered in blood, my shoulder thinks it's a noodle, when I stand, my legs are like rope. I think it's all good."

Moreno smiled at her.

"Don't worry about me," Izzy said. "The victim needs an ambulance stat and you need to cuff this one."

Moreno stood over her and handed her his cuffs.

"You do the honors," he said.

She took them with her left hand and said, "Thanks, Moreno."

The paramedics arrived and loaded Lolly up. Izzy objected, complained profusely about going to the hospital in an ambulance to have her arm and shoulder checked out. In the end, she went.

Lying on the stretcher, she watched Mark and Sarah as they were escorted toward separate vehicles on their way to headquarters for processing.

Moreno leaned over Izzy, his dark eyes soft. He touched her cheek.

"You acted like a big girl cop in there, Izzy O," he said. "I may have to stop calling you newbie."

Chapter Forty-Seven

Izzy walked into the back room of the bar. Her arm was still in a sling, so she couldn't move the table, but she could start pulling the chairs out of the corner.

Everyone started to arrive. They all pitched in moving furniture, fetching Spencer and the cards, getting the first round of beer. It felt good to be at home around her friends. The door opened and Norman bounced in, followed by Apple who was carrying a homemade cake decorated with a police badge. The upper layer sat askew atop the bottom layer. It started to slide and Apple stuck her thumb on it to push it back in place, leaving a hole in the icing.

"What's that?" Izzy said.

"Well, I made a cake to celebrate your nabbing this guy," Apple said. "Norman said you liked chocolate."

Izzy laughed. "Thanks, Apple."

Apple set the cake down on a small table nearby and gave Izzy a big hug. "Congratulations, Izzy. Good job."

Everyone clapped for Izzy. Cal tapped his glass to get everyone's attention. All eyes moved in his direction.

"I just want to say that Izzy worked hard on this case," he said. "She had to put up with a killer and me. I'm not sure which was worse."

A chuckle went through the group.

"Doing the right thing isn't always the easy thing. Especially when it comes to bringing evidence that implicates one of your partners."

Cal's words made Izzy blush.

"Cal, nobody really suspected you," Izzy said.

"Maybe not, Izzy, but it took guts for you to do what you did," Cal said. "And you kept digging like a puppy after a root—until you cleared my name. You *all* stuck by me. I know I haven't been very pleasant lately. I'm here to say two words I don't use very often: I'm sorry."

Izzy almost dropped her beer. Cal never apologized.

"Apology accepted, Cal. Thanks," Izzy said. She tipped her mug to him.

Cal raised his glass to her and said, "To Detective Izzy O'Donnell."

Doctor Dan, Moreno, Apple, and Spencer all followed suit. "To Izzy," they all said.

Izzy felt heat rise in her face again. "Thanks everyone. But it was a team effort. It wasn't just me. We did it together." She raised her glass to them.

Spencer's glass remained in the air a second longer. "I'm proud of you, daughter," he said.

"Thanks, Dad."

Dr. Dan's lapel pins winked in the light when he turned toward Spencer. "So, Spence, how do you like your new digs?"

"I like them just fine," he said. "When Apple found out the woman on the first floor below her apartment was moving, the office manager didn't stand a chance. Izzy and Apple nailed it down that afternoon."

"It's nice that you're so close to the bar," Moreno

said. "Half a block isn't bad."

Norman hopped over to Spencer and jumped up on his lap. Spencer rubbed him behind the ears.

"And I do believe Norman enjoys sharing my courtyard with me," Spencer said.

"Like it?" Apple scoffed. "He *loves* it. He gets to hang out there during the day and when I come home after work, he hangs out with me upstairs. He's got the best of both worlds."

Right on cue, Norman nudged Spencer's arm. Spencer reached into his pocket and gave him a bunny treat.

Izzy's heart swelled. She couldn't ask for a better best friend. Nobody but nobody could top Apple. She helped walk Spencer to the bar every day and didn't even act like it was a big deal. The doctor had switched up Spencer's meds, and he seemed to be having fewer bad days. With Moreno's help, she and Apple had rearranged the storeroom and put a futon in it so Spencer could rest if he wanted to. Izzy always set something out for dinner and if she ran late, Spencer watched the bar while Apple cooked and brought it downstairs to eat. Unable to contain the love and gratitude she felt swelling in her chest at that moment, Izzy sniffed back tears, hoping nobody would notice.

"And what about you, Cal? How's the wife like the new job?" Spencer said.

"She seems to be happy there. Now that Heather won't have to change high schools, there's less drama around the house. All is well in the world. And I actually like my new desk job." He paused and raised his glass to them. "It's going to feel good to put those people behind bars."

They raised their glasses to him and mumbled, "Here, here."

"Whatever happened to that Lolly Glad person?" Dr. Dan said.

"Well, she called me the other day. She didn't buy that house," Izzy said. "But her husband is fixing her face right up. She e-mailed me a picture, and with time and a little makeup, you'd never know about her ordeal. Of course, she was advertising her husband's good work and inviting me to another one of her parties." Izzy said with a wink.

"Look, partner, you don't need to go to any of her parties. You scare the crooks just like you are," Moreno said.

Izzy gave Moreno the stink eye. "Cork it, Moreno."

"You gonna deal or what?" Moreno said, playfully tossing a fork at Izzy. It bounced off her collarbone.

"Owww," she yelped.

"Sorry, but I missed your sore arm," he said.

"But you got my stitches."

"Wow, Izzy, I am sorry. How is that healing up?"

She pulled her shirt down to reveal the wound on her collarbone that was stitched in the perfect shape of a "V." "It's okay so long as nobody hits it," she complained.

"Enough show-and-tell. We've all got scars from the job," Cal said. "Deal already!"

"Cal," Izzy said. "I'm surprised at you. Don't you know that patience is a virtue?"

A word about the author...

Jocelyn Pedersen is an award-winning, AP-published professional journalist with hundreds of published clips in various newspapers and magazines. A lover of the mystery and thriller, she eats popcorn while watching documentaries about serial killers and huddles under blankets on the couch while watching *Criminal Minds* with her friends and family. She enjoys her kids, the beach, teaching writing at the University of Oklahoma, and being a former sheep farmer, considers herself a sheepie slipper aficionado. She has more animals than brains and wouldn't have it any other way.

Check her out at www.greatwritingworks.com, and on Facebook, Twitter, LinkedIn, and Pinterest.

CPSIA information can be obtained
at www.ICGtesting.com
Printed in the USA
LVHW022308100619
620818LV00009B/215/P